W9-BMI-984

BETWEEN

the

TIDES

BETWEEN

the

TIDES

SUSANNAH MARREN

ST. MARTIN'S PRESS ☙ NEW YORK

FIC
Marren

This is a work of fiction. All of the characters, organizations, and events portrayed in this novel are either products of the author's imagination or are used fictitiously.

BETWEEN THE TIDES. Copyright © 2015 by Susan Shapiro Barash. All rights reserved. Printed in the United States of America. For information, address St. Martin's Press, 175 Fifth Avenue, New York, N.Y. 10010.

www.stmartins.com

Designed by Steven Seighman

Library of Congress Cataloging-in-Publication Data

Marren, Susannah.
    Between the tides : a novel / Susannah Marren.
       pages cm
    ISBN 978-1-250-06673-2 (hardcover)
    ISBN 978-1-4668-7462-6 (e-book)
  1. Married women—Fiction.   2. Suburban life—Fiction.
3. Domestic fiction—Fiction.   I. Title.
    PS3613.A76874B48 2015
    813'.6—dc23

                                        2015015601

St. Martin's Press books may be purchased for educational, business, or promotional use. For information on bulk purchases, please contact the Macmillan Corporate and Premium Sales Department at 1-800-221-7945, extension 5442, or write to specialmarkets@macmillan.com.

First Edition: July 2015

10   9   8   7   6   5   4   3   2   1

For my family

for we were born by the sea,
   knew its rose hedges
      to the very water's brink.

—WILLIAM CARLOS WILLIAMS
from *Asphodel, That Greeny Flower*

BETWEEN

the

TIDES

PART ONE

Lainie

ONE

The selkies are sea creatures, half woman, half seal. They wiggle out of their seal skins on the rocks to lie in the weak winter sun. One fisherman watched with his binoculars from his fishing boat and waited."

"He loved the prettiest one!" Claire interrupts.

"That's right, darling girl," I say.

Jack sticks out his tongue. "Who cares about some stupid sealy lady?" he shouts.

I stop the story. "Jack, please sit down."

Jack returns to the couch beside Tom, his big brother, who is on his iPad. Jack yawns and props his eyes open wide with his fingers. "Boring, Mom!"

"More! More!" Claire screams. She jumps off the chair and starts dancing around the den, waving her hands like flippers in her crazy water dance on land. "More!" she screeches.

Matilde, my solemn child, interrupts, "Mom, are you a selkie?"

I laugh and look out the den window that faces west. It is too dark to see anything. "No, darling girl, I'm not a selkie."

"But you love the water and you swim every day. When we go to Cape May you lie on the jetties just like the selkies. You never answer us when you're on the beach . . . it's like you're not even there. . . . Remember last February when—"

"Matilde, I am *not* a selkie."

"Mommy," Claire cries, "the sealy skin! The fisherman! Finish the story."

Perhaps Charles is right and I ought to quit this tale. It isn't *Cinderella* or *Snow White*; there is no prince with whom to live happily ever after.

"Mom?" Matilde is waiting.

"Okay . . . well . . . the beach is empty in December when the fisherman sees his chance. He sneaks up near the rocks and comes close to the prettiest selkie."

"He takes her skin, Mommy! The man takes her seal skin!" Claire begins to sob as she always does at this part in the story.

"That's true, Claire darling. The man takes her seal skin while she is in the icy sea. When she comes back to the shoreline, frantic to find her sealy coat, he is holding it in his hands. He tells her she has no choice but to go with him, without her coat she will drown. But he promises to love her forever, that they will marry and have a family. That's the deal." The "forever" part gets to me.

"And she marries him!" yelps Claire. She begins to dance again. "She marries him and they have babies!" Claire is the cheerful one; she bounces from one side of the room to the other. She passes Tom and Jack, who watch her as if she were an alien creature. I wonder if Jack and Claire will ever share a thought, an interest. Fraternal twins are not a matched pair.

"Until one day . . ." I look up. "Jack, are you listening?"

Jack covers his ears. "I don't care about seals and babies. It's gross!"

"A dull story for the boys," says Charles. He is in the doorway, appearing out of nowhere, as usual. He is so stealthy, Charles, more burglar than surgeon.

The children race to him and grab at his arms and hands, his legs, anything that is their father. Except Matilde, who stays close to me.

"Lainie, how about another story? Something more realistic? You could read to them from *Tom Sawyer.*"

Matilde leans in toward my ear. "I know why you like the story. I know you're a selkie. I saw your sealy skin."

Everyone is waiting.

"What sealy skin? What are you talking about, Matilde?"

"In the hall closet, hanging in a zippered bag. A black, thick coat," she answers. "Hairy."

"Oh, that. That's from my grandmother. You're right, it is made of seal, a long-dead seal. I wouldn't wear it. I don't have the guts to ditch it. I guess I'm sentimental."

No one else speaks. Claire is frozen in mid-dance. Matilde says, "The sealy needs her coat to go back to the sea. She has a land family now but she misses the sea."

"That's right. That's how it works," I whisper. "The days become flat for her, days without any sun."

"Until she finds the coat!" says Claire, twirling around in circles.

Charles enters the room now, fully present, taking up the oxygen. His loafers make a clicking sound on the wood floor.

"Forget the sealy coat," he says.

He is tall and strong, buff. He lifts weights, runs through Morningside Park in rain or shine. Sometimes he wakes me predawn and invites me to run with him. "C'mon, Lainie," he'll say, "shake up your schedule and run this morning. Forget the pool every day."

"Okay, Charles, soon." Although I don't mean it.

I walk the reservoir, around the track slowly, only to be by a body of water. I want water, any kind, like a vampire wants blood. Matilde is the one in the family who understands. She is only twelve but she realizes that if I didn't paint pictures of water, I wouldn't exist. If we didn't live by the Hudson River or go to the ocean every summer, to my hometown, I'd wither and die.

Charles sits down in "his" green leather chair next to the fireplace and faces my largest and best-known work of art, *Trespassing: Drift-wood*. The six-by-eight-foot painting has overwhelmed the living room these years, making me proud, sad, regretful, and attached to Charles. His eyes are on the piece as he speaks. "I have big news. Might as well talk now, while we're together."

I tilt my head and Matilde sits next to me on the couch. "Claire," I say, "come here." Claire pushes between us and I put my lips to her damp and clammy forehead.

"Tom?" says Charles. "Can you settle down with Jack?" Jack slides out of Tom's reach and runs to Charles's lap, clapping and yowling. Charles gives me one of his "Can't you control these children?" looks while he tousles Jack's hair and hugs him. Who can blame Charles for choosing order; he is a famous surgeon, skilled, popular, a perennial Best of the Best in *New York* magazine. When he dons his scrubs, patients and nurses swoon. He is booked years in advance. *Dr. Morris, Dr. Morris, Dr. Charles Morris.* At home with his children, he softens—the only place and only time that he is soft.

"I've got a surprise for you," says Charles. "A big surprise."

"You know how I hate surprises, Charles," I say.

"Finish the sealy coat story," Claire says. "Mommy, please?"

Charles glances at Claire and then turns to me. "Lainie, you must stop with these stories before—"

"What is the surprise, Dad?" Tom asks.

"Before what?" Am I missing something here?

"Surprise! Surprise!" Jack jumps up from Charles's lap. They have the exact same eyes, neither the color of water nor the color of the sky. Instead, they are dark blue, the color of dusk.

"Hush," says Charles, and I become very still to set an example. I put my fingers to my lips and stare at each of my four children. The only sound is of Candy out in the kitchen, opening cupboards to start the children's dinner.

"What is the surprise, Dad?" Tom asks again.

"Well, I wonder if you see anything different about me?" His voice becomes light and self-satisfied at the same moment that my heart starts to race.

"You have on blue!" Jack shouts. "A blue jacket, Daddy!"

Charles is wearing a navy blazer, and he usually wears a suit to work. A darkish one or grayish or striped, the same as the other surgeons.

"Yes, Jack, I'm in a blue sport coat."

"You're home early, a half hour earlier," Tom says.

I nudge Matilde and then Claire but neither attempts to guess what is different.

Charles keeps it going. "What else? What is different about me today?"

I close my eyes and wrap my arms around myself as if a wind is coming through.

"I don't understand," I say. "What are you telling us?"

"Lainie, you and the children are looking at the new head of orthopedic surgery at the Elliot Memorial Hospital. The chief of the goddamn department!"

I don't think I've ever seen Charles so euphoric, his bottom teeth show when he smiles. The children and I stare at him.

"Elliot Memorial in Elliot, New Jersey? How will you commute with your schedule?" I ask. "You get to the hospital now by six in the morning most days and it's twenty blocks from our apartment."

"Well"—Charles clears his throat—"that's the other part of the surprise. Remember a while back when we were in Rye to look at houses and then went to Playland? How Jack loved the Ferris wheel? Then we went to New Jersey and went to a McDonalds drive-through?"

I stare at my work and admire how it is illuminated by the changing hours of the day and the slant of light through the windows, especially at twilight.

"That was more than a year ago, Charles, and we nixed it. We nixed the entire idea of moving out of the city," I say.

It was a troubling time when Charles had a yen to look at houses. Those car trips were revolting and slow. Claire was always carsick. Matilde was sullen because she was missing entire Saturdays with her friends, with whom she was no doubt sneaking cigarettes and having makeout parties at a terrifyingly early age. Charles and I would speak in the front seat, assuming that the children couldn't hear, evaluating each town and community, the pros and cons of life beyond the city. Charles's many laments about New York cluttered my head.

"Let's not move," I told Charles after Jack fell in love with a tree house in some unknown suburb. "I have a feeling it isn't right for our family."

"Tree house! Tree house!" Jack screamed on the ride home. "Climb the tree house."

Charles let go, one of the only skirmishes he's ever lost in his lifetime of wins. "No tree house, Jack. I'll build you a tree house someday, don't worry."

That was the last discussion about it until today when Charles was offered this plum job. What better ticket out of Manhattan than that? Who would dispute such an imprimatur for my husband?

"Actually, we *should* be moving to Elliot. To Somerset County, New Jersey, Lainie. How else can I manage?" Charles asks.

Tom, taking his cue from his father, grabs Jack's arms and they swing around the room. Is Tom serious, is he okay with leaving everyone behind in New York for his father's new position? Doesn't he view his father as famous enough already? Then again, Tom has wanted what his father wants since the day he was born. I'm sure that Charles wishes that the rest of us would be as pleased as he and Tom are. Yet we're not. Suddenly my toehold in the downtown art scene, albeit a tenuous one, is in jeopardy. My chances of reclaiming the spot everyone thought I was destined to occupy could be obliterated by a move to a suburban nirvana.

"Lainie, you'll love it. A place with woods, sprawling grounds, acres . . . You say that you want to spend more time in nature."

"Woods? Grounds? Is there any water in Elliot? Anything like Coney Island or the Rockaways, where I go to paint?"

I walk to the window and stare fourteen floors below to the Hudson River. Has he ever understood that I require water twenty-four hours a day? It matters little since my husband has decided for us anyway.

The boys are celebrating because they believe that Charles is able to do anything. Claire comes to where I stand and reaches for my hand. Hers is sticky and I wonder if someone gave her ice cream. Not Candy, who is under strict orders not to give the children treats before dinner. Matilde? Probably. She has a tendency to please Claire.

"How did this happen, Charles? How could you get a job without my knowing that you were looking for one?" I ask.

"Serendipitous, I suppose. I was at that faculty dinner, the one at the UN dining room that you decided not to attend. Gerard mentioned the opening to me and one thing led to another. . . ."

"And you interviewed without saying a word to me?"

"I didn't expect it to go anywhere." Charles clears his throat. "You know that I could never be head of surgery here, Lainie."

Charles, who has a new job and gets to displace his entire family in the process.

"Lainie?"

I'm silent, a statue. The children watch their father.

"Lainie?"

"I'll be fine." My voice is crushed and strange. Matilde's gaze is far-off—as if she's pretending that we've all met tonight for the first time.

"Of course you will be fine," Charles says. "What a move for our family! This is what people aspire to, Lainie. More space, a more gentle life. The Elliot hospital is challenging . . . fresh . . . exciting. The city has become . . . tougher and we need a bigger place. The children will have a finished basement to run around, to play Ping-Pong. Lainie, you'll have a real studio. No more painting in the alcove or the laundry room . . ." *One man's poison, another man's cure.*

Then the reality of the situation hits Tom. "What about school? Where will we go?"

"New schools for everyone," says Charles. "Claire and Jack will begin kindergarten in a public school. A very fine public school. The school system in Elliot is stellar. The college entrance rate out of high school runs at ninety-seven percent."

Matilde shudders at what's next. She and Tom will be going to a public school too—Tom for ninth grade and Matilde for seventh. Still her brothers are cheering and their father is the winner. On our side it's misery and fear. Matilde's rising panic is palpable. She goes everywhere in the city with her posse of friends—I'm sure that I don't know the half of it. She's never been the "new girl," but she knows what happens to them.

Meanwhile, Charles and Tom seem to be trading thoughts in airwaves. What are they imagining, that I'll become a suburban mother cloaked in khakis from J. Crew, carpooling like my cousin Agnes does in Fairfield County? For Tom, the fantasy of the right mother is fast approaching.

"Your mother is on board, aren't you, Lainie?" Charles asks. "You're on board, aren't you, Matilde?"

On board.

Claire walks over to Tom and tugs on his shirt. "Piggyback?"

"Not now, Claire." Tom moves beside Charles.

"Would anyone like to know something about the town or how far it is from the city?" Charles asks.

No one answers. He stares in my direction. "Any curiosity about where we're going?"

Tom says, "Sure, Dad, tell us."

Would anyone want to know that it's all hills and valleys? Would anyone want to know it's landlocked—another world completely?

"Well, it's about an hour outside the city, in Somerset County. Right next to Bedminster, New Jersey. Horse country. Very horsey."

Horsey? Charles couldn't possibly be thinking of getting one, could he? None of us seems to understand what he's saying. He is talking about over an hour of travel to get to the places I love: the Seventy-ninth Street Boat Basin along the Hudson, the promenade at Carl Schurz Park that flanks the East River. Places where I sit and paint or meditate on the composition of a new work, a place where one might hallucinate waves out of small ripples. "It's not the sea or the bay," I say to the girls every time we visit a New York waterway, "but at least it's better than no water. On a boat you can buck the current and that's an adventure." Now there will be horses instead of boats, woods instead of rivers. I shake my head.

"Did you hear what I said, Lainie?"

"I heard. Why horse country?"

"There's nothing more lovely," Charles says, as if we're discussing the Impressionist wing at the Metropolitan Museum of Art.

"The rolling hills, the privacy. Maybe you'll want to take riding lessons, Lainie, with the girls."

I twist off my wedding band and twirl it on the end table. The inscription reads *Love Is Eternal,* not that Charles thought it up. It's what Abe Lincoln had written in Mary Todd's ring. I've often thought that the jeweler must have suggested it to Charles along with a few other ideas.

"The commute to New York is fairly painless," Charles continues. "As long as you get yourself to the Summit train station, the trains run often enough. Plenty of express trains."

"How far is Elliot from Summit?" I start pacing.

Charles waves his hand and doesn't answer. Claire starts more water dancing. Matilde puts her hands on her shoulders. "Claire, stop, please, Mom and Dad are talking."

Matilde smiles at Charles. I imagine that she doesn't want to take sides. Charles is a cool dad, a fine father. He picks her up later at her friends' apartments than I would like. He stays and chats with the parents on a casual Sunday afternoon while I'm always rushing home to get back to work. Charles permits Matilde and Tom to skip Sunday school, claiming they have too much homework to be pressured. He is the handsomest father and he's never too tired to take the children wherever they need to go on a weekend. He takes them to musicals, to the Hayden Planetarium, to ride bikes in Central Park. Matilde loves to walk on Upper Broadway with him, stopping at Starbucks.

"When do we move, Dad?" Matilde asks.

"That's a very good question, Matilde. A logical question."

Matilde shoots Tom a triumphant glance.

"We'll move sometime during the summer," says Charles. "So you'll have a little time there before school starts to get to know the place and meet some kids."

"Charles," I say as calmly as I can, "what about the Shore?"

"We'll have to skip it this year, Lainie. Everything is changing. For the better."

"Charles, we always go to the Shore for the summer, that's the deal. That's always been the deal." My voice is hard, crisp. I'm counting on the jetties, the strong sun of summer, the smell of seaweed, the clam beds, surf fishing. Swimming.

My husband stands up and Tom and Jack do the same. They are directly in front of my work, and although it is enormous, they are ruining a view of the lower frame made of seashells and sea glass, turtle backs and debris.

"Well, maybe we could rent the house out for a month. I'm thinking aloud. . . . Maybe put that money toward the house in Elliot that we'll rent first . . . while we shop for houses. . . . Getting some income from the Shore house would be useful."

"Useful," I repeat. I walk over to the couch to sit between Matilde and Claire. The three of us melt into it, our human skin branding to the fabric.

"I'm tired, Mom," says Matilde. "Like a grandmother must feel."

"I know," I say.

"Mommy, what happens to the prettiest selkie?" asks Claire. "Where does she go?"

Charles is at the doorway and the boys are beside him. Candy is outside holding up a wooden spoon and the lid to a pot. "Do I need to bang?" she asks. "Dinnertime for the little ones!"

Charles looks at his watch. "Dinner, Lainie?"

"Yes, we have an eight-thirty. With Jane and Robert."

"Don't go." Claire grabs my arm. "Mommy, please don't go. You have to finish the story. Where is the prettiest one, the selkie mother?"

Charles turns to us and then he leaves without another word, moving down the wooden hallway with his methodical step.

"Ah, the prettiest one." I straighten up.

"Hey, Mom? Do you think you'll have to wear nail polish once we move to this place?"

"I'm sorry, Matilde?" I examine my short fingernails with their residue of charcoal.

"You know, be like the other mothers. Dad said he's going to have a big job."

"Mommy!" Claire shouts. "The selkie mother?"

"She has children and she loves them very much, Claire. For years she tends to them and is a good mother and a good wife. There are days when she almost forgets her sealy skin and she seems resolved to life on land. Other days she visits the rocks and remembers her selkie roots: a distant memory for her until one morning there is a rainstorm and the ceiling starts leaking. The mother climbs up to the rafters to plug the leak and she finds her sealy skin that her husband has hidden away. She cries over her old coat that has stiffened and is withered and dry. Her sad salt tears moisten the coat so it looks more like a seal coat."

I stop speaking and the room gets cold.

"Then what?" asks Claire. "Mommy, what?"

"Later, Claire," Matilde says. "Claire. C'mon, Candy has dinner on the table and the boys will eat up the good stuff. Mommy and Daddy are going out with friends. Mommy has to get ready."

"The prettiest one jumps into the ocean!" says Claire. "I know she does, Mommy. I know already! But she has to come back, right, Mommy, back to her children!"

Matilde scoops Claire into her arms. Claire is struggling, pounding on Matilde's shoulders. Matilde looks at me and I give in.

"She does come back, my darling girl."

Claire cries anyway; her face is blotchy. Then Matilde cries and so do I.

"No, Charles, not tonight." I am as far away from him as possible in our queen-size bed, not far enough to keep me from his ever-magnetic pull. Lying in bed with Charles is a reminder of our shared history and the private currency we trade in. Before children, before the *idea* of children. Those days we used to trek along the coast, those nights we read Yeats, mostly "The Song of Wandering Aengus" and the

Maud Gonne poems to each other. Sometimes there were no stars in the sky and only a silver moon. He pledged to be my friend, my best friend. Charles, who once kept me safe.

He sits up, switches on the light, and looks at me. I look away. He takes my head in his elegant surgeon's hands, runs his fingers down my jawline, and turns me to face him. He leans down and kisses me.

"Lainie. Lainie. We're not moving to Minnesota. We're moving an hour out of the city." If only what Charles said could influence me.

"I don't want to leave New York," I say.

"You might change your mind," Charles says.

"I don't want to leave my life."

"What life? What will you be giving up? You can have anything you want. You can have everything you want, Lainie." He starts kissing my earlobe, a preliminary move.

"Why is that?" I ask.

"You would have your very own studio. A large studio." A smart bait for me, his first method of conviction. I've worked at my dressing table or in a corner of the living room ever since we converted my studio into Tom's bedroom two years ago.

"You'll make new friends. There's an Arts Council right in town to join, get to know some other artists. Elliot is where people go when they are successful, Lainie. You'll be getting a new life, a greener life—isn't that what we strive for?"

I grew up on the Jersey Shore and know nothing of a backyard—who needs a backyard when your front yard is the beach, the ocean, infinity? A place I stay in the summer with the children while Charles comes and goes, bobbing on his own raft and never a swimmer. If Charles is not enamored with the seaside, he appreciates Cape May enough for our family to go every summer.

There I spend hours painting by the jetties, facing the open sky. Along the coastline I'm in search of scraps of beach life. Each day I swim wherever and however I can. If it's the ocean I do the Australian crawl beyond the lifeguards' buoys and fight the undertow; in the bay I swim on my back and the minnows beneath tickle me. In a pool I take over the fast lane. I smash through, doing a butterfly, while dreaming of bodies of water, the ones you cannot claim as your own.

Charles is neither a New Yorker nor an island child and has been a bystander since he arrived in the city. That's what comes of growing up in Utica, on his grandfather's dairy farm. He has some twisted form of Heidi inside him. He drinks whole milk with abandon, not fat free, eats Swiss cheese, and believes in a simple life that he isn't able to define. He was going to be a veterinarian until he realized the only way to be a luminary in medicine was to be a surgeon. Cutting humans, not animals. While Charles hungers for farm life, to this day I long to jump out of bed and race along the ocean. I want nothing more than to dive in and swim until I forget about places enclosed by land and privilege.

His eyes bore into mine. He begins his mantra, one I have heard for what seems years but with a new spin. "Lainie, we have our chance. The city isn't an ideal place to raise kids, you know that. Remember the pervert on West End Avenue when you were with the twins? Wasn't there that child stalker by Gracie Mansion? Tom has been mugged twice. Matilde sees a rat family right on Broadway and Ninety-first Street almost daily. The children need fresh air, room, nature, pets—a real life. New York isn't real. I have been asked to chair a department."

I listen to his persuasion, knowing that when Charles speaks to an audience, most heads in the room nod in approval at his words, whatever they are. I've been in the marriage for too many years; I have radar for false promises, I'm not part of his constituency. Besides, what is he talking about and how does he know where the other artists will be?

He tugs at my camisole and pushes my boxer shorts to the floor. He starts stroking my breast. I open my eyes and his face is precariously close to mine. I can't recognize his bone structure in the shadows and I'm confused for a brief second. Has Charles's affection not seen me through the ups and downs of our marriage? Being close to Charles is a sensation that I crave, a method of outlasting the lost hours, the frictions over money, children, his work, my work, in the same order. I settle in. Sex has always worked between us. I surrender to his caress partly because I'm hooked on the sex, partly because I won't win this one. I want to be like other wives, where the passion fades first, not last.

His voice has that raspiness that I know too well in sleep or in the waking hours. "You are beautiful," he says.

The moonlight is low through the largest window to the right of our bed, facing west. Charles doesn't appear to be in husband mode. He climbs on top of me and I place my hands on his neck and then on his biceps. I move toward him, hoping he means it about being beautiful since yesterday he remarked that I was tired and wan. My body yields to what was; I sell out in the midst of Charles's master plan. I bend into him as best I know how.

After Charles falls asleep and exhales a rhythmic, satisfied breath of a paramour, I have a sense that I'm on a sailboat that is rocked by the winds that blow in an unpredictable direction. I close my eyes and float on my back against the tide.

I decide it's okay to put our apartment on the market, a home that we both love, despite his complaints. Charles wins as if I have no free will. Or too much free will. I hand over the only existence I know, remembering a lesson of my grandmother's is that the future is pre-ordained. Nothing is coincidence, each of us experiences many lives.

TWO

⨳

"*Elliot, New Jersey?*" Isabelle asks the next afternoon. We are at the Guggenheim to see the Zarina Hashmi exhibit *Paper Like Skin,* a retrospective of her work since the sixties. Having perused the show, we are now sitting in the restaurant, ordering espressos. The group—Isabelle, Cher, Gillian, and I—meet weekly to talk about our art, our lives, and artistic integrity. We usually choose women artists to view and then fantasize that women artists garner more and more authority.

"You aren't pregnant, are you, Lainie?" Cher asks. "You're not moving because you need more room in the city, right?"

"No, no, I'm not," I say. "It's Charles. He has a new position."

"Your keeper," Isabelle says. "Every goddamn year Charles is more and more your keeper."

"Am I missing something? Lainie is okay . . . she *is* working." Gillian defends me since she has three children and is forever trying to finish a project herself.

"You shrunk *because* of Charles. Men are jealous," Isabelle says. "They want wifey. Charles doesn't care what it costs you. You should have been a rock star. . . . I've watched the entire landslide—from day one Charles didn't grasp your talent or how close you were to fame."

Cher turns to me. "Lainie, tell Gillian since she's only been with us for what . . . a decade? Isabelle and I were there at the Cosmo Gallery eighteen years ago. That's how we met—in a group show. Lainie was the youngest."

Isabelle scrolls around on her iPhone. "Look, here's what they wrote about you, Lainie—I've googled your first review. 'Lainie Smith transports water and natural elements in a style that she owns. In her largest work, *Trespassing: Driftwood,* her magical use of sea and shoreline creates an emotionally charged tale. This is shown to us as a hybrid of canvas, collage, and sculpture. We expect more thrills ahead from this vibrant young artist.'"

"Charles and George were medical residents at Columbia Presbyterian who came to the show. Roaming around with the serious collectors." Cher clucks her tongue.

"Right, and Charles asked about my medium, the figures in my work—why the piece was massive. . . . He cupped his hand in mine and didn't let go. I told him the form encompassed the story—the theme was loneliness for women . . . women as travelers . . . boundaries, driftwood as a barrier . . . the sea, sky. . . ." I look at my three best friends, who are neither nostalgic nor convinced of Charles's early enthusiasm.

"Love is blind," Isabelle says.

"You should have known then, right then," Cher says. "He was just flirting with you."

"I'm the one who let go of his hand—to meet the Greys. Patrons who launched young artists. I thought for sure they'd buy my work. Then the three of us went to the Odeon after the opening, and Charles and George materialized—they came to our table. Charles announced that he'd bought *Trespassing: Driftwood,* that he'd paid more than anyone else and the gallery owner couldn't refuse. George said that Charles would be piss-poor for the foreseeable future—they were both in their second year of residency," I say.

"I called Charles a turd that night while Isabelle decided his purchase would *not* benefit Lainie's career," Cher says.

"So she married him a year later," says Isabelle. "You know the rest, Gillian. Lainie's masterpiece hangs in her living room, where no one except family members and friends see it."

"I had my first child. . . . Somehow it was easier to have fewer accolades, fewer collectors chasing me. The smaller scale—I began my twelve-inch squares with flora and seashell frames, and while not exactly incendiary, they seemed more . . . manageable. I could do it while Tom was napping when he was a toddler and I was pregnant with Matilde. . . ."

"Lainie, your compromise is somewhere between a Hallmark greeting card and a lightweight painting," Cher says. "You were the next Judy Chicago in size and scope."

"I'm working. . . . I'm selling the miniatures on Etsy. I'm repped by a quiet gallery that gets the job done. . . . It's fine. Besides, the children . . ."

"Etsy? A form of paying for your sins." Isabelle shakes her head.

"You might as well move to goddamn Elliot," Cher says. "You'll have tons of clients there."

"I hope that you'll come back for our group meetings," Gillian says.

"I'm not so sure. Now I'm never more than a subway or cab ride away. Once it's a commute of over an hour in each direction, especially with the twins in a half day of kindergarten, it won't be easy."

They are looking at me with pity in their eyes, and an unspoken fear creeps into my soul.

The time until we move to Elliot is like clamming in muck and mud, clams buried under your toes and the crabs nipping at your ankles. Finding a pediatrician and a dentist, moving the children's health records and school records, and giving away clothes and old toys becomes a furious nightmare that infiltrates my waking hours.

Within a week of Charles's announcement we are house hunting sans children. A constant humidity trickles into the sterile, purified interior of Charles's vintage BMW those afternoons that we roam the streets of Elliot. His car is much neater than my vehicle—why wouldn't that be, given who drives the children around the city? Elliot is already etched in his mind while I despise looking at houses I never want to rent, let alone buy. I have two paintings due by the first of next month, both for private clients. I should be working.

Instead we arrive at these properties, drive forward, back up, and narrow it down to two minimansions, one Dutch Colonial and one Georgian. My imagination is filled with silhouettes and shadings of backyards for potential purchase. The Elliot broker, Christina, a woman about my age with blond hair, long legs, and stilettos, is extremely peppy and enthusiastic. We travel through the famous horse country. Every few acres produces another perfect house flanked by assorted flower beds, making its own statement. While she and Charles sit in the front of her car to chat endlessly about school systems, barbecues, the beauty of neighboring towns—Bedminster and Far Hills—the easy commute, I try to conjure up what people do in these houses all day. Christina pushes for us to skip the rental house and commit to buying now. At least Charles is sensible enough to reject that plan, to explain that the move is a process.

He is drawn to the elitism of Elliot, like a moth to a flame. It deludes him and eludes him—the high ground and sprawling if understated homes—and he believes that he has arrived. The many acres between houses—a breath of fresh air after apartment dwelling. The brew of doctors, nurses, administrators in a pristine hospital, saluting his surgeries.

"I don't want to live here," I divulge to no one who could hear me or could change the course. "I love the city."

Elliot has a small but real artistic community. On our second visit there, Charles and I walk an open field where local artists are showing. We check out the stalls together—the work is high quality and varied—portraits, landscapes, oils, watercolors.

"One day, I hope, Lainie, you have a one-woman show in Elliot. It could be a big deal," he suggests as we walk around. I briefly wonder how it would be to live in a place that is tame enough to have your art count.

The windshield wipers make a soothing swish/swipe sound as we drive back from Elliot. I'm considering that Charles's thoughts today about big fish, small pond might be prophetic. Talent in the town, unlike the city, where it is cutthroat and competitive, where artist friends might or might not be enamored of your success. Is it possible that Charles is right? That in Elliot one stops pushing for a gallery and embraces the purity of painting without tension? Is it of another order than merely papering an art opening with faces you know? Charles surely wants me to believe it is so.

He who earns the gold rules, my grandmother always said. Although he has cornered me, Charles continues to cheerlead and cajole. He stirs the pot to get me to concede, to forget my favorite haunts, those that can't be replicated in the middle of New Jersey.

⬯

The last morning, when the movers come, I imagine being carried with my mouth taped shut, kicking and screaming, into their large, overstuffed truck. I imagine that I'll be craning my head for my final views of the river from the fourteenth floor of our apartment. Views that are soon to be forever erased.

I have purposely saved *Trespassing: Driftwood* to be packed last in order to avoid any problems or obstacles. I have asked repeatedly if the movers are assured about packing it up. Custom art movers who handle only paintings and sculpture and come highly recommended. "Make sure that Derrick, the head mover, is personally responsible for your work," Isabelle said. "Use *only* Derrick," Gillian recommended. "No one else at the company is as good or as careful."

Weeks before the move, Derrick himself, freckled, strong, and tattooed, came up to the apartment with his foreman to measure the piece. He came back a second time with two assistants to measure and re-measure the angles. "What a singular shape, Mrs. Morris," he said. "What a rare form. We'll design a custom container for it."

Today Derrick and his crew are carrying several moving blankets. Two men climb up on ladders to carefully, expertly place them over the outer corners and top ledge of wood before they dislodge it. Two more movers set up two more ladders. The four men heave and sigh as they carefully remove the work, and as they do the driftwood, canvas, shells, and sea glass catch the sunlight. On the faded wall where Charles has showcased my work a dirty rim is left behind. A shrine to the career I might have had, the one that got away.

Then the piece is completely lifted and the heavy wooden frame begins to shatter. The wood continues to splinter, as if it cannot hold together if it isn't affixed to the living room wall, where it has hung facing the Hudson River these last nineteen years. The more that Derrick and his crew try to steady the unwieldy piece, the more it fractures and breaks. The shellacked algae fall on the floor and burst; the canvas appears too taut and then tears in the middle. Derrick and one other mover attempt to stop the motion when what is left of my work begins to disintegrate crazily. Huge slabs of the frame crash to the floor.

"Oh my God! Please! Stop!" I scream. "What are you doing? Stop walking like drunken sailors!"

The movers fall side to side against the walls, thumping into a door. Long jagged wood turns to a white mix that covers the entire floor. Derrick holds his hands up for his men—capable, strong, muscle builders—to halt. They make an attempt, then keep rocking with wedges of my once famous work in their arms, unable to halt the cycle.

"Stop! Stop!" I scream again. "Please!" I fall to my knees and start clutching my heart. "Oh my God, it's falling apart!"

"Mrs. Morris?" Derrick says. "We're doin' the best we can."

Candy comes into the living room carrying her fiddle with Claire and Jack behind her. Tom and Matilde are in the bedroom wing and come in from the opposite door.

"Mom! Your work . . . *Trespassing: Driftwood* . . . Mom!" Matilde slips and slides on the baby shells, fish bones, and smallest particles of sea glass. She is on the floor frantically collecting the pieces. She stands up and starts to skid, then steadies herself.

"Matilde, don't," I say. "Please. I'll do it. I'll pick it up. Please don't, you'll get hurt."

Candy starts to pick up the larger pieces with her free hand. Then Claire jumps around, missing the sharpest wood slats by an inch. Nails protrude—rusty nails.

"Claire, my darling girl. Go with Candy. Jack, you go too . . . into the kitchen. Candy will play a song, won't you, Candy?"

Candy stands up and steadies the fiddle on her left shoulder and lifts the bow to begin. "'Ready to Run'?" She starts to play as if she is part of the Dixie Chicks. Claire and Jack hop up and down, mesmerized, and follow her away from my work of art, which keeps fracturing before my eyes. Matilde drops back to the floor and starts accumulating the shells and algae.

"Matilde, wait," Tom says.

"Why, Tom? We have to help Mom." The movers place it carefully on the floor while it keeps imploding. The largest part of driftwood on the bottom falls off and breaks into more withered wood chips.

"What do you want, Mrs. Morris?" asks Derrick. "At this rate, we won't be out of here until noon, and then to drive the truck to New Jersey . . ."

"I want to collect every bit, every sliver of wood and chipped paint and every shell . . . and put them in these boxes wrapped up in Bubble Wrap. The frame, although it has broken apart, can go in a big crate, Bubble Wrapped too. The bigger pieces can go in moving blankets. That was our original plan."

"Mrs. Morris, I'm so sorry . . . your collage . . . is more or less ruined. I've never moved something that's in a state of disrepair," Derrick says.

"No," I say. "Not exactly ruined, not totally in disrepair."

He holds up the large parts that have crumbled. "Mrs. Morris . . ." Minute seashells fall to the floor. Some of the shells are no bigger than a thumbtack. Larger shells have fallen into mounds. Then the paint turns to dust where Derrick places his rubber-gloved hand. A mermaid's face is eradicated.

"Pack it up, everything—all of it—whole or broken, please."

With her hands Matilde has swept a high pile of debris. I point to it. "For example, what my daughter has collected could be put in a box marked 'fragile.' I'll know what it is."

An hour later they have finished packing up the shards of *Trespassing: Driftwood*. Our other possessions have been packed and ready for what seems days. I stand next to the fireplace and survey an apartment as empty and impersonal as it gets between former and future inhabitants. What has graced the mantel above is a pair of bronzed baby shoes for each child: Tom, Matilde, Jack, and Claire. Days ago they were packed along with my grandmother's candlesticks, the Lalique crystal flowers, the entwined Baccarat crystal hearts. The latter had been wedding gifts, the kind that make you wince once you are deep into the marriage.

Charles comes in from making early rounds at the hospital, an unannounced gesture on our moving day.

"Charles, you missed what happened."

"I heard. I saw the other movers in front of the building. They're hanging around, waiting for the art movers to finish."

"You heard. *That's it?* Charles . . . it's shattered . . . ruined. . . ."

"I'm sorry, Lainie. I find it very disturbing." Charles is using his best "doctor delivers the news" voice. "Maybe, Lainie, the nature of the piece, the pounds of driftwood and the ornate frame . . ."

I don't respond. Charles takes his iPhone out of his pocket.

"Lainie, we have to go." A foot on my soul. Has he forgotten that he bought my painting another life ago? How he had to have it, had to have me?

"I can't leave, not quite yet, Charles."

I pat at the wall where the art was hanging. There is the bottom rim that has formed, about a foot wide, where the frame was. How hollow the room is without it. I move to the mantel and hold it so tightly that my fingers turn white. When I let go my life as I know it will be over and unredeemable. I should never have agreed to leave the city, to move to Elliot. What a grave error. A knowledge fills my being, a kind of slow drowning. Charles could have commuted instead of uprooting our entire family.

"Lainie?" I hold on more tightly. My fingers are peeled off the mantel and Charles's hand is on my arm. Not strong, only forceful. Not a guiding hand, just a male hand. Still I agree to go to the country, a pseudo-suburb, a place filled with greenery and ersatz lakes and fish ponds. A town that is rife with women who opt out of the workplace and are left to their own devices. I might succumb to life in an antiseptic hamlet if I paint my way to freedom while adoring my four children. Although my only hope is in making this gesture, I am abandoning my own skin.

THREE

After I slam down the trunk door of our Grand Cherokee in the sultry August heat, I weave down Columbus Avenue toward the Lincoln Tunnel. I stare longingly at every storefront instead of concentrating on the road. The city is being crushed behind me. I'm leaving my entire life without a compass for where I'm going or a guarantee that I can ever get back. My devastated *Trespassing: Driftwood* is a sign—a warning. No wonder I don't consider my marriage en route to a glistening town across the river to begin what Charles calls our new chapter.

Candy, bow in hand, is playing "It's Your Love" on her fiddle while I hand out gummy bears and small lemonade cartons. Each child settles in with an electronic babysitter—my iPad, a DVD, Tom's smartphone—in order to get through the hour-long trip. Matilde is in the front passenger seat. I resist talking to her about how the future is obscure, how regret is an awful emotion. We're too crammed in for it, the four children and Candy, who is squeezed into that third seat, which faces backward.

"Jesus, Lainie, I might be a martyr, but you're taking it too far," Candy says. "My legs are going numb."

"Candy, I'm sorry. . . . It's been quite an ordeal, in case you didn't notice."

"I noticed all right," she sighs. "Like there's nothing ahead for you. Or for me."

I should say, *Let's not talk about it in the car;* instead I agree. "Right. Like everything has been taken away from us."

"I'll say, Lainie," Candy agrees. "I can't imagine how it's going to be."

"Mom, if you pull over, I'll switch with Candy," Matilde offers.

I decide. "Let's keep going since the traffic isn't heavy."

"Yup, we're avoiding traffic on the way to nirvana," Candy says.

Candy twists her head around. Her eyes meet mine in the rearview mirror.

"Let's not be negative, Candy."

"Oh, sure, Lainie. Whatever you say."

The rain starts, first a drizzle and then a downpour. The proof that the city dwellers are at the Shore is how I hurtle through the tunnel. Although I'm only going sixty-five, it feels like I'm speeding. The Jeep bumps along, the GPS guides us through the labyrinth of highways, the New Jersey Turnpike to I-78 West until finally we are on I-287 and near Elliot, "a grass-laden jewel of a town," according to Charles. The rain becomes a deluge as we turn onto our street. "Maybe the rain counts as a car wash," I say as we pull up under the portico. Then we face the house. "A Colonial, children. We'll see how we like it; it's a rental." None of my children speaks.

As I start looking around for what might keep me from falling apart and weeping, I notice Charles walking down the garden path. How has he arrived ahead of us—was there a better, quicker road to Elliot, one that only true believers know about? I'm relieved that he's here to do what I won't and can't do—boss the movers around and get serious about how the furniture should be arranged. That's when he announces he has to get back to the city for one last day.

"Why bother to come, Charles?" I ask. Tom and Matilde wait for the answer too, knowing it has to be a good one.

"For you, Lainie. I mean, you were so unnerved about your work collapsing. I thought I'd come for moral support, if only for a few minutes."

"Do you remember, Charles, when we first bought our apartment? You said that you'd oversee the hanging of *Trespassing*. And you did, and it stayed intact. . . . We only had two small children then and were only moving from downtown to uptown . . . not as dramatic as today. . . . It was gallant of you. . . ."

Charles is kicking at the dead shrubs and looking away. I'm not sure what he sees beyond except more shrubs, a slightly overgrown garden, and a property line. I know that he will tell me in a matter of minutes that it needs to be pruned since the last tenants paid no attention, particularly around the sides of the house.

"Dad, everywhere is so . . . grassy," Matilde says.

"Yes, Matilde, plenty of grass. With plenty of charm. Give it a chance. Your mother is planning to, right, Lainie?" Charles is moving in my direction as he speaks.

We ignore our children for the briefest moment. Charles gathers me into his arms and lifts me to the front door. Claire starts clapping. "Pick me up next, Daddy, pick me up!"

Charles's mouth is on my ear. I'd like to wipe out the day and the place except for an exquisite piece of time with him.

"Lainie, do you have the key handy?"

The carrying continues. I laugh and he kisses me. The rain has stopped and the sun is shining. For a second we're in some black-and-white movie that Charles loves and I've never seen. Charles puts me back on the ground and takes a few steps toward the children. He hugs each of them quickly and moves in liquid motion toward his BMW. He disappears quickly, the mirage of Charles—husband, father, surgeon—is gone. I start fumbling for the key in my purse, which is a patent-leather bucket. Charles once announced there was an animal who died in my bag from food poisoning. He said that the amount of old Polly-O string cheese and opened bags of peanuts in the lining could kill our enemies.

We stand outside looking in and then I turn the key in the lock. Surreal how it seems that I've done it a thousand times before—that we live here.

"At last!" My voice sounds metallic. I open the door and we face a gigantic box, with trees and earth around it. No doormen, no elevator, a vast open space that's ours to fill.

"Where are the movers, Lainie?" Candy asks. "You know, the regular movers . . . Furniture, flat-screens . . ."

"I don't know. The whole day is confusing," I say.

"They're jerks, those movers," Tom says. One never knows whose side he's on.

"You're doing well, Mom," Matilde says. She turns to Tom. "Elliot is very far away from water for her."

Tom rolls his eyes. Then Jack runs through the empty front hallway in his sneakers and makes an echo.

"Tom?" I say. "Could you please go after Jack?"

Tom runs into the house and disappears, shouting, "Jack? Jack, come back."

Candy picks up her bow and starts playing "Fisherman's Blues" and sings.

"Candy! Please!" I say.

She stops. "Matilde? Are you ready? You're next. Kind of like the haunted house at the rides down the Shore. C'mon."

Matilde shakes her head and remains outside the door.

"All right then, I'll leave this open slightly." Candy clicks the dead bolt and the heavy glossy wood door is left ajar as she walks into the unknown.

Matilde sits down next to Claire on the brick steps.

The rain starts again, a late summer rain, more stickiness. Sometimes I believe that Matilde would like to scream, *Shut up,* but that has never happened. Claire begins to cry, holding a small sketchbook that I've made for her. She opens it up to the last page.

"Who is that man? Who is that lady?" She begins to wind her "blankie" around her right thumb.

"Claire," Matilde says patiently. "You and your stinky blankie. Maybe in Elliot you can start fresh, put away your blankie on a shelf. . . ."

"Won't." Claire sucks harder on her blankie and looks at more sketches. She finds one with the ocean at sunset. Then she flips the page back to a portrait in charcoal, a portrait of a couple.

"Who is this, Matilde?" she asks.

"Let's see, Claire. Hold it up so I can see." Claire pushes the sketchbook to Matilde.

"Claire, that's Mommy and Daddy in front of the new house. Our house. Mommy drew it for you and Jack last night, remember?"

Claire traces her right forefinger along the lines of the rendering, over and over in a circle. Then she falls asleep on the doorstep.

CRACK

The first day at the house that we rented without understanding anything about living outside the city, I pay attention to the art movers, who are carrying what's left of my precious work of art into the basement. The other movers are being bossed around by Candy or left on their own. I care little about the rest of the belongings—clothes, coats, books, coffee cups.

"Please be careful, Derrick, please make sure nothing more happens. Please beware the boxes. The parts of the frame that you wrapped—can those please be brought to the living room?" I almost beg.

Candy and Matilde are in charge of the twins, who are sitting on the floor eating Twinkies—my concession for the afternoon.

"Matilde, please begin with the book boxes in the family room," I say.

Matilde begins unpacking, almost an automaton.

"Candy? The plasma televisions? Can we get them up and running?" I ask.

Candy keeps playing any song that comes into her head, including "#41" by Dave Matthews. The youngest, cutest mover holds up the plasma on the wall to the right.

"I dig the music," he says.

"Candy?" I say with my eye on Derrick and another box of shards from *Trespassing: Driftwood.*

Candy shakes her head, her eyes on the youngest, cutest mover. "Not there."

"Here?" he asks. His muscles ripple.

"No, not there," Candy says.

"How about 'Two Steppin' Mind'?" he asks, still holding the television in his arms.

"Over there. The couch will be on this side." Candy points. She takes her bow and strikes a chord for him.

The twins are exhausted to the point that they've become limp. Derrick appears again, back from the basement.

"Derrick? Maybe it's safest if we place the crates together downstairs?" My request is strident to my own ears.

Tom, who is supposed to be in the garage going through boxes, comes into the family room.

"Tom, I thought you were busy. Do you need something?"

Matilde gives me a quizzical look and it triggers a wave of guilt. I remember that we are in the country.

"Children, go outside," I decide. "The sun has come out. All of you. And play . . . catch. I'll need Candy to help with Derrick and the boxes. We're deciding where the best place in the basement is to keep the parts."

No one moves. "Matilde?" I say. I point to the windows and the vista of flower beds and berms. "There's a swing set and sliding board—like the playgrounds." I point to the right edge of the property.

"Who is going with us?" Matilde asks.

"We're not in Central Park," explains Candy. She's standing with an armful of children's books and two torn-up Barbies. "You don't need me or your mother."

"I'll stay inside and help you with the broken painting, Mom," says Matilde.

"You know, there's a rose bed in the back yard," I say.

"Yes. Yes, it is beautiful in late summer with the lawn and the terrace. A little like an English garden," Candy says. Then she starts playing "Greensleeves," the song that Henry VIII wrote for Anne Boleyn. Or might have written for Anne Boleyn. It is my favorite "old song," one that I sing when Candy plays it. We are not a singing duo today.

"Children in the suburbs run around the backyard," I say, wondering if Charles failed to emphasize such an advantage.

Derrick comes into the family room and Candy stops playing.

"Mrs. Morris? We've put the boxes of your broken picture where you asked. Want to come check and make sure it's okay?"

I wave my hands at the children. "Go. Go ahead. Matilde? Tom?"

"Thank you so much, Derrick. I'm following you." I move quickly out of the room with him, ready to focus. Although I don't look back, I sense Matilde's eyes on me as she leads the twins to the swing set.

⚬⚭⚬

At twilight the doorbell rings. We're shocked, too accustomed to apartment living to know how to react or what to do without a doorman to intercept. Tom and Jack race to the front door.

"Don't open it, boys, wait." Candy is on their heels. Matilde and I stay in the kitchen with Claire.

"Mom," says Matilde, "really, Claire is eating too many gummy bears. After the Twinkies."

"I know, Matilde. Only a few more."

The door opens and we hear Candy. "Dr. Chuck! You're home early!"

Charles detests it when Candy calls him that and she does it whenever she can. Charles comes into the kitchen with Tom, Jack, and Candy behind him.

"What's for dinner, Lainie?" he asks.

"Oh, hello, Charles." I do not look up from the counter where I'm still unpacking. "I don't know what's for dinner. I mean, there's no pub or French bistro around the corner."

"Family dinner! Family dinner!" Jack shouts out. A prize event in the city where parents are delineated by those who do family dinners and those who are always out at that hour. I prefer family dinners to any evening event, the idea of twenty-five uninterrupted minutes of collective civility. There are rules: no name calling, no reading at the table, including iPads, iPhones, and actual books, and no food throwing. Toward the end of the meal when at least one child is nearing a meltdown, we play charades in teams, miming and hamming it up for the "guessers." I doubt the game will last much longer since Tom has conveyed how boring and out of style it is. Either way, by the end of these dinners, despite how I believe in them, I'm usually there in body only, dreaming of watercolors or oils, of frames consisting of sand glued on wood.

"Dinner?" Charles asks, checking out the scene. The twins have scattered jigsaw puzzle pieces and LEGOs everywhere. Tom ordered the first *Harry Potter* movie on Netflix and is blaring it although no one is interested. The regular movers have signed off, having shoveled boxes into every room as well as the entryway and garage.

"Dinner. Sure, Dr. Chuck, nothing special about today," Candy says. "All good around here." She's got an armload of pots and pans and is looking for the best storage place. She bends down at the cabinet under the stovetop.

"Maybe we should order a few pizzas," Charles suggests.

"That's a nice thought, Charles." I'm wondering what he's missing about how exhausted we are. Or the possibility that we've already thought of it.

Candy moves to the island where her iPad rests and taps on the screen. "We live in the Monroe section of Elliot. No one delivers."

"Charles? Why don't you go into town with the children, Candy can go too, and eat at the pizza place. I'll stay at the house. . . . I'll keep unpacking."

"Too dark, the streets are very dark by now," Charles answers.

"Dr. Chuck, you're the one who wanted to move to the country!" Candy says. "Didn't you know there are no streetlights here?" She starts making up a song. *"Pizza! Pizza! Pizza!"* she sings.

Charles starts rummaging around the cupboards. "Where's the gin?"

"We didn't find it yet," I say. "I don't know where it is. . . ."

Was it only this morning that Charles carried me to the front door and swept me away? When Charles slides into a mood I remember that my grandmother used to tell me that we are born alone and die alone, although no one ever wants to be alone. She advised me to marry the right man, a man who would be my friend, first and foremost.

Charles traipses toward the back entrance and then turns to us. "Are the boxes marked in the garage? The boxes for the wet bar?"

"Dad, what about the pizza?" Tom freezes *Harry Potter.*

"Ask Mom." He disappears into the garage, slamming the door behind him. A half hour later Charles pulls my Jeep to the front of the house. I watch from the window as my children and Candy pile in to go into town for dinner. Charles shines the light from his iPhone app as they buckle up, illuminating each of their faces. Then they are progressing, my family, whom the move has rendered unrecognizable. I am alone in the empty house, as desolate as I've ever been. Derrick has neglected to place the last box of shells and shards from my broken work with the others. I open it, overcome with grief.

PART TWO

Jess

FOUR

Just my luck, a newbie at the front desk and Stacy is taking her own sweet time registering her. Why this transaction, which is more the Stacy Power Show than anything else, has to affect me is beyond my belief.

"Is it possible to get a locker and to leave my things here?" the newbie asks, holding a gym bag that appears dreadfully dense—possibly loaded down with a blow dryer, soap—filched from five-star hotel bathrooms—John Frieda shampoo, and two accompanying conditioners, Nivea—the extra-rich version—and La Mer for her face. A brew of immaculate and high maintenance. She shifts her weight and the gym bag thuds to the floor. Beyond the desk, by the snack bar, sits a bevy of young mothers who have purposely arrived early for their toddlers' ten o'clock swim class. They chat it up—the complexity of motherhood is riveting and perhaps unique to them.

I turn back to the raven-haired woman and her narrow body, the profile people always thought was the result of a plastic surgeon. Without having this glimpse or having heard her voice, I'd know her anywhere. The high pitch, the slightly pleasing tone, the confidence. *Lainie.* A wave of nausea ripples through me. There she is, standing in front of me, and as usual, doesn't notice that I'm here. What the hell is she doing in Elliot? For twelve years I've built it into my turf. My husband is a big man in town, my soirees are the coveted invitation. Lainie the righteous, Lainie the beautiful, whose mere actuality trumps the rest of us.

"No, not right now." Stacy, with her downturned mouth and weak chin, is and always will be behind the desk. Her eyes fall upon Lainie and her bulky gym bag. "I can put you on the waiting list for a permanent locker."

"Thank you."

Stacy will do nothing of the sort. Who acclimates to such abuse but the locals? No surprise that transplanted New Yorkers fall into a quick and deep depression when they relocate. Voilà, the latest of the batch. Lainie. The one who constantly wins while feigning she isn't in the game. I would leave immediately and get my swim in at noon if I could work it into my day. Besides, why should I move aside for her—those days are long gone. I watch anyway, mesmerized as Lainie is handed a small key while Stacy files her check away in the drawer and gives her a membership card, handwritten, not computerized.

I flash my own card and walk on Lainie's heels into the locker room, which has the aroma of clean soap and Lysol. An unfriendly locker room that is more sterile than the one she left behind in the city. How I know without exchanging a word, let alone a glance, is easy. When you're married to William and ensconced in Elliot, you've seen everything. New York women expecting the same level of women as the Y buddies they left behind. That would be the camaraderie of women, young, middle-aged, old, rich, and poor, those who complain constantly, others who give unsolicited advice on any topic. It comes back to me, that kind of mix that is not possible in Elliot, the crème de la crème capital of New Jersey. Lainie takes small key to locker 74 and begins to strip out of her black Theory pants, white button-down shirt, and jean jacket into a Speedo swimsuit.

Who wouldn't be thrilled with the Elliot Women's Y Olympic-size pool, painted a cool aqua and filled to the edges? Who wouldn't overlook how the water splashes onto the tiles when the aggressive swim-mers are there and the humidity causes your goggles to clog up for the thrill of the swim? Most newbies sneeze from the up-to-the-minute chemicals. Lainie plunks herself down at the end of the fast lane and sits at the side of the pool, tucking her heavy hair into her latex cap and spitting into her goggles. Odd how she hasn't so much as glanced in my direction. Is she kidding?

I've seen more aggressive butterflies, although none more fluid or stoic. I know the feeling—this respite is how to endure the rest of the day. She's at one with the water. Her buoyancy is enviable; then again, it has always been true. Whatever Lainie did was enviable. Lainie Smith Morris, who went from cause celebre to cosmic dust in less than two years. I wasn't sorry when it happened, right after college. While her work may no longer be the "visceral, evocative collage-scapes of the sea" of the early reviews, she's not hidden from sight. She travels in a tamer circle of miniatures and quiet paintings. All that raw ambition and then a bait and switch. Wouldn't it have been better to have fallen off the face of the earth? Then again, Lainie never disappears. The proof of that is at the pool.

She has no idea that I've wondered about her these years—followed her without reaching out, a perverse curiosity that would not result in a "friending." Why friend someone who has always gotten what she wants? Specifically when I was on the sidelines, the antiwinner. That gnawing sensation begins again, plucked from the recesses of my mind. I remember vividly that Lainie is preferred, that whatever she wants she gets. She was known to catch the lifeguard's eye at the Shore or the best guy of the summer. I have not forgotten her victories nor have I forgotten her parents' beach house, how every-one filed through there barefoot in wifebeaters. The boys drooling for Lainie, the rumors that she invoked, how every teenage girl had to be her friend. How her popularity was random, almost shocking to her, not hard-earned and challenging to keep up. Lainie situated at the top of the heap. I'll need a good look at her skin to check out her crow's-feet—perhaps she's gone scot-free.

Then I realize that today is different. Today she is the outsider and I understand what that entails better than she does. I know what she has yet to learn about Elliot, that the supposed payoff is the house, emblematic of one's success in the world. With the house comes the accoutrements of success—educated, attractive wives who burn their brain cells arranging playdates, tuning up their SUVs, bossing around their full-time household staff and a gardener or two.

Did I not hear her tell Stacy that she lives on Longview Way? Has she stormed into town and planted herself in the Monroe section of Elliot without so much as a few years in a more modest area—the price the rest of us have paid? No, Lainie arrives, catapulting herself among the social elite, five-acre-minimum neck of the woods, slam dunk. Yet I know the house that she's in, and it's a rental. The owners practically abandoned their home when the husband was relocated last minute. Not that Lainie would pay much attention. After our long separation, I doubt that Lainie's take on the glittering prizes has altered, that Lainie in her own quiet way views it as where she is supposed to live. I can't imagine how she'll acclimate to time spent with women who mention their horses and houses, their pit bulls and Dobermans before their children, when immersed in deep conversation at the Ivy, the restaurant on our main street.

In the fast lane Lainie remains the connoisseur of water. She passes me at least ten times—the only other butterfly swimmer—without so much as a bit of interest. I jump out of the pool, check out the crowd's whereabouts since a good shower is hard to come by. I beat her to the locker room, minor victory that it is.

Most of the women congregate at the open showers—I wait for a private stall, but the large clock on the wall reads 9:45. Obviously Lainie is also feeling too fraught time-wise to concern herself with privacy. She peels off her bathing suit and soaps up in the very public middle shower on the left. The women of assorted ages and shapes, vigorously scrubbing themselves while chatting about recipes, children, dinner plans, and the weather take notice of a stranger to town who doubles as an exhibitionist. That's before she starts her Academy Award–winning demure. Time to make myself known.

"Lainie? Lainie, is that you?" I shout in her direction from the opposite end.

I turn the spigot.

"Jess, is that you? I can't believe it!" Lainie is astonished. "Do you live here?! What luck! I never imagined I'd find someone I know. But to find you again, Jess! We just moved in. We are in the midst of unpacking. . . ." She smiles. "A crazy time . . ."

Is it her emphasis on "moved in" and "unpacking" that gets to me and causes the past to bite me in the ass? She shuts her eyes and water pours over her face and body. I squeeze out my hair, which feels suddenly inadequate in its blondness and wispiness. Lainie's hair always weighed ten pounds. She races across the shower path with too much ardor, standing unclothed, lanky and smooth, dripping wet. Clearly she drinks some kind of Pollyanna Kool-Aid, not much different than back in the day. Without exchanging a word, I know that Lainie will welcome memories of our shared summers at the Jersey Shore and one year together at RISD before I transferred out. Not everyone has Lainie's talent and her Zen attitude. I admit over the years she's been infuriating. That's why I feel like shaking her by her shoulders and shouting, *What makes you so special?* I bring it down a notch, in the spirit of "there is nothing like an old friend."

"Aren't you a brave soul," I say. *Oh, la-di-da.* I wrap my towel around my head, but I do not cover my body. I do a puffed-up march toward the dressing area.

I note with satisfaction that her locker is in the last row, the one saved for newcomers and paltry visitors. It will take her weeks to realize that mine is in the desirable part of the locker room. I dress quickly and saunter by in jeans and a leather jacket.

"I'm in such a rush to pick up my daughter," I say. A sincere sentence, not calculated or untruthful.

Lainie's eyes light up at the mention of my daughter and I hate myself for giving her the opportunity to gush. "Oh, Jess, how nice! How many children do you have?"

"Two," I say. "A girl and a boy."

"How old are they?"

"Nine and eleven," I reply. I would offer up more details but I'm late.

"What are their names and where do they go to school?" She's interested but it's a turnoff. Damn, I'm rude.

"Another time, Lainie. You know how it is. . . ."

"Well, I'd love to get together. I don't know a soul in Elliot. I thought you lived in Princeton. I guess I wasn't up to speed. . . . I should have done an Internet search. . . ."

"You mean Facebook?" I ask.

"I suppose. What has happened these last ten—no, fifteen years for you?"

"A saga," I say. "Except I have to go."

I could explain quickly as I search for my car keys that we moved to Elliot because William, my husband, had a hard-on for the suburbs and for stately towns. William thought that running a hospital here would be pleasant enough, believing there isn't the kind of stress in Elliot that seems to shorten one's life expectancy. Not to say that life isn't taxing around here or that being the quintessential Stepford wife isn't limiting. Still, there are plenty of opportunities in Elliot. The Elliot Junior League could stand some new members. Especially a woman from the city, I'm sure. She could volunteer as class mother for each child, although that might push one to open a vein. Only yesterday I had to say to William why I won't be a class mother for both children; I relinquish that honor to someone who truly wants it, it's only fair.

I say none of the above and she looks discouraged anyway. She'll be worse when she witnesses how unfriendly everyone is, how insular and full of themselves. How they are full of shit.

"Call me, Jess, and we'll catch up, have coffee."

There is no pity party for Lainie. *Lainie, the heartthrob, Lainie, the genius artist in college, Lainie, the innocent, Lainie, the one and only.*

Nonetheless I do take her card when she hands it to me.

"That's my cell. Obviously I no longer live in the city." Again the damn smile.

I begin rooting around for a card and come up empty-handed. That's what happens when you let yourself go, when the idea of your son's soccer match outshines your own ability to work so much as part-time. Losing oneself in Elliot is inevitable. I will be kind, I will not mention how the days get frittered away.

"You'll reach out? My info is there."

I look at her eyes once more. "We'll get something on the calendar," I reassure her, although we both know how slippery I can be. Or has she forgotten—a case of selective memory—how she had the boyfriend I had to have, the friends I had to have, the body and face I had to have. Yet she never had the hair or the coloring. Even today it remains a plus to be a frizz-free blonde with blunt ends and sporting a tan. Who would want that pale skin and mass of tangled dark hair around her face? No matter that on Lainie it's exquisite.

In a millisecond I'm gone, dragging my towel and bathing suit in a canvas bag that reads GO HERONS for the local girls' basketball team. I move fast through the swinging doors that lead to the lobby.

FIVE

On Saturday morning, not two days later, I find myself in a line of vehicles on the long private drive to the Crawford estate. As I glance in my rearview mirror I realize that Lainie Morris, in a worn, nasty Jeep, is directly behind me.

We're several miles beyond town for a swim party. Both of us are with our sons; Billy is invited as the best friend of the youngest of the Crawford boys and Lainie's son must be in ninth grade and one of the guests. I wonder if Lainie understands that the mothers are expected to mingle for the first half hour.

Lainie catches up to me in the center of the wide circular driveway where we are idling, abreast of each other.

"Never mind, we're here now, Tom," I hear her say to her son. "Let's go." They open the doors to the Jeep when the butler comes running toward them, waving his hands.

"Miss." The butler points to Lainie. "You'll have to park behind the guesthouse. You aren't allowed to leave a car in front. Not that vehicle. The nannies are dropping off, only the mothers are staying and allowed to park."

"Excuse me? I'm with my son. Aren't we at the drop-off area?" Lainie's voice sounds strained, tight.

"Mom! Mom! Stop being embarrassing," her son is muttering. She motions for him to walk with her and they troop up the stone steps together, disregarding the butler.

There is movement behind us as other mothers pull up with their sons to the front door. I quickly relinquish my Mercedes sedan to the valet and watch as sedans and SUVs are whisked away. The mothers congregate outside the grand front door to greet one another while waiting to step inside. To Lainie they might appear clannish, although I welcome a social morning. What is the point of Elliot if not for these get-togethers? Billy runs ahead and I mark time alongside the mothers who stand at the entrance.

In a surge we move into the anteroom with a throng of mothers and a few straggler sons who haven't yet gone to the pool. Lainie is behind me, I notice, and I'm torn. Should I be inclusive, welcoming, or should I gravitate toward the center of the crowd and make the most of the hour without the burden of Lainie and her strange ways? Her outfit alone is enough to disgrace me.

That is when my friend Tia, who is walking ahead of me, turns to Audrey, another mother, and says, "Who is that woman, dressing as if she's in SoHo? The wrong address in SoHo?"

"Well, I don't know," says Audrey, taking her in. "It's refreshing." She marches up to Lainie, and I stand to the side.

"Excuse me," says Audrey. "What cute boots. I've never seen anything quite like them in mid-August. Although seventy-five degrees does remind one of how imminent autumn is."

Lainie smiles doubtfully at Audrey. They are incongruous together, Lainie in her garb and Audrey in her purposely understated sheath and sandals, a cardigan casually draped over her shoulders.

"Please come in," Tia says. "I'm sure that Christie will want to meet you."

"Christie?" Lainie asks.

"Christie Crawford. You know, the host." Tia leads Lainie into the center of the anteroom. Lainie stiffens and I remember that she could become awkward in a millisecond, ungainly rather than graceful.

I'm about to make myself known to Lainie and to be sympathetic when a glint of activity catches my eye. Christie's two golden retrievers are charging her, separating her from the surge of guests. The dogs start pulling at her clothes, chewing at the beaded hem of her Indian-print skirt and the fringe of her purse. They drool on her booties, yapping at her.

"Help! Somebody, please . . ." No one so much as faces her direction. "Someone, please?"

I watch, frozen, as the first retriever puts his entire mouth around her ankle, his slobbering tongue slipping inside her bootie.

"Please, I'm being attacked. . . ."

I watch with a perverse fascination as the dog gnaws at the suede and at her flesh at the same time.

"Lainie," I say. "Move back."

"Jess! Please . . . do something."

Christie Crawford comes after the dogs, putting a hand on each of their collars. "There, there," she coos. "Down boys. Down!" Christie proffers Lainie an indiscernible smile. "Maybe they like you."

The dogs withdraw as if the incident never happened. Neither of the retrievers so much as pants or lolls his tongue. Both sit at their mistress's feet. She is patting their heads.

"Christie, you saved the day," I say. I hope that Lainie appreciates my going out on a limb for her.

"Yes, thank you so much," Lainie says. She holds out her hand to Christie, the dog lover. The gracefulness returns—she is ethereal.

"My dogs are being friendly. . . . Your booties seem a shoe toy. That's all. . . ." She leads them away with dog biscuits up her sleeve and they become docile, their tails wagging as they follow her. Her entourage is behind her and the place thins out. I'm the last of the women to leave when Lainie's son appears, gorgeous boy that he is. He stands against the wall, almost in tears.

"Mom!" he says. "What are you doing?"

Lainie walks over and speaks softly, as if to set an example. "Tom? You should go back to the party."

"The party? I'll never be invited anywhere ever again, Mom!"

"You saw what just happened, Tom? I've just been attacked by the host's dogs."

"My life is over," Tom says. "I'll have no friends at school. Thanks to you."

He clutches his SwissGear backpack as he disappears into the fray.

SIX

Lainie texts me the morning after the machinations at the Crawford estate, to see if I'll be at the pool. *Sure,* I text her, *9:30.* I'm right on time when I observe her from across the lobby. She's firmly situated at the snack bar with her twins and older daughter, a clone of Lainie's for certain, a reminder of our childhood, as if I'm looking backward.

I'm a pro, and since it takes one to know one, the way that she is fortifying her younger children with Luna Bars (is there a child around who eats them?), books, and iPads is familiar. She's frantic to be in the pool and hardly able to pay attention to them in her quest to be underwater. That's why those twins are bickering loudly—it's their chance to show Lainie that they exist.

I come over. "Hi, Lainie. Hello, children."

"Jess!" She's utterly enthused. "I'm almost ready."

"She kicked me," the little boy says. "Mommy! Claire kicked me!"

"Can you tell me your name?" I say to him.

He scowls.

"Jack?" says the Lainie-carbon-copy daughter. "Can you tell the lady your name?"

I extend my hand. "Let me introduce myself. I'm an old friend of your mother's; she and I go back decades. I'm Jess Howard."

The daughter shakes my hand as if she's had a few lessons, not too firm but no pushover. "Hi. I'm Matilde."

"Matilde. Lovely." I smile at her and then at the younger twin sister. "I know that you are Claire because I just heard your brother shouting your name."

Lainie is riffling through her gym bag, the one with endless creams and hair products. She takes out two lollipops—the freebies from the bank, which should be banned in America.

"Here, Matilde, please distribute these."

Matilde dutifully hands one to Claire and one to Jack. Jack looks at it and promptly drops it on the floor. Claire begins to rip at the plastic wrapper and Matilde intervenes. Claire misses her mouth and slides it against her cheek. She starts to laugh and Jack laughs too.

"Jess and I are about ready for the pool, Matilde," Lainie says. "Why don't you take your sister and brother to the little snack bar and get them something nourishing. They must be hungry." She reaches into her pocketbook and hands Matilde a small packet of nifty wet wipes and a credit card.

Instinctively I know that Matilde finesses breakfast better than her mother and if there is no brown sugar in the house, it would not be the daughter's fault.

"Well, shall we?" Lainie motions for us to follow her toward the pool desk.

Matilde leads the twins and Jack begins to do a jig, then Claire does the same. Lainie ignores them while Matilde is keenly concerned that there are too many people noticing them, including other children. One of the twins drops her mother's iPhone on the floor.

"Stop, please," Matilde whispers to Claire. "A few kids from my class have come in. They're by the food with their little brothers and sisters. Their mothers are about to swim laps. Or yoga. Please?"

A line has formed at the snack bar despite the fact that what they serve is inedible. Have I not force-fed my children their grainy egg salad, tuna fish with coagulated mayo, and packaged chocolate chip cookies? Standing there are a boy and a girl who are most likely Matilde's classmates. *The girl.* I know it immediately, a blond, curvy number whose hair swings when she walks. Matilde must want to disappear, must be praying that they don't notice her. Circumstances would be different had she washed or at least brushed her hair today. Moreover, she is wearing what looks like her older brother's sweatpants. Lainie owes her daughter a few lessons in public appearance.

"Where is that charming son of yours?" I ask Lainie as we close our lockers.

"He's at a father/son Rotary breakfast in town. They're doing it to meet people. My husband isn't a member, but he could join."

"Matilde doesn't mind being here? I would imagine that some of the girls from her class will be at the football field in about an hour."

"Oh, she doesn't mind, Jess."

"Well, she needs to be with the girls in order to have friends, Lainie."

"Sure, sure. My nanny left last night for the city until tomorrow. Without a swim I'm useless—I can't think. Matilde is missing Sunday school for this. So are the twins. Once I'm finished, the day will be Matilde's."

"Why didn't you drop them off first, Lainie?"

"I tried. The twins wouldn't leave Matilde to go into the class. Besides, if Tom can miss it, why can't the others?"

It is too early in the game to explain that it doesn't work in a pristine town, a holier-than-thou suburb, to make your own rules. Should she care to know, my children were both dropped at Sunday school on my way here.

"Let's swim," I say.

While I collect my paraphernalia from the side bins—flippers, weights, a kickboard—Lainie jumps in. She's careening through the water, outswimming the swimmers in the fast lane in a dizzying swim to tomorrow.

I pause at the side of the pool to observe as Claire and Jack run down to the bottom of the bleachers with Matilde at their heels. She plies them with cookies and they become surprisingly docile. Then the lifeguard walks toward her. He is pure machismo—total crush material, although I doubt he ever finished high school. When he smiles at her it is evident that he hasn't had proper dental care.

"Who ya waitin' for?" he asks Matilde.

"My mom." Matilde points to Lainie, who is flipping around like a dolphin. Her muscles ripple more than the water does.

"Wow. Do you swim that fast?"

"Me? No, no. Almost like that."

He smiles with his crooked teeth and points to a wide chart against the long wall. "Well, maybe she's swimming the Raritan River."

"What?" Matilde squints to read the chart. "What is it?"

"For swimmers to get to the other end of the Raritan River. Maybe she's part of it, one of the ones swimming the river."

"I don't know," Matilde says. "She didn't tell me and she usually tells me stuff like that."

"What's your mom's name?" He's holding a black-and-white grainy notebook from the year one, the kind that would date me if I dared to bring it out in public. This one is marked "YWCA" in pink Magic Marker on the front.

"Lainie Morris. Lainie Smith Morris."

He thumbs through the pages. "Yup," says the lifeguard. "She's in it and . . . hmmm . . . since she started she's swum farther than anyone else. Anyone. Farther than the men who are in the competition." He closes the notebook.

"Yeah, that's about right. She'll probably win," Matilde says.

"The last two years the men swimmers won. The winner and runner-up."

Matilde watches Lainie's crazed swimming, then she taps Claire and Jack, who look slobbery, even from a distance. "We have to go. We'll go back to the snack bar and wait. Mom will be finished soon."

"Soon?" Claire asks. At the age of five this child knows that it isn't true. And signing on for the Raritan River swim makes the swim longer and more enthralling. I glance at Lainie and remember her tireless swims, her indefatigable devotion to water. I resist telling Matilde that it's another forty minutes at least. Matilde leads the twins to the wall and points to Lainie's name.

"Look, Claire and Jack, Mom has the most filled-in blocks to show how far she's gone. Thirty miles so far."

How could I have not known? Would I have not learned it sooner or later since little passes me by when it comes to the stratagem of Elliot life, including what happens at the Y?

Claire starts to cry. "I don't want her to swim away, Matilde!"

Matilde points to the map and speaks in a soothing, adult way, although she looks distraught herself. "Claire, look. The river is three hundred and thirty miles. Mom has a long while to go. See the parts that haven't been swum yet?"

"No, Matilde, she's swimming away!" Claire is too loud; everyone can hear her unless they are underwater. As Lainie's head is—Lainie, who is absolutely missing her own daughters' drama. I resist the urge to rush to Matilde and explain that many days will pass, months, a year, for Lainie to get to the red-flagged finish line. Instead I strap on my flippers and within seconds I'm also moving through the water.

SEVEN

With the unseasonably warm October weather, I stand on the front step of my gray stone and green-shuttered home, sneaking a cigarette. Lainie pulls up in her Jeep, and while nothing could be more unlike the beachy summers in Cape May that Lainie and I shared, she is blasting Bruce Springsteen's "Rosalita." As she claims her parking place in our driveway, she backs up and lurches forward, one of the worst parking jobs I've seen in ages. How could she possibly parallel park in the city? At the same time, she pumps up the volume and sings along, unaware that no one in Elliot drives with the windows down.

Tom is in the passenger seat looking bored out of his mind. Matilde is sitting in the back between Claire and Jack.

"Mom!" Tom says. "The song. Stop!" He switches it off.

"C'mon, everyone out of the car." Lainie turns off the engine and waves at me. She adjusts her rearview mirror and applies liner and lipstick so quickly it has to be uneven. I'm more conscious than usual of my glamour—had they wanted to cast a refined version of *The Real Housewives of New Jersey,* friends tell me I'd have been chosen.

There is the possibility that the Morris clan is on good behavior. Lainie has Claire and Jack dressed in twin outfits, the kind most people would save for Easter and family birthday dinners that include grandparents.

She turns to me. "Hello, Jess. How nice of you to invite us all tonight."

I give Lainie a hug and kiss and a lukewarm hug to each of her limp children.

Tom disarms me with a smile. "Hi, Jess. We meet again. Cool house. And guesthouse. I noticed your striped awnings. Dad loves those, right, Mom?"

I lead the way into the kitchen. My own children, Billy and Liza, are hovering beside me. I do the introductions as if I'm entertaining long-lost cousins from out of state. Lainie's blandness today in those tan jeggings and cream cardigan looks incomplete. I'm managing to move around the kitchen in my stilettos, a cream lace T-shirt, and the tightest jeans that I own. The message being that I'm not rushed, I'm stylish, a mother who balances her life skillfully. I put out the food that's been prepared by Therese, our cook, while our nanny, Norine, engages the twins with packets of Silly Putty.

Therese hops between the kitchen, where she shapes hamburgers, lines up the hot dogs, and slices the marinated chicken into breasts and thighs, and the gas grill on the back porch. Tom's and Jack's eyes light up at the blazing red coals.

"Mom?" says Matilde. "Is that carving board made of wood? We're not allowed to use wood carving boards and plastic bowls for raw meats. Right? Won't we catch some kind of bacteria?"

"Matilde, it's fine. Don't worry, darling girl." Lainie laughs a tinny laugh. "Jess, your outdoor table is wonderful . . . very wide and long. It would be perfect for our family. Whenever we sit down to eat we become a dinner party."

"Another perk of Elliot life—large spaces, large tables. Do you like the sloping hills, Lainie? How about you, Tom, what do you think?" I ask.

"Since I don't care about a water view, it's good. My mother and

Matilde like creeks and rivers . . . at least creeks and rivers . . . the sea . . ." Tom says.

"Mrs. Howard?" Therese calls from the porch.

I walk gingerly in my stilettos toward the screen door. "Yes?"

"Are we ready?" Therese asks. "If not I'll be transporting food the night long."

I'm about to remind her of what her job entails when Norine comes to her rescue, dragging the platters outside.

"That will do, Norine." I point to the side table. "Right there."

I do my best at charming drill sergeant, smiling as if I'm in an ad for Whitestrips, the two-hour application. "Everyone, sit down." I point to Lainie's children and then to my own.

"Lainie, you and I will sit at the head together—there's room. Claire is next." I snap my fingers. "Matilde, you're with Claire and then Jack is across. . . . Tom, I'm certain my children would appreciate your company. Perhaps you can squeeze in between Liza and Billy."

Liza is excited, she does a young-girl flirt look and Tom is ridiculously pleased.

"Perfect, Jess," says Lainie.

Tom, tonight's VIP, a singer in a band, my favorite of the Morris children, smiles at Billy as if he means it. Matilde, so Lainie-like it's frightening, asks where the bathroom is.

"Down the hall, dear," I say. "Do you want somebody to show you?"

Norine is on top of it. "Here, Matilde, follow me." She motions for her to follow. "Why don't you use Liza's bathroom instead of the guest bathroom?"

"Thanks, Norine. I'll be fine."

I watch as she moves toward the bedroom wing.

"Excuse me, Lainie," I say, and get up to go into the house. Lainie nods and begins to cut Jack's chicken.

Matilde is sneaking into my bathroom with the stealth and flare of a robber in a bank vault. I admire her instincts as she opens my side of the medicine cabinet in a bathroom larger than most master bedrooms. She's a pro as she sorts through the pills. Pills that I doubt her mother has, pills that I'm confident other mothers in the city have.

I sense that she has seen them before and that she is in search of Klonopin, the drug of choice. I'm about to make myself known when she pops two into her mouth and places a handful in the pocket of her jeans. She is ready to return to the dinner table, certain that no one has noticed. That's when I stop her, my right hand held up.

She is indignant and the blood drains from her face.

"Is that what you need, Matilde?" I ask. "A few pills to get you through the week?"

"Jess, I'm not—"

"Matilde, please. Don't insult me. Are things that bad?"

"No, I'm okay."

"What's in your pocket?" I hold out my hand.

Matilde forks over perhaps six pills, probably not all of her stash, yet I've made my point.

"No matter what you think, Matilde, I'm your friend." The way that Matilde looks at me, the word "friend" sticks in my throat.

PART THREE

Lainie

EIGHT

She's pretty, Mom, prettier than your friends in the city."

"What do you mean, Tom?" I'm speeding. The sooner I get home, the more time to be in my studio. "There are plenty of pretty women, pretty mothers, in New York."

"Right," Tom snorts. "The ones at those piers with your painter lady friends." He pronounces piers "peeeers." "Cher? Gillian? Isabelle? They're dogs compared to Jess."

"Tom, what are you talking about?"

"Jess! Jess is cool, Mom. Really cool, really pretty."

"She's not that nice," Matilde gurgles. "She wears tons of makeup, Tom. Did you see it caked on her face and neck?"

"Okay," Tom laughs. "Let's look up-close at the waterfront friends. Nice, huh? Those crevices and lines."

"Tom, I haven't heard you speak negatively about a mother before," I say.

"She's a mom, Tom, not only an old friend of Mom's," Matilde says.

"Duh, Matilde. She's a babe!"

"Tom! Stop it!" Matilde says.

The car curves through the streets of Elliot.

"Yeah, stop it." Tom gives Matilde the finger.

"I'm not going to finish your Spanish paper tonight," Matilde announces. "I heard you tell Jess that you speak Spanish fluently. That means you can do the paper yourself."

"You'll do it since it's easy to write a paper for *any* teacher in Elliot, Matilde, and you promised. I don't care what you write, but you owe me, Matilde," Tom says. "Just do it. Knock yourself out."

"Tom! Matilde! What are you talking about? Who is writing a paper for whom?"

"*El Guardian entre el Centeno, The Catcher in the Rye*. I thought I'd write about how Holden Caulfield is a dweeb who wants us to feel sorry for him. Tom wants another angle, maybe about the girls who Holden calls along the way." Matilde is slurring her words and I'm not sure why.

"It sounds interesting; both takes sound interesting. But why wouldn't you be writing your own paper, Tom?" That feeling washes over me—my children aren't like this, my life isn't about morality or being a referee. "Matilde has homework of her own, Tom," I say.

"Let's bring the whole story to Dad, see what he says. I guess he won't care that you write my paper, he'll care if it's late and I'm inconvenienced," Tom suggests. A petrifying thought, that Charles might condone the idea for Tom's sake.

"Tom? Why are you bringing Mom and Dad into it?" asks Matilde. "Dad will call it cheating—plagiarism. We shouldn't tell him."

Matilde and Tom fall silent and it occurs to me that they'll work it out on their own, without much consideration for our conversation. The worst part is that I'm relieved. I look in the rearview mirror, where I see Claire is asleep and the strip of candy buttons, another Jess present, has fallen on her chest.

"Matilde, please wake up Claire. If she sleeps in a car at night she won't fall asleep in her bed."

"Claire. Claire, wake up." Matilde is moving like a rag doll.

I look again in the rearview mirror. "Matilde, are you all right?"

"Matilde is fine," Tom says. "So Jess, she's your friend from the Shore, huh, Mom?"

"The Shore . . . college until she transferred . . . a long time ago." I pause. "You know, Jess's husband, William, is the CEO of Elliot Memorial. He's Dad's boss."

"Dad's boss? Dad has a boss? I thought Dad is the boss," Tom says.

"Dad is head of orthopedic surgery. Jess's husband runs the entire hospital."

We pull up at the house and I want to apologize for how hackneyed it must seem to the children after being at Jess's.

"Matilde, darling, let's start unbuckling the twins," I say.

Tom jumps out of the front seat and slams the front door. In an unusual moment, he opens the back door for Matilde. She almost falls out.

"Tom?" I say, trying to see Matilde's face in the dark. He is holding her up as if she's depleted and I wonder if we each ask too much of her.

"Leave her, Mom. It's okay. I've got the twins, don't worry."

NINE

⁂

"Shouldn't Matilde be with her friends?" Charles asks. He is ready to leave for the third Saturday morning in a row for an early round of golf.

"Maybe, Charles."

"No, seriously, Lainie, Matilde needs to be with the girls in her grade. Today is a Saturday, for chrissake!"

Perhaps he has forgotten—if he ever noticed—how Matilde spent her weekends in the city. From the age of five, she divided her time between painting and learning about artists, playing with Barbie at her friends' houses, and being a guest at manicure/pedicure birthday parties. As she grew older, she continued her balancing act. "She'll figure it out. Charles, she'll be fine," I say.

An hour later Matilde is on a stepstool, facing the unframed canvas, six by eight, that she and I are going to paint together, a brush in her hand. What I love most about the studio is that it faces to the north and the sun filters in during the day. I have two easels; one is new for Matilde and then my own.

"Mom. I called Grandma. She said she is proud that Dad is the 'chief.' She said that he is revered and that he changes people's lives."

"Ah, yes, she would say that. He's her son." I kick off my booties and put on a smock. "Matilde, people are in line for your father to do their surgeries." I find my flip-flops by the closet. "I don't have to call Grandma, do I?"

"I don't know, Mom," Matilde says. "She didn't ask about you."

"We'll take advantage of the quiet in the house," I suggest.

I look at the size and the breathtaking emptiness of the canvas. I haven't worked on such a scale for years. "Let's finish the ocean first, Matilde."

Matilde keeps on painting the jetty that she's started. We should talk about the hue of sunsets. Instead I reconsider what Charles said. "Matilde, wouldn't you prefer to be with girls from school today, wouldn't it be more fun?"

"No, I want to paint, Mom. We've never had a big space before. . . . We can put mothers and their children in our picture. Cape May families."

"Yeah. Mothers who are lucky enough to not get sentenced to life in Elliot." I sigh. "I don't know what I'd do without the studio to come back to . . . the retreat that it is for me . . . the only good thing about the house except for the space and the fact that there aren't cockroaches. Or water bugs. They only inhabit the city, where the fun is. . . ."

"Mom . . . please don't be . . . this way. . . ." Matilde stops working and is about to console me when I censor myself.

"You're right, Matilde, women at the shoreline—with their children. That's what we should have."

Candy and the twins come back from children's hour at the library by midafternoon, race up the stairs, and crash into the quiet. Within a matter of seconds, my studio feels crowded and the questions are fired at me.

"Where's Daddy?" Jack asks. "Where's Tom?" His hands are grubby and I don't want him to graze anything in the room.

"Golf," Matilde answers. She's preoccupied with the angle of the jetty and has changed it twice already. "Tom's out with his friends. He's got lots of new friends. . . ."

"Tom is out! Tom is out!" Jack starts to stomp around. "Mommy! I don't like this room."

In my dreams my younger children are occasionally muffled, toned down, silent. Or better yet, I take a break at a faraway seaside resort. My family doesn't notice, doesn't care, and the shoreline resembles the isolated resort in *The Thorn Birds* where Meggie meets Father Ralph and they have their secret tryst. The best part about it, since Father Ralph turns out not to love Meggie enough to forfeit his love of God and the glamour of priesthood, is the place itself. I want to skip along that very beach at daybreak and twilight, without any children in sight. Obviously, I keep my thoughts to myself.

Then we hear Charles's voice. Candy and I look at each other since his return is earlier than expected and not what I have in mind. There are footsteps up the stairs, Charles's first and then Tom's, both home too soon and ready to invade.

Charles knocks as he opens the door. Tom is beside him.

"Why, Dr. Chuck! What a quick game it must have been," Candy says.

The room becomes gloomy. Charles puts his arms around Jack and reaches for Claire, who half slithers away, half comes toward him. Matilde and I stop painting. At any second Charles will dismiss the twins and Candy while Tom will remain in the room. We are a family of gender divides and gender sidekicks. Tom's face is lit up—it's going to be them against me.

"Dad!" Matilde runs to Charles. "Look at what Mom and I are working on together!" Matilde the politician, attempting to win Charles's favor with our work. She persists, "Dad, look at what we've just started, our wall mural, the first work that we've ever shared. See it?"

Charles nods and gives Matilde a pained smile.

"Hello, Charles, hello, Tom," I say. "How did it go today?"

Tom puts his hands on his hips.

"No big deal," Charles answers, "I shot a ninety. No one was Tiger Woods. I was good enough." He clears his throat. "You know there's a dinner coming up next Saturday. A dinner with wives—the same group, at the country club."

"What country club?" I ask.

"The one where I played a round of golf an hour ago, Lainie."

"Of course, Charles." I keep mixing the colors. "Just text or e-mail the details."

Charles has a beer in his right hand when he sits down on the wrought-iron love seat that I found last week in the Elliot consignment shop. He pushes at the cushion. "Lainie, why did you buy this? It's very uncomfortable, too stiff and wiry."

"I know why, Dad," Matilde offers. "It reminds Mom of summer . . . the bayfront and cookouts. The furniture she likes to keep outdoors."

"I love it, Charles. It reminds me of the sunsets at the Shore."

Charles tries to adjust the cushion. I'm tempted to say, *Why don't you rent a wife, Charles, the kind of wife who would suit you?* I've mentioned it before; sometimes we laugh at the thought, sometimes we don't and the room is filled with tension.

Charles stands up, then sits down harder in the chair; the floorboards squeak when Tom moves back and forth.

"Mom? What's that over there?" Tom points to the miniatures on my worktable, the commissioned painting propped up on the easel.

Matilde races to the miniatures and gathers them together. She opens the single large drawer beneath and starts stuffing everything away. "These aren't ready to show, not yet. Right, Mom?" She closes the door with a thud.

"Nice job, Matilde," says Tom. "But I'm sure Mom can handle things."

"Aren't those your commissioned work? Due soon enough, Lainie, yes?" Charles asks.

"Yes, they are commissioned work," I say. Matilde's eyes turn inky.

Tom's hands are still on his hips. If Matilde and I seem in cahoots, Tom and Charles are twisting their faces the same way. In the seconds before their dissension, both of their lips disappear.

⚮

Charles starts to pace. "So there was a scene last week that has just come to my attention."

"A scene," I say. "Well . . ."

"Well? Well?" Charles slams his hand against his thigh.

"Tom, what have you told Dad about the drop-off that day?"

"Nothing, nothing really." Tom stands robotlike.

Matilde puts her hands up as if she's swatting the scene away and yells, "How could you do that to her, Tom? You aren't fair. She's not who you think she is."

"You embarrassed Tom, Lainie. At a party that he was invited to, in a new town," Charles says.

"That isn't what happened." My voice is very clear.

"For chrissake, Lainie." Charles sighs. "What did happen?"

"You think I'm the chauffeur, don't you, Charles?" I stand against the wall; Matilde comes beside me, she could be superimposed into the picture.

"Tom! Matilde!" Charles says. "Go downstairs. This minute."

Tom scuffs his loafers on the wood floor. Old wood that I appreciate.

"Tom, please go downstairs to the family room where the little ones are with Candy," I say.

Matilde waits against the wall; perhaps she hopes that I've forgotten to send her too because it's about Tom.

"Matilde, join your brother." Charles is fuming.

"Isn't it horrible enough? Isn't Tom sorry yet?" Matilde is crying. "Don't you see that she's awfully sorry today, Dad? Can't you make her laugh again?"

Charles points. "Go. Now."

"Matilde, you should go," I say.

Tom and Matilde leave. Charles fumbles with the door handle in search of a lock.

"I had that changed so that Claire and Jack wouldn't accidentally get locked in or out," I say.

Charles pushes the door and it thuds shut. "What in hell's name is going on, Lainie? You've made a mess for Tom."

"Don't you understand, Charles, that I don't want these people in my life? People with mean dogs, people who judge you by your car, your wardrobe."

"Mean dogs? They were golden retrievers, Lainie!"

"They were slurping at me! Then they actually started to bite. I was frightened!"

"We have a different life in Elliot, Lainie. There's no question that with four children it involves presenting yourself a certain way. It involves driving. You've known that from the start."

"Driving," I repeat. "Presenting."

"Yes. You have a responsibility to wear suitable clothes. To be quiet about someone's fucking golden retrievers."

Charles's mouth moves. "Let me remind you of how lucky we are to be here. I've provided for our family, haven't I? Is there something you're missing, Lainie? Are the children without something?"

"Compared to whom, Charles? There are plenty of entitled tortured people around Elliot. Have you rambled along the main street, have you ever seen it in play on a weekday around noon? I have met the women, I have watched them. They complain at the dry cleaners, they are sour at the pharmacy, they steal a parking spot in front of your eyes. They check me out when I walk down the street. When I pick up the twins no one speaks to me. They were mock friendly, not truly friendly when the dogs were attacking me.

"I don't want to burst your bubble or your vision of country life, but there's a torment . . . despite the size of the houses and golf courses at every turn. You get to escape the everyday. . . . You're in a hospital where nothing has changed for you. Except you are chief, headier than ever."

"Since when did you become a sociologist, Lainie? What makes you think everyone is miserable? Not everyone wants to be an artist. Some people enjoy coming home from work and kicking back with a drink and an hour of HBO. Some people want to put their work behind them at the end of the day. Other people want to spend their days shopping or having lunches out. Maybe they don't think their lives are miserable. Maybe they would view you as miserable."

"I'm not one of them," I whisper.

"What are you denied in Elliot that you had in the city, Lainie?"

"Everything. My friends, my art classes, the waterfront. People who are open-minded and kind."

I remember our apartment in New York City, the windows open to the street, the herringbone wood floors, the eggshell paint on the walls, the orderly living room and not-so-neat bedrooms, the peanut butter sandwiches without crusts, the deliveries up the back elevator. Bolting was much easier there. It feels so thick living in the country, as if I'm swimming against the current to reach the other side. As if getting to the Shore will be a heroic feat.

"Matilde's happiness, that's a concern," Charles says. "You see the girl isn't getting a chance, you're sapping her energy. There are boys, boys who will like her, there are friends for her to meet."

"I agree, Charles. I do."

"Do you, Lainie? Because you are her *mother,* Lainie; she watches *you.* We have three other children who need your care. We live in Elliot and each of us will create a new reality because of how it is. New friends, a new rhythm. Perhaps you won't book countless visits to the city."

There is no sound after he speaks. With nothing left to say, Charles walks out, taking his usual meticulous steps. As I'm closing the door behind him, I see Matilde standing in the narrow back hallway, cast in an ultraviolet light.

"Why are you and Dad together?" she asks.

"Many reasons, Matilde," I say.

"Such as?"

"Well, he's a good dancer. Your father can twirl me around to an Al Green song anytime, anywhere, Matilde."

Matilde wrinkles her nose. "You mean 'I'm Still in Love with You'? I've seen you and Dad do that in the living room. Gross."

"Well, Dad knows the end of a John Grisham novel when he's only at the beginning of the book . . . and he's funny. He knows the best jokes. I mean, your father could *write* comedy, Matilde."

"Well, he won't, Mom. Maybe he *was* funny. He's not funny anymore."

I think of other reasons, ones that might convince a twelve-year-old daughter.

"He knows the galaxies—Bode's Galaxy, Cartwheel Galaxy, Hoag's Galaxy, Sunflower Galaxy—on a summer night. A summer night at the Shore, Matilde."

"Yeah. Well, on Sunday when Dad and I were at Starbucks, he told me that he married you because you're pretty. He went into a long thing about how you're talented but beauty matters the most. How he had to have beautiful children."

I am silent. Hasn't Matilde enough to sort out without details of her father's priorities?

TEN

After what went on in the studio today, I'm wide awake, bordering on insomniac.

I'm tempted to interrupt Charles's sleep, a confident sleep. He lies on his back; the moonlight dribbles in despite the blackout shades he has to have. I have the urge to cut right into his snorting/breathing/inhaling gig. I've never awakened him out of respect for the number one rule, *Thou shalt not disturb the sleeping surgeon between the hours of one A.M. and six A.M.* If a child cries, it is my responsibility. The caveat is if a child or two has a fever of over 102 or is projectile vomiting. Fair enough.

Tonight he is unconscious; perhaps he has sleep apnea. He is so heavily asleep he could be dead. I poke at him, something I would not have done in the city. New place, new rules. I tug at his shoulder.

"Charles? Charles?" I give it a go.

"What is it, Lainie?" he mumbles.

I hesitate.

"Christ, Lainie, I have four surgeries lined up starting at eight tomorrow, followed by two staff meetings. In by six-thirty. Is this an emergency?"

He sits up and switches on his bedside light. I'm stricken with conscience.

"No, no emergency." A fog of loneliness surrounds me.

He faces the direction of the bathroom, which is a long way off in our bedroom suite. In a second he is snoring again, maybe dreaming of the lawn and garden as the season fades, bookended by deciduous shrubs and evergreen trees.

I'm at the end of our bed. I take the pocket flashlight from the night table. Although it's obvious that Charles won't awaken, I'm very careful. I tiptoe downstairs. I walk through the kitchen door that leads to the finished basement. While I'm thankful that it's not too creepy and the owners of the house have gone to great lengths to fix it up, it still feels like too dark a space—a hole in the earth. I hit the light switch on the wall and the steps are illuminated.

I descend quickly to the adjacent storage space, where three custom cases and eight large boxes hold strips of driftwood and hundreds of shards, cracked bits of my treasured work. There is only a hazy light where Charles's ransom of me remains. A flawed, sullied ransom. I see well enough to begin tearing open the cardboard boxes stuffed with shells, whole and broken, large and small. I load them into kitchen garbage bags and begin to carry them up the basement stairs and then the front hall stairs and into my studio.

Next I take the hammer from Charles's "family" toolbox, which is conveniently sitting to the right of the last crate. In a crazed frenzy I begin to pry open the crates, dismantling the driftwood that is too unwieldy to be dragged into my studio. As if I alone appreciate what it takes to escape a house that suffocates itself. As if my creation has been starved for visibility and the hours are evaporating.

I stay up most of the night dragging the sections of driftwood and carrying the loads of shells and dried sea animals, bones of birds, and fish scales in shopping bags. I feel that I'm one of those people who saves someone's life through an unprecedented act of strength in a crisis. I keep going up and down the stairs, from the inner room of the basement to the floor of my studio and back. The heavier the parts, the happier I am.

In my hushed studio I open the cupboard and pile in the bags full of my broken work. I carefully lean the driftwood against the wall where Matilde and I are painting our large canvas. More dust falls. I snap pictures on my iPhone of everything that has been transported. Before closing up, I fill four letter-size envelopes with a handful of clamshells, baby turtle shells, sea glass, broken crab claws, and dried seahorses. I take the crushed conch shells and small sticks of wood, which are almost powdery, and add them. Then I roam the house and tiptoe into my children's rooms. The children sleep as if being uprooted and miles from any body of water is insignificant. I place an envelope under each of their pillows.

Afterward I go back to Charles, whose snoring hasn't ceased. I climb in beside him. Yet I no longer mull over the rooms in a house that is not quite a home. If these rooms have seemed cavernous, an impossibility in the city, where families live in the largest box they can afford and call it an apartment, it no longer matters. If the playroom can't be kept neat with the large orange rubber ball that gravitates to the center and pleases Jack, so be it. If there is a huge kitchen with the promise of ambitious meals and a computer center that no one in the family cares about—except Charles—let it rot. If I find Claire and Matilde sometimes sitting there together, staring into the abyss, that's how life is in the suburbs. If I fear it's ennui, I might be wrong. Perhaps the girls are planning their future on our state-of-the-art couch that faces the swivel chairs, anticipating at what angle their future boyfriends will kiss them ardently. These boys of tomorrow who will try for second and third base while watching the latest equivalent of *Twilight Part Three*. These boys will hold my daughters' hands and statistically and ultimately they will break their hearts. I close my eyes and imagine *Trespassing: Driftwood* as it sits in my studio.

Last week on the news I learned that wives, more than husbands, have worrisome dreams about their marriages, about what they do right and what they do wrong. While that has not happened to me, I think about it as I fall into a deep sleep. I dream that I'm doing flips at the edge of a pool. Next I'm at a window and there are stars on the horizon. The room looks to the sea and beckons me. Charles's snoring begins to subside. The only sound is the water rushing against the Shore.

ELEVEN

I walk into the kitchen, where Jack has his shells and crushed wood chips in his fists and is throwing them on the floor. He starts unloading the dried-out jellyfish. "Listen to the sound they make!" He laughs.

Matilde looks up from her iPad. "That tiny crunch, the way it sounds when you step on ants."

Candy sweeps them up. The more she sweeps, the more Jack has in his pockets to scatter around. "You see how busy I am, Jack," she says.

"Candy, how come you don't laugh when things happen anymore?" asks Matilde.

"Right," Tom says, showing up with his book bag strapped through his finger and then across his back. "Candy, you used to wink at us and wiggle your nose so we'd laugh. Does anybody remember?"

Tom glances in my direction. "Mom, what are these duds?"

"She's just in some black cape and jeggings," Matilde says.

"Children, we have to go." I speak in a commanding tone. I try out the Elliot drunk or drugged mother smile that I've recently learned. "We need to get into the Jeep."

I push back my sunglasses that Charles calls my "Jackie O specials." Definitely not good form for Elliot school drop-offs. "Okay, everybody. Ready?"

"I have a ride," Tom announces and is out the door too swiftly for me to ask questions.

"The morning is really strange, Lainie. . . ." Candy shakes her head. "You're so chirpy. . . . What's that about . . . these broken clamshells and other shit? You know Tom will complain that the wood is under his skin, that he has splinters. Wait until Dr. Chuck learns about it. . . . Your ruined work . . . parceled out to your kids."

Jack comes toward me, holding a seahorse in his hand, which he gleefully cracks in half. "Ha!" he shouts.

"See what I mean?" Candy says.

"Candy, where is Jack's knapsack? Matilde, are you ready?"

Matilde nods and holds out her arms to help Claire off the kitchen stool.

"Claire, where are your shells, the ones that were under your pillow?" she asks her.

"I put them back. Back in Mommy's drawer."

"Mommy's drawer?"

"Back where Mommy wants them, Matilde. By her bed."

Tonight Charles is already home when I pull in, having picked up Matilde from Latin Club. Charles and Tom are on the couch in the kitchen, eating potato chips. Jack sits between them watching *SpongeBob,* as usual. His mouth is half open and he's hypnotized.

I walk to where Charles and the boys sit. Charles says, "Lainie, we can't be late tonight."

I rush upstairs to my bedroom to find Claire sitting on Candy's lap at the built-in makeup table. Matilde is behind me.

"The mothers in the city would love an area to do makeup and get dressed, right, Mom?"

"I know. What a space to try on dresses and high-heeled boots. The walk-in closet could be a playroom for Claire," I agree.

"That's it for me, then," Candy says. She lifts Claire and stands up. "I'll go start the chicken fingers."

"You like it a little, right, Mom?" asks Matilde. "Having this."

"Well, tonight it works." I sit on the corner of the upholstered bench.

I pile my hair on top of my head and twist it into a donut shape. "Up or down, Matilde?"

I reach into the vanity drawer and take out an envelope and start doling out the shells and starfish.

"Mommy, that's mine," Claire says.

"No, Claire baby, it's mine. I gave an envelope filled with the same sea treasures from a sea garden to each of you."

"I gave mine to you! I told you so!" Claire slides off the seat and runs to the night table stand on my side of the bed. "See! See!" She pulls an envelope from the drawer and everything flies out.

"Look!" Claire catches two starfish.

"Thank you, Claire darling. May I please borrow your two starfish?"

Claire water dances back with the dried-up starfish in her right hand.

"Matilde . . . I'll need more sea life," I say. Matilde hesitates, then reaches into Claire's envelope and hands me a small conch shell and a seahorse. I add two starfish and one seahorse from my own envelope. "Matilde, what do you think will make the shells hold in my hair?"

"Mom . . . you know it might be too much for tonight. . . . Aren't you going to a dinner with other doctors and their wives? I mean . . . I'm not sure that . . ."

"Well, let's see the full effect first." I stand in front of the three-way mirror in a drapey blue dress that is a bit too neon and blouson. I place the shells next to the starfish.

"I know!" I walk back to the vanity. A wide velvet hairband, one that I use to keep my hair off my face when I'm painting, is there. "Let's put the bitsiest shells on this with Krazy Glue!"

"Mom . . ." Matilde says.

"Krazy Glue . . . I must have some, Matilde. Do you know where it could be? I don't quite have my bearings in the house yet. . . ."

"Are you sure that you want to add *more* to your hair, Mom?" Matilde asks.

"I do, I most certainly do." I try to fix the starfish by lining them up behind each other in my donut-shaped bun.

"The Krazy Glue is in the studio," I say. "We have it for the ordered miniature from the lady on Long Island. The one with the triplet daughters. Could you please get it, darling girl?"

A minute later Matilde has the Krazy Glue and I hurriedly start squeezing it along the hairband to set the smallest clamshells in a single line, alternating them with slits of wood. "What do you think, girls?"

"You look perfect, Mom, just not for the night."

"What the hell is going on?" Charles is in the doorway. "Lainie?"

"I'm ready, Charles." I pat down the hairband. "All set."

Charles is quiet for a second and then he starts to scream, "What the fuck is in your hair, Lainie? What the fuck are you *wearing*? We are going to a business dinner! I've told you already. We are invited to a country club by the CEO of the hospital. *Tonight matters.* Look at you!"

The girls and I freeze. I hear Matilde breathing. "Dad, you can't talk to Mom like that. Stop it!"

"Matilde, it's okay," I say. She should know that Charles's words don't hurt me, that I'll sign on for the night—for his sake. I wait for him to continue.

"Get that crap out of your hair, Lainie. God knows you have the ability, the wardrobe. . . . Why can't you do it the right way?"

Matilde grabs Claire by the shoulders. "C'mon, Claire, let's go. Let's go help Mom."

"Hurry up, girls," Charles says.

"Claire, c'mon." Matilde carries her toward my closet. "We'll find Mom a plain black dress."

Charles stations himself on the settee and frowns.

"We have twenty minutes, Lainie. Matilde, twenty minutes to help your mother."

"Don't worry about me, Charles. I'll be ready." I'm almost floating toward my girls.

⁂

Matilde holds up a choice of sheer stockings or black tights. Next she finds my pearl stud earrings and matching pearl necklace in the bottom of the jewelry box. She favors the first black dress that she finds, a sheath that I used to wear in the city for back-to-school night. Matilde hands me a pair of black stilettos.

"These are the kind every cool mother wears," she says.

"Not those," I say. "If I'm doing safe, let's go all the way." I point to a two-inch heel. Matilde nods—I slip on the second pair of shoes and she zips my dress.

Claire puts her hands on my legs and hides her face there while Matilde holds up an evening bag with a whalebone handle, a "find" at the fair in Cape May last summer. "You could use it," she says.

"Too funky." I have completely converted. Matilde hands me the plainest black suede clutch. Then she hands me a gray-blue pashmina. "What about your hair, Mom?"

"My hair. That's the real problem, right?" I take off the hairband and pull out the starfish. As my hair falls down some of the shells that weren't glued well enough clatter on the floor.

"Maybe a ponytail or a knot. To make Dad happy?" Matilde hands me the hairbrush.

Claire opens the suede purse and finds a pinkish lipstick and a kohl eyeliner pencil.

"Give it to Mom, Claire."

I use the lipstick and ignore the eyeliner, dropping them both back inside. Then I brush my hair for a second before tugging it into a thick coated rubber band. In the three-way mirror I am as wife/mother as possible.

"Okay, Charles, I'll let Candy know that we are off." I sail past him and notice that he's pleased. For tonight.

PART FOUR

Jess

TWELVE

B y the way that William's office has assembled the dinner at the Wintergreen Country Club, a Thursday Rock 'n' Roll Night, I get the picture. Two new chairs of divisions and two other longtime chairs are mixed together to make a table for ten. William and I are pros at these evenings and we don't discuss the guest list until we arrive at the club forty minutes early.

"I know one of the wives, William."

"What wife, Jess? What are you talking about?"

"The wife of your recent hire—chief of orthopedic surgery."

Wives are fungible for William and rarely count, let alone have jobs as heads of departments at Elliot Memorial. They appear for hospital dinners and act relevant for the evening, that's the deal. He yawns.

"We were together when we were young," I say. "In Cape May. Later on in college too—we overlapped for one year."

William takes out his iPhone and moves his forefinger around the screen, then he holds it up to me. "Here he is, Charles Morris."

I take the phone and angle it away from the light or else it reflects too much to see his face or read about him. He is alluring, fine-featured with brownish hair and a square jaw. That Dr. Charles Morris is quite accomplished I already know since William wouldn't have it otherwise. Without warning I'm slightly anxious and slightly intrigued, wondering if Lainie has him in a vase on the table as she had the lifeguards years ago or if her knockout husband takes the lead. I would bet buckets that Dr. Morris hopes to join Wintergreen. I'm sure that he's been told that the golf course is excellent and should he become a member by spring, his wife will be taking tennis lessons as will their children on the grass courts. Dream on, unknown husband—are you aware of your phantom wife? It's not likely that she'll be quite as eager. Yet it is a fine club or else William wouldn't belong. *Put that in your pipe and smoke it, Lainie.*

Lainie and her husband are punctual, the first to arrive. I lean against the carved wood bar of the cavernous grill room as they sashay toward us. Four children, unending glue, yet the space between them is more than two feet wide. What an observation, a reminder of how time passes and the seismic shifts that become plausible. Lainie, who has been immune to how other women feel. Had she made an effort, tried to win us over those summers, we might not have hated her for her beauty and popularity.

"William." I sound stinging. No impact. His right index finger moves over the little screen that rules so many lives. William, rude as hell, doesn't look up. Hasn't he always been rude? Then they approach us and William's interest is piqued. He places his iPhone in his pocket and while Lainie is invisible to him, his face lights up at Charles's presence. He beams at Charles as they shake hands heartily, nabbing the other's fists in glee. William, the kingmaker, Charles, a young king in the kingdom.

I look at Lainie again and it takes less than a minute to scrutinize her outfit—the uninspired, safe clothing of a surgeon's wife, a chair of the department's wife. The getup pleases him, the black sheath, the strand of pearls, the medium-heel Manolos, the angular face. Her hair, in a smooth knot at the nape of her neck, has an otherworldly sheen. Her lips are closed tight and I wonder, is she praised then vilified? A question that arises as I stereotype her husband, another overly confident, immensely important surgeon.

Then my gaze shifts to the actual man. He is a husky, hunky, brainy man. That's a first. A man I have imagined who has yet to exist. I smile the fervid Elliot smile that I know by rote. Charles holds out his hand to greet me and it runs right through me, an electric charge that ignites us. We have never been introduced before, not in this life. Lainie watches, her head tilted to the side, her eyes wide, perplexed. William radiates success at his latest conquest, who might be more appealing tonight than he was during the interviewing process. *Lure those doctors out of the cities and make them yours at Elliot Memorial* is William's slogan. I'm too busy with Charles to care. I'm too stupefied to breathe.

"Shall we?" William motions. "We'll have our other guests sent along."

It's as if my husband is in some other country. I can barely hear him.

We exchange superficial greetings while we meander as two couples into the cocktail reception, but it's lost on me. Country club living has never been this perilous. At the bar Charles orders a Glenlivet and William follows suit. I need something very potent—I wish to be drunk for the foreseeable future.

⌾

Having tossed back two apple martinis during our cocktail hour, I find myself surrounded by wives. Wives who owe me for carpooling, invitations to charity luncheons and elite dinners that only I can arrange, discretion when it comes to their spending secrets, my ability to look the other way when their children have been unkind to others. Most important is how I "Henry Kissinger" the herd of women; at least once a week I play the role. Everyone sitting down bows to me and no one gives a rat's ass that the most beautiful player has just landed, *Lainie*. Tonight she has this wild look in her eye—or is it simply that caged-bird demeanor of the ill-fated wife?

Now she's just like everyone else and she hasn't anything special to bring to the party. There isn't a woman at the event who exists as more than an accessory.

Wind yourself up, Lainie, for the arm-candy duet. Ha, she can't escape it any more than the rest of us. *Husbands, houses, children.* I imagine Lainie at the Y pool about to start her regime, Lainie at the Wintergreen Country Club, Lainie driving the curvy country roads in the rain—my topography.

Of all things, William notices how I've guzzled the drinks and am about to order a third. He gives me a quizzical look that stops me. As soon as we are seated at the dinner, the band plays. A woman in an ill-fitting black skirt and tank top is the lead singer and she chooses a Karen Carpenter song, "Superstar," as the first slow number. William, to my right, is robustly scouting the perimeters, taking inventory. Charles pushes back his chair and holds his hand out to Lainie. She stands up and follows without moving her mouth. They approach the dance floor, where she halfheartedly places her hands on his shoulders. Charles is facing me and I take his cue. William is sifting through the guests when I leave my chair and levitate toward the dance floor, solo. There is no playing nice or suggesting that my husband break in and dance with Lainie, thus producing Charles as my partner. It's up to me.

"May I have this dance?" I ask. Lainie backs off; her arms, those swimmer's biceps, go limp. Charles first puts his arms around me and then flexes his body into mine. It is stifling when he pulls me closer. I owe no one anything.

THIRTEEN

C offee today?" I ask Lainie as we are about to leave the Women's Y locker room. There is a mad exodus, as if everyone is on the same weekday schedule, although we aren't. She gives me a look as if she's torn about what to do and I realize that she is counting down to time at her drawing board. On the other hand, she ought to say yes or she'll never have a friend in Elliot. I'm not convinced that she knows how salient it is to join me. She might be the "artiste," compared to mere mortals, but each of us compensates for lost hours—let her stay up the night long if need be to paint.

"Lainie? Coffee?" I ask again.

She nods. Bingo. "Let me check to see if Candy is on the train." She squints at her screen. "Yes, she confirmed a minute ago. I am good to go."

"I'll drive," I offer.

Lainie sits in the passenger seat as the baby hills of Elliot show the first signs of autumn, a burnished top inch of every blade of grass and shrub. I take the road in one slick move, spiraling for a millisecond. Then we are there, pulling up in front of the Corner Books, as close a parking spot as one might wrangle to the Tea Tree. I lead her through the glass doors and commandeer the front table facing the window and overlooking Main Street.

She becomes anthropological, watching the women on the sidewalk, some swishing in the chicest day clothes, others sporting yoga gear. Their fast robotic motion—as if they are about to save the day, as if their mornings are complicated—can't be newsworthy if you've lived in the city.

"Where is everyone going?" Lainie asks.

"Appointments," I say.

"Doctor's appointments?"

"Hair, nails, pedicures, Pilates . . . some women work," I say. "You know, at home, freelance, part-time . . ."

"The very idea of *not* working on a canvas or on a sketch sounds so . . . easy," she says.

"Sure, it has an enticing element to it. Think about it, Lainie, you could be sipping a macchiato and nibbling at a scone guilt-free."

"Is that how it is, Jess? Is there a lightness to the days when they belong to you and your family and place is *enough*? When you don't need anything more?"

I am the wrong person to ask. I am one of them at a price. She too could cross over, run hither and yon, to the shoemaker, wine shop, tailor, the vegetable market. She too could be in search of organic apples, the best goose liver pâté, the triple crème cheeses sold beside the low-fat Gouda. But it's ridiculous to expect this of Lainie, who is at one with sea grass, how the river bends.

"Well, some women like it more than others," I say.

"Charles would love it if I could be involved with the community. . . . He'd like me to let go of my . . . I don't know . . . my commitment to my work. Ever since we moved here he seems frustrated when he sees me in my studio."

During Lainie's lame confessional, I remain heavily invested in the others who are congregating. I welcome the women from the other tables who descend upon us, who pay homage to me.

"Jess, Jess!" they exclaim in these rehearsed tones. *"Jess!"*

The tables are designated by age groups. Mid-thirties to early for-ties are seated by the window while those between forty-five and fifty-five are behind us. The older women have settled in the back of the Tea Tree. Everyone is coiffed and polished to perfection, hair is beau-tifully colored and foreheads are frozen in place. If anyone had a reason to furrow her brow, it would not be effective. A few women wear Hermès scarves around their necks and others broadcast their décolleté. Similar to the ladies who lunch in the city, I'm sure, ex-cept that there is no buffer, no diversity of street life once you step outside the restaurant. Lainie notices as she pulls the collar of her jacket around her neck.

"Cold?" I ask her.

"No, I'm fine."

I sip my macchiato and am stunned. Evidently there's been a mis-take made in my order. I motion to the server, who knows me very well. "Greta?"

Greta rushes over, harried and worn although the day is begin-ning and she is only in her mid-twenties.

"Yes, Mrs. Howard?" She should be repentant since it has unfor-tunately happened before.

"Greta, meet my friend, Mrs. Morris. She's moved to town and now that I've brought her here, she'll be a frequent customer. Right, Lainie?"

Greta is discontented with the idea but silent, knowing there is more to this than an introduction. She gives Lainie a doleful look.

"Greta, I asked for skim milk. Always skim milk." I frown in a way that gives away my Botox. If anyone asks, I say that I do it for my headaches. I'm too young to have begun for any other reason.

"It is skim milk, Mrs. Howard. Your regular order," Greta defends herself.

"I don't think so." I push my cup toward the periphery of our tile table.

"I'll order another, Mrs. Howard."

"Yes, please do."

Greta scoops up the cup and vanishes. I turn my attention toward Lainie.

"I suppose she's never heard that the customer is always right," I sigh.

Lainie waits, knowing as well as I do why I've invited her. We want to hear what each other has to say about Saturday night.

"My husband doesn't dance, thank God yours does," I say.

"Yes, Charles is a good dancer," she agrees, sipping her macchiato. "Jess, do you remember the summer that we worked at my father's marina?"

"How could I forget. I haven't done a stitch of clerical work since," I say. "There was the one small window that faced the boatyard and the bay. To this day when someone uses the word 'repair' I remember keeping track of the boats, the endless follow-up system we had to follow 'to please the clients.'"

"We talked incessantly about what we'd do on our time off. I was always trying to sketch at Higbee Beach."

"No, you also swam before the lifeguards were on duty. Your father used to go nuts. He'd say, 'Every year, a local drowns, Lainie. Promise me you won't go beyond the markers.' Still you did; you would have lied and cheated for those swims."

We both laugh.

"Didn't you work at the Pier that summer?" she asks.

"Yup, by the waterfront. I was seating customers and my grandmother kept saying I should waitress instead for the tip money. I wanted the prestige of hosting, it appeared to be classier. Then I'd go with friends to the different beaches—not to swim or with a charcoal pencil and pad—to be the babe in the string bikini."

"You were. You and your friends had that contest, whose bikini bottom stretched most across her hip bones."

"I won. I didn't have an ounce of extra fat on my stomach." Three espresso machines make a loud swooshing sound at once. Greta returns with the skim-milk macchiato.

"You showed up sometimes in the early mornings when the life-guards did their aerobic workouts. Mostly to flirt with Matt."

"Ah, Matt. I'm not sure we should go there, Lainie."

Matt, captain of the Cape May lifeguards, whom I've pushed out of my mind for years, along with much of my experiences in Cape May. Once our repeated trysts were known up and down the beaches, Lainie announced how little she cared for him, how his swagger bothered her.

"Don't you see that everyone likes him, everyone wants him, Lainie, everyone?" I had said to her. She warned me that my fling with Matt would end badly, and it did when I swallowed sixteen of our friend Alice's birth control pills in Lainie's mother's guest room. Lainie was my confidante first and then my nurse that afternoon I spent almost bleeding to death.

"Oyster roulette," Lainie had said while I cramped and writhed in pain. "Matt makes me think of oysters, you know, irresistible and almost sly going down your throat. People act like they're winning when they devour them. Not everyone wins."

"The summer of '90 . . ." I say now, as if none of it had been that traumatic.

I take a thin purple plastic hairband out of my purse and point to it. "Liza's. Three for two dollars at CVS." I put it on and push back my hair to remind Lainie that my widow's peak, my one feature she ever commented on, is intact.

"We go way back, the two of us, Lainie, lots of history." I lean toward her. "How is it being in Elliot? The Y is the best pool, right?"

"I love the pool, Jess. It's been a saving grace."

"The water is oxygenated, and that's much better for our skin, our hair. I was on the committee to get that kind of filtration."

Women are getting up again, exiting, others are entering as if it's a directed play and the first round of performers concede the stage to the second. Every one acknowledges me with an extensive wave. Half of a new round of women come to the table and interrupt our conversation. *"Let's get something on the calendar! So glad to see you.*

Will you be at the luncheon on Thursday? Do you need any more volunteers? How is next week looking?"

They move beyond us and settle in their chairs. Then the pause. "Where were we, Lainie?"

"We've gone from Cape May to the Y pool." She looks at her phone and then away, toward the window.

"Hey, Lainie, I'm able to help you. Elliot is a standoffish place—you're in the room with me, I don't need to tell you. It must be tough on you, on the marriage—a move. *All the driving.* I know, and I'm used to it—it is *too* much. By evening I'm exhausted half the week. That's with two children, not four. *Four children,* Lainie! How do you keep track? Well, at least your husband has a good position at a very fine hospital. William has made Elliot Memorial the caliber it is, you know."

"You must be very proud of him," Lainie says.

"He's well respected and smart, if a bit deficient in emotional intelligence. I admit, I *had* to marry him."

"I know that feeling. I felt that way too about Charles. I had to be his wife, had to have him as my husband. I thought he was my best friend."

"And? Is he?"

Lainie laughs a dry laugh. "Well, he would like me to be his pal when he watches cable TV or a Jets game. He thinks that a room with a seventy-two-inch plasma television is a badge of family life—bigger, better, and improved. He loves the den so much that it hurts his feelings when I try to escape it. Little does he know what it's like to be a referee there earlier in the evening, or else maybe he too would avoid it. What he gets is a room that the children have vacated. The other night he was watching Sean Hannity on Fox News. I swear that Charles was a Democrat when we met. He used to watch CNN."

"You are a wife and mother, Lainie. That's what we do," I say.

Lainie holds up her hand to stop me. "We've lost years, Jess. I don't remember how long ago we were last sitting together. I brought Charles to Cape Henlopen, where he caught more sea trout than the fishermen. He was tossing back the sand sharks. I'm trying to remember . . . that was after we'd graduated college . . . after your grandma died and you said you wouldn't be coming down the Shore again."

"I meant it. I haven't been to Cape May since she died. . . ." I say. Still I haven't forgotten Lainie, nor does she disappoint since she appears remarkably the same and unscathed by time and childbirth. I must have had a hunch that it would be like this if we were ever to cross paths again. I have resisted googling her too frequently and I haven't paid enough attention to her husband, it turns out. That is what happens when you land a successful one of your own and you live in Elliot. Then again, Charles on the dance floor not two nights ago. One of the few surprises of my life that doesn't seem overrated.

"How exactly did you meet Charles?"

She squirms and squeezes Aquaphor onto her lips from a small tube. "He came to my first opening. . . . He bought my largest piece of art ever. . . . He claimed he couldn't live without it, without me."

"Well, that's inventive." I smile encouragingly while fantasizing about his shoulders and his V waist. Although I have no basis for knowing, I'm confident that Charles uncorks a bottle of wine without a hitch, that he understands the crux of the topic before the speaker is finished explaining. He has sparkling surgeon's hands.

I repeat what she said several minutes ago. "Your best friend? That's rich. No husband is a best friend to his wife in Elliot."

"I thought that Charles could be that to me. . . . It was years ago. . . . Tom is fourteen, Jess."

"Marriage works on another plane. If you need a best friend, I'd be the one, not your husband." I glance at my iPhone; almost an hour has elapsed.

"I'm fine in Elliot, Jess. All okay."

"I don't believe you." I pour my macchiato down my throat. "Around here every adage we consider out-of-date holds true. Wives depend on husbands, wives look the other way if they have to. Children are not egregiously spoiled, just privileged. Charles needs to be happy, meaning you need to be happy. I offer help."

"I'm sorry? Help for me or help for Charles?"

"Lainie, if I bring you into the Elliot fold, Charles will be pleased. Trust me, Lainie, that is very important. And I've had the chance to speak with him—during the dance on Saturday. That's what I mean by help." I feel rushed. Greta is at our table, her face unreadable. "A check, Greta, and a splash more?"

Back to Lainie. "I offer my help."

"Sure," she says. I watch her compute her reality. The rivalry rises in both our guts. She pushes it back down while I position myself most expediently.

"You should come to the Arts Council kickoff meeting next Tuesday, Lainie," I suggest. "As my guest; I can arrange it, I'm on the board."

"That would be appreciated, Jess." She sounds lyrical. Because whatever our reunion conjures up, I'm her only friend for miles around, for better or for worse.

FOURTEEN

The sun still isn't shining by midmorning and a pall is cast over the center of town when Lainie and I meet in the parking lot of the Arts Council.

"Lucky for us that they decided to call this for early in the day—much easier with our kids. I honestly believe this is the one place that you'll find your niche."

"Thank you, Jess!" Lainie is almost giddy. "Charles has been saying all along that there could be an opportunity in Elliot for my work to be shown. I'm very hopeful."

Lainie carries her iPad close to her chest, undoubtedly loaded with her latest pictures, and her portfolio is tucked beneath her arm. The building, a Victorian mansion, stands alone at the top of Birch Street. Outside is a sign that sums up the council's mission, to fan the flames of culture. There is a signboard to the right of the large oak door that reads ESTABLISHED IN 1898 TO NURTURE YOUNG ARTISTS IN THE TOWN OF ELLIOT. There is a list of advisors and board members, thirty people in total, including three heavyweight women artists and two men who paint portraits, whose work Lainie would know. I adjust my best

Gucci sunglasses to better appraise her. Maybe she won't be as disappointed about the move to Elliot. Maybe her husband will be off
the hook if this happens, and while it is early in the game, I'd like to
see Charles less burdened.

I push open the heavy front door. We are three minutes late for
the meeting and members are already engrossed in a tacit conversation; they've been at it a while. I count fifteen women and eleven
men, the old-and-retired constituency.

"I'm sorry that I'm late," I say.

They stop talking to ooze their hellos. "Jess, we are *thrilled* that
you're here," calls a man from the back. "Excellent, Jess!" calls a man
to his right. "Jess! Jess!" Everyone is effusive, including the dourest
of the bunch.

They watch Lainie, who comes well recommended in her own
right. Apparently her friend Isabelle has arranged that Lainie be introduced to Edna Abre, the director. Isabelle and Edna were together
years ago at Skowhegan as artists-in-residence.

Edna, a sage docent for patrons around town, is fifty, with gnarled
fingers and a long neck. She adjusts the knot of her Hermès scarf.

"Hello, Jess. Good to see you!" Edna says. "And Lainie! Lainie
Smith Morris! We are pleased to meet you." She spreads her hands
as if to explain her position. She is the one to promote art, to invite
artists in, to include a precious few on the council. The group qui-
ets as she clears her throat. No one mirrors her welcome, rather
they are stony, unkind. Lainie looks stunned.

"Listen, they aren't as bad as they look. Behind their facades everyone here has the same everyday worries the rest of us share—
children, health, money," I say.

Edna claps her hands. "Everyone, I'd like to welcome Lainie Smith
Morris. She hails from New York City and has recently settled in
Elliot with her five small children. If you can believe that. Why, you
look like a child yourself."

"Four," Lainie corrects her. "Four, not five children. Two of them
are not that small—more in the middle. Thank you for your welcome."

No one moves.

"Lainie, have you shown your work frequently? Isabelle has e-mailed some information. A few illustrated books, graphics, logos . . . You seem to have had success in both fine arts and commercial art. That's not easy to finesse."

I wonder where Edna is taking her point. Is she critical of book illustrators, or showing her group that Lainie is versatile?

"I've shown at a few galleries over the years," Lainie says. "Most recently at the Paul O. Gallery. I do illustrate children's books from time to time. I have a book for three- to five-year-olds that will be out next June."

"Excellent." Edna beams. "Exactly what we are looking for, Lainie! Perhaps you can describe your settings for the group. I know you paint the sea, seascapes. . . ."

"I started with large forms. For a long time I've been painting smaller canvases, collages. Whatever size, miniatures, twelve-inch squares, the theme is the same—water. Not only the Atlantic Ocean, but the New York waterways. I'm influenced by the locale. I'm drawn to the Upper New York Bay, the Gowanus, Red Hook. I love the Narrows, the Hudson River, the East River. My favorite is the town of Cape May—the Jersey Shore. I view water as the story. Sometimes the sky blends with the water and it becomes a huge part of the canvas. I imagine Turner skies while I do this."

"I thought that your focus is on women and the sea," says Edna.

She has done her research, and Lainie realizes that she has a shot at something. She might fall into Edna's arms in gratitude.

"Well, yes, always women." Lainie opens her iPad. "I'd like to take a few minutes to show my latest work. If there's time."

"Yes, there's time!" Edna points to the screen that is already set up.

In the minute that it takes Lainie, the women start semiwhispering to one another, and the men aren't much better. One of them, the seriously craggy Mortimer Alexander, scowls at the first image that Lainie shows. She quickly moves to the next frame and to the next.

"These seem more decorative than we anticipated. . . ." Loretta Raine, dowager, comments.

"Do people pay you for these paintings?" Mortimer asks.

Lainie is about to respond to his disparaging question when Nan Ogily, a too-tall woman whose eyes are close together, asks, "What would a membership at the council do for you, Ms. Morris?"

Nan wears solid black and a gold circle pin and gold clip earrings and has smooth gold hair. Altogether I find her elegant, Elliot-style elegant.

"I'm sorry?" Lainie says.

"What are you looking for in a membership?" Blakke Willsin chimes in. She's smaller in scale with the same attitude. "We are very selective about our members. We don't take anyone in willy-nilly. The council serves the community, while the members themselves, well, we nominate our artists very carefully and rarely include decorative art. We hold the bar very high in a competitive atmosphere."

Edna shakes her head at how the power has shifted and is being drained from her by the second. She gestures for Lainie to take a seat in the second row on the end. The others are pulling their chairs next to one another as if Lainie is contagious. Her response is too earnest; she doesn't understand their indifference or how her husband's position at Elliot Memorial could garner respect at every turn. I mean, why not drop a line about how the family relocated because her husband has been named chief of orthopedic surgery?

In these last ten minutes Lainie has gone from hope to despair. It isn't easy to become one of us, that combination of self-concern, purse shopping, achieving children, successful husbands, and the arts.

That's when I stand up and move toward Lainie. The sound of my stilettos tapping against the hardwood floors causes a hush across the room.

"Lainie, aren't you a member of the National Arts Club in the city? Don't you show with a group, at the very least, almost yearly?" I ask.

"Yes, Jess, I do." Lainie nods and it reminds me of how talented she has always been. She's out of her element and won't do well with false starts and false promises.

I slip into the chair beside her and trace my right hand over her right hand as if it is some sort of pact we are making. "Hey, Lainie, what can I do with the dead wood around here? I'm sure there's something to do," I whisper. "I'm the one who schedules the spring events."

The paradox of it is not lost on either of us. The tide has turned. I have become the prom queen, the "It girl" who has a voice in the town.

"Jess . . . I would be extremely grateful."

"We'll see." I cross my legs. "We'll see about squeezing you into what will be a group show, most likely an early spring or summer event. Based on your new works. Would you be able to offer enough unseen, fresh art by then?"

"I can do that!"

An assignment, from me to her. One that she welcomes, no matter what my ulterior motive may be.

FIFTEEN

J ess?" Although I'm intrigued the next day when I see the name CHARLES J. MORRIS come across my iPhone screen, the pitch of his voice tells me that this is no seduction. Instead there is a palpable fear in his voice and I cringe at the sound.

"Charles, what's wrong?"

"Lainie's disappeared and won't answer her phone. She can't be located. I thought she had a doctor's appointment, but it seems she's roaming around the New York waterfront. . . . She isn't accessible. . . . I don't believe she'd allow this to happen." He's pissed.

"I haven't heard from her," I say. "What did she tell Candy? I'm sure that she knows where Lainie is. Candy knows what to do with the children after school, Charles, doesn't she?"

"Candy has had an accident on the way to pick up Claire and Jack. She's totaled the Jeep. She'll be fine but she's in the emergency room now. The children are stranded. I'm at the O.R. about to start another surgery."

Out of the blue I become the savior and Charles is relying on me. I imagine him in his scrubs—Charles in his fiefdom. An orthopedic surgeon who specializes in spinal fusion, his brute strength is combined with skill and a portion of brain power. William believes that orthopedic surgeons are not often rocket scientists, rather a population of men who played football for an Ivy League, a brew of discipline, talent, muscles, height, and an uncanny ability to concentrate and cut bone. At the top of the heap is Charles—a feather in my CEO husband's cap, a fine addition to the staff. William views Charles as able to administrate, teach, and conduct research, along with his busy operating schedule. A chief among chiefs, Charles hasn't more than a moment for the call.

Although I've been fairly clever my entire life at how *not* to get siphoned into situations, the arrival of Lainie Smith Morris and her family is proving a major challenge. Regardless of the advanced stage of my social career in Elliot. In a matter of seconds, I find myself weighing the intricacies of after-school scheduling of four children. I have become part of the Lainie and Charles world, where they seem to be counting up their children in order to grasp the enormity of it. Another notable is that Lainie is too smart, I know, too caring in her own way, too much a mother. I'm confident that everything was in order when she left this morning.

"Jess, is there any way that you can pick up the twins? At the elementary school? They are waiting in the principal's office."

Those feisty children whom I scarcely know. Plus the fact that they were on good behavior that evening at my home. Would they recognize me in a lineup?

"Of course. I'm on way."

"I don't know how to thank you, Jess. You are a saint."

A saint. I've been called many names, but never this.

"Charles, you are most welcome." How I love to say his name. He hasn't hung up, so I gild the lily, let him know how far-reaching are my talents.

"What about the older two? Can I help out with their afternoon?" That snooty, spooky Matilde who is a younger version of Lainie gone unbridled. The eldest, Tom, is destined to be a heartbreaker. His father's son.

"I've texted them and called Elliot Taxi. They'll be okay, thanks. They'll take a cab back to the house together."

"Oh, Charles, not necessary for the older ones to wait in an empty house. Let them take the taxi to my home. Let them stay until this is resolved."

"That would be great, Jess." He sounds rushed.

"*I'll* text them—I have their numbers. Lainie gave them to me. For emergencies." Ha!

Before I pull into Elliot school traffic, I work the food chain—texting the two pleaser mothers who beg to carpool my children. Within three minutes we're set, and my children, who also need to be picked up, dropped off, cajoled, spoiled, and placated, are also set. Norine is on call, making me a hundred percent available to subjugate myself to Lainie's children for the afternoon. This underscores my pledge to Lainie and reminds each of us of her absence. I'm choreographing everything so thoroughly that I almost miss the right turn into the Elliot Lower School.

The parking lot is empty, the other mothers have come and gone. How fondly I remember when Liza and Billy were in kindergarten.

I turn off the engine and unbuckle my seat belt, yank down the rearview mirror to primp a moment.

Charles, don't hold anything against her. I practice in the mirror, sounding saccharine to my own ears. Why not throw Lainie a bone—another bone after the Arts Council meeting? At my end life is moving at an unanticipated clip.

PART FIVE

Lainie

SIXTEEN

As soon as I leave Penn Station I load my reusable T.J.Maxx oilcloth shopping bags into the backseat of an Uber town car and climb in. The driver, young with an accent I can't quite place and a shaved head, skillfully navigates us toward City Island. These sandy stretches are the best getaway, close to the city yet a historical, beachy part of Long Island Sound. We cross the bridge and I open my window to smell the salt air and to view the disparate group of boats moored on the western shore. The color has bled out of the sky by this time of year and the water is a stone blue.

With two uninterrupted hours to spare, I unzip my boots and switch to my waders, tucking my hair into a tattered baseball cap that has an insignia of the Cape May Fire Department on the front. I ask the driver to drop me at the Eastchester Bay side, where I unload my goods. First a faded beach towel that was once striped in lavender and yellow, two glass jars, a shoe box, three Ziploc bags, and a square jewelry box from Tiffany that housed Charles's last gift of gold petal earrings—all to collect what the tide brings in for the second panel of *Triptych*.

Three pairs of mallards skim the water as if they are married couples. The male ducks with their vivid green heads are followed by their gray and plainer female counterparts. The geese and white egrets are farther out, fluttering and straining their necks. I take my Olympus from my pocket and angle for pictures of sandpipers and gulls overhead. My waders barely crunch into the hardened sand as I kick aside a used condom, a dead blowfish, and a patch of dried seaweed. I hold my arms out against the light wind and wallow in the rush of water at knee level. I gather the mussel shells, snail shells, and a few slugs with my strainer and drop them into the Ziploc bags.

Two solitary hikers, a woman and a man, walk behind me and then pick up their pace. I wave to them from where I stand and they wave back; they are holding hands. I sigh and breathe in, imagining their day, their afternoon. While not Cape May, it is a homecoming, a path back to the water and the swaying sunlight.

⬤

I sit on the train to Elliot in a late-afternoon reverie. How deficient a weekly visit to the city is, a far cry from when we lived on Riverside Drive and I could at least view the river each day. I was able to go to Fresh Kills with Isabelle and Orchard Beach with Cher and be home in record time.

Out the window the stations appear and disappear; Newark Broad Street, Highland Avenue, South Orange. I lean back against the worn leather and consider my slight lie to Charles last night in order to have had a brief respite. Who knows where the truth gets mixed with the lies—saying that I had a dermatologist's appointment when what I planned was more photographs of the midday light across the water. What I dared not reveal is how important these visits are, how I'm making my comeback to the large canvas, to collages that fill entire walls. Today is proof of my intentions.

Then that sense of unease and guilt rises within me—anything might go wrong with one false move. With a wave of panic I realize the peacefulness is partly because I haven't checked my iPhone in hours, years. Nor have I cared to while I collected whole shells, sea-weed that scrapes the barnacles. I start digging around in my can-vas bag for the phone. I panic until I find it at the bottom, lodged between my sketchbook, pastels, and camera.

The train lurches forward to Summit, my stop. I glance at the texts first, before the calls or e-mails. Charles has been texting every fif-teen minutes for the last two hours and so has Jess. Why not Candy, who was meant to assure me that the children have been collected for the day and are safe at home? My head spins and my heart beats in a queasy rhythm. *I'm being punished for my sins.* I read Charles's texts as an out-of-body experience. They begin, *Lainie, where are you?* followed by more imploring messages: *Lainie, Call me, Important; Emergency; Lainie, Call home at once.* Oddly enough, the texts from Jess are practically alongside Charles's texts and also have the same immediacy. *Lainie, please call; Lainie, call me; Lainie, don't worry but check in ASAP; Lainie, this is critical.*

I get off the train and trudge through a personal tsunami where the damage and remains are only evident to me. I'm a perpetrator, a thief in the night, the one wanted by the law. My ankles are wob-bly and I have double vision. *My children. Tom, Matilde, Jack, Claire.* On the kind of adrenaline that allows a person to lift a 3,800-pound car off a child, I hail an Elliot cab in a matter of seconds and beg the driver to drive as fast as he is able, to speed me home.

"Lady, I'll get a ticket," the driver says. "Plenty a' cops around."

I toss a twenty-dollar bill at him and he hits the gas, doing seventy-five in a forty-mile-an-hour speed zone. I arrive at the appointed hour for my original plan, the one I had made with Candy.

❧

Charles's BMW is parked in the driveway. Jess's gunmetal Mercedes sedan is directly behind it. The muscles in my legs twitch and I'm too terrified to open the front door. Jess opens it from the inside and although her face is somber, she is composed.

"Lainie," she says. Charles appears. They stand together.

"The children?" I ask. *"The children?"* I screech.

"Everyone is fine, Lainie," Jess says. Charles moves in front of her and she is eclipsed.

"Where the hell have you been? Is there some reason that you can't answer your cell? That you don't answer *all fucking day,* Lainie? Do you know what happened, that Candy crashed your Jeep and—"

"Let me see the children! Are they okay?"

Again that wooziness I've never known. I go tearing past him. In the den the children sit quite still, staged by Charles. There is nothing new in the way that Tom faces the big screen, his head lolling back and his hands on his iPad. Jack is close enough to him that they could be glued together; he is watching *SpongeBob SquarePants* on the TV with intense concentration. Matilde is sitting on the opposite end of the couch with Claire neatly beside her. She is reading *Great Expectations* and Claire is trying to imitate her, listlessly turning the pages of a Dr. Seuss book, *Green Eggs and Ham.* My children are from another place and time because I left them alone and have become the voyeur, observing without participating. They are beyond my reach. Charles's wrath weighs down the room.

Jess insinuates, ". . . over an hour away . . . hadn't checked her phone in five hours . . . trusted this Candy . . ."

"Am I invisible, Jess?" I say. To Charles I ask, "What happened?"

"Candy totaled the Jeep, Lainie. While you were out of town." He is in the unaccustomed role of worrier and gatekeeper, more exhausted than after four surgeries packed into one day.

"Is she all right? Was anyone with her?" I know it matters although Charles won't allow it to matter. I'm in a position I've never been in before. I have abandoned my children for my own preservation. City life with city children would not have yielded such a catastrophe. Jess abreast Charles, Jess taking his side, Charles smirking at his superiority. He wins the best parent award.

"Matilde," I say.

"Mom?" She drops *Great Expectations* and hurries over to me. Up close she is wispy when we hug. "Mom, can you believe what happened? About Candy and your Jeep?"

"Yes, yes, I heard."

Claire collides into my arms as I bend down. "Mommy! Where were you? Mommy, Mommy, we made an angel food cake!" I stand up and she starts her water dance. I resist the urge to warn her, *Not now, my darling girl.* Yet why should I? Her eternal optimism is one reason that I've returned. If only it could be bottled and sold.

"Candy wants to talk to you," Tom says without moving.

"Where is she?" I ask. Then Jack comes racing toward me and practically pushes Claire down when he grabs my legs. He puts his head against my thigh.

"Jack, dear Jack." I put my hand on his curly brown hair, hair that reminds me of Charles that first year we were together. Chestnut, thick, unruly.

"Everyone should go back into the room," Jess purrs.

Her eyes and Charles's eyes meet for a brief second. Tom grins at Jess in a way he hasn't grinned at anyone in at least a year or two. Charles folds his arms in this O.R. move—he's top dog.

"I've fired Candy," he says. "Although she might claim that she's quit. She'll be leaving any minute. Her one friend in Elliot has agreed to drive her to the station."

"Fired her? I don't know what you mean, Charles."

Jess straightens up in that "running for office and next at the podium" style.

Charles is glaring at me, a glare he reserves for strangers who offend him, those who are clueless to his fame.

"Candy doesn't have to leave. I don't want her to. I'll go speak to her, Charles." I'm submerged in a wave of terror. He is taking away my chance to fight another hour, another day.

"Too late for that, Lainie." Charles's face is slanted away from the light. "I'm the one who was here in the crisis today. Candy smashed the Jeep. She's irresponsible. I won't allow her to drive *my* children."

"She isn't irresponsible. She's been with us for eight years, Charles. Candy was twenty when she first came to babysit. Candy left *Juilliard* for us. She moved in to be with our family!"

"More fool she," Charles says.

Jess sighs dramatically. "She left Juilliard for a babysitting job? She must not have been that good."

"She taught Matilde how to play piano. . . . She taught the children songs. She taught them a bit about the fiddle. . . ." I try to defend Candy.

"That's enough, Lainie," Charles says.

I can't stop. I can't let it happen. "We've left her in Cape May with my mother, Charles, while we were at those four-day conventions. Those vapid doctors' conventions in California. In Arizona. We trust her; she's held it together for us."

"I won't dispute that, Lainie, I won't dispute the past. What happened today while you were off in the city doing God knows what shows that Candy isn't working out in Elliot. I don't want her in the house. She could have killed the children."

Why would he say such a thing in front of them? "Well, she didn't, Charles, she didn't have them in the car. She had an accident, Charles. People have accidents every day. It doesn't mean she's inept. Do you know whose fault it was? How the accident happened?"

"Apparently she lost control. The Jeep spun around twice. That is the police report," Jess says in a flat voice.

"That's about it," Charles says. "She isn't welcome anymore."

I let go of Claire and Jack and that swirling sensation behind my eyes intensifies. A free fall from grace.

SEVENTEEN

C andy's tenure has come to an end and neither she nor the
children seem able to wrap their minds around it. Jess has
decided to plant herself squarely in the middle of it, helpmate
to both Charles and to me. While Candy is in her room packing, Jess
calls a caucus in the dining room. Tom comes along in his recently
acquired adult comportment; both he and Charles seem quite taken
with Jess. I hear Matilde and the twins making noise in the back hall.

"Let's go see Candy because she has to pack and move away for
a bit," Matilde explains.

Claire starts to cry—she knows better than anybody how it will
be without Candy. She and Matilde. Had we stayed in the city this
might never have happened unless Candy fell in love, married, and
left the country. I suddenly appreciate how much Candy sacrificed
for me, for us. So that I could do my miniatures and keep up a semblance of my career, Candy put her own work on hold. The center
has fallen out in Elliot since Candy is not equipped to drive the children around. She resists plugging in addresses on the GPS and she
is too cautious for back roads and alternate routes. I have heard her

frustration when houses that she's meant to find for drop-off and pickup can't be located. I'm starting to suspect that she resents big homes with curving private roads and being in the car in constant if small traffic jams.

I walk downstairs to Candy's room, where Claire is latching herself on to Candy and almost falling to the floor.

Matilde and Jack stand and watch Candy rapidly fill two small suitcases. She opens a tote bag that I painted in pastels for her last summer. It's a scene of the boat runners at Cape May Inlet on a summer day. That's when she starts tossing her belongings, her rage surfacing.

". . . in my fuckin' life," Candy is saying into her cell phone. "Piece a' shit."

Candy kicks a boot, a black leather number with a wedge heel. We bought it together about a year ago.

"I'm sorry," Matilde says. "So sorry, Candy."

Candy stops for one moment, a pair of Under Armour workout shoes in one hand and her charcoal Lululemon yoga pants in the other. She places them in the bag, grabs her fiddle, and opens the case.

"I love you children, you know that. Matilde, I'm going to miss you. . . ." Then she starts throwing books in the bag, seeming more angry than before. That's when she notices that I've come through the kitchen side of the basement to stand close to the wall.

"Sometimes I've envied you a room downstairs, off the beaten track, Candy," I say, walking in.

"Lainie." I can't see her face in the shadows but I know those dark circles under her eyes that could be from her kohl eyeliner. I have learned to ignore the many ear piercings that grace her ears, usually adorned in hoop earrings.

"Lainie, I'm sorry. So sorry."

"I know. I know, Candy. Matilde was four and Tom was six the day that you came to meet us. How you looked at them . . . that's why I hired you, you know. I knew you were young, a student. . . . Life is going to be a mess without you, Candy. . . . Candy, whatever today was about . . . please don't go. Let me salvage this."

"Don't come in!" Matilde says, looking over my shoulder. "Mom is so . . ."

I turn around and there is Charles, yet again standing in a doorway, this time with Jess behind him, her arms crossed.

"Mom is so what?" I ask. No one is listening.

"Candy, your friend is waiting outside." Charles holds out his hand and there is a wad of cash. "Here is two months' pay."

I start shaking my head as I hold up three fingers. That's when Jess begins to shake her head at me.

"Charles? Can we speak alone for a moment?" I ask.

"Look, I don't want to get in the way but it's rare that we end up firing someone," Jess begins. "We don't work in corporate America. Your idea is overly generous, Lainie."

"Jess," I say, "please. What's happening isn't about you." To Charles I say, "Three months. It's the least we can do for Candy."

Charles looks at me and I look away. He is very familiar with how infrequently I pick and choose my battles. Charles opens his wallet for the extra month in hundred-dollar bills. Candy opens the door and the house becomes dark and dreary; the days stretch before me in a soulless town.

"No. No! Candy isn't leaving, Charles. I won't have it. She was with us when the twins were born, she was with us when Tom broke his leg on the Sunfish. She is part of our family, Charles. You have no idea, Charles; Jess has no idea!"

"Candy, your ride?" Charles holds the wad of money.

"No, Candy, listen to me." I press my hands together, my fingertips turn white. "Candy, tell me this nightmare is ending. Promise me that you'll stay."

Candy puts her arms around me. One last time we share the mom/nanny language that was expedient in the city, where nannies are practically "wives" to the mothers.

"I'll call, Lainie, I'll call you. Maybe it's for the best since this place isn't for me. The house . . . the driving . . . I miss New York."

Who wouldn't feel that? Yet there is little more to say and I resist being disloyal to Charles. The fight is over and we both know it. Candy climbs the staircase while Matilde follows, guiding Claire and Jack. I shift my weight up the stairs with Charles and Jess at my heels.

The moon is low and shines through the glass windowpanes of the first floor. Jess switches on the overhead light. Everyone's eyes flutter.

"Fight back, Lainie, those are my parting words to you." Candy lugs her bags to the front door.

"Candy, may I help in any way?" Jess asks.

"Doubtful." Candy puts her purse over her shoulder and glares at Jess.

Tom leaves his father's side and lines up beside Matilde. Candy throws her arms around each child, kissing them. Matilde starts to cry and then Claire believes that she should cry.

"You're stuck, you know, Lainie. Being here. S-T-U-C-K," she spells it out. "I'll miss you, I'll miss the kids." She sighs, she kisses me last.

Then she looks at Charles and Jess. "The truth is, I won't miss the losers in Elliot."

Within seconds of Candy's exit, Jess says, "Don't worry, Lainie. Finding another nanny is right up my alley. I've already lined up a few interviews while you were gone today."

I'm about to respond when I notice that Claire has discovered my stash from City Island, which I'd tossed on the credenza in my haste. She is shaking the Tupperware that holds the clamshells.

"What does Claire have in her hands?" Charles asks. The Tupperware pops open. "Is this crap from today? Weren't you at the dermatologist? You lied to me about your plans in the city, Lainie!"

"Well, Charles," Jess interrupts. "I have been trying to get Lainie an appointment with Dr. Evans—she's the best dermatologist in town. As good as anyone in the city. The wait . . . it's awful." She turns to me. "You *had* to see your own doctor in the meantime. . . ."

Matilde is becoming quite pale. "Mom, did you go to the—"

"True, Jess," I say. "I had to stay with my doctor in New York until an appointment breaks in Elliot."

I begin to drift, floating back to the afternoon that is being snatched from me. The mallards, my precious findings—parakeet feathers at

the end of the visit—the tranquility. Jess and Charles continue bab-
bling as if what they speak of counts. Jess is raving about her many
resources, the twins are shouting. I walk into the living room with
Matilde and the twins following me. The twins press their noses into
the bay window.

"This reminds me of the living room on Riverside Drive, Mom,
for special occasions . . . holidays. But it's like a balloon has popped
or the party's over. . . . C'mon guys, we should leave." Matilde tugs
at the twins.

"By all means, Matilde, stay where you are. No special occasion
necessary."

"Because the house is rented, Mom?"

"No, because I don't care," I say.

∞

I realize that it is seven o'clock and Candy would have already fed
the twins, who must be starving. "They're acting out. They're hungry," she would say.

Ten minutes later Matilde and I start rummaging around in the
refrigerator. I open the freezer door. "How about we microwave a
frozen pizza or chicken fingers?"

Instead Matilde starts scrambling eggs with a whisk, putting too
much milk in, and the eggs are watery. I hoist Claire and Jack onto
the barstools at the granite island where they watch *Dinosaur Train*
on the kitchen flat-screen. As they begin to eat with their eyes glued
to the show, Tom materializes.

"Oh, Mom?" he says. "Dad wants you to come into the dining
room."

I move quickly before anyone chokes or falls off a stool.

The lights are low and Jess and Charles are immersed in conversation. Jess stands with her thighs pressed against the long dining
table. Her upper body is tilted toward Charles, who is across from
her, sitting in one of the Queen Anne chairs.

". . . in twenty-four hours . . . forty-eight at most. Pronto," she says.

"That's impressive, Jess," Charles says.

"Yeah, good stuff," Tom agrees.

"Tom?" I say. Tom, who I thought would remain in the kitchen. "Tom, don't you want some dinner? Matilde and I have thrown together—"

"No thanks, Mom. Not yet."

"That's the point, Lainie," Jess says. "Tom might not want what you've 'thrown together'—eggs, I believe, with ketchup for good measure? I can help, I can recommend a fabulous nanny, someone who will change your life."

I look out the window, although there is nothing visible—mounds of land and suburban homes covered in darkness.

"Lainie," Charles says. "Listen, we'll have someone else and be right on track. Just make sure that she drives, Jess, please. Confidently. That she's familiar with the area."

"I would only find someone with those skills. Leave it to me."

Charles is pleased—I've never known him to be interested in the hiring of a nanny before. I resist any remark that might break the spell, appreciating that I'd be worse off without Jess's input. Without an old friend who knows how to fix things—including the Arts Council—in a town that might as well be Mars. A friend who has the ability not to be bogged down with kids day in, day out, rather to move irreproachably through the morass of drop-offs and pickups. I shudder at the thought of life without Candy, and that enhances Jess's offer. Let Jess put her money where her mouth is.

I nod. "That's brilliant, Jess. Truly brilliant."

I cede the day to Jess without a fight. She takes over our family's future as flawlessly as if it were her own. Gratitude surpasses rage. For now at least.

EIGHTEEN

⁂

The next morning I'm slow to resume work. Too aroused and confused from last night's events with Charles, I'm stuck staring at the large unfinished canvases. That's when the landline rings with startling clarity. *Matilde,* I know before I answer hello.

"Mrs. Morris?" A voice I've never heard before. Authoritative, teacher-like.

"Speaking."

"Ms. Wagner calling. I'm a gym teacher and one of the swim coaches at Elliot Middle School."

"Is everything all right . . . is it Matilde?" My heart thrashes against my rib cage, the sound swooshes through my ears.

"Mrs. Morris, would you be able to come to the school now?"

"What has happened? Please . . ."

"Matilde is okay. Only we cannot get her out of the pool."

I blame myself when I lay eyes on Matilde doing flips at the edge of the twenty-five-meter-long pool, alone. Mostly since I'm the only one who realizes what she's doing. I myself yearn to stay in the Y pool for hours on end. Vapor is coming from the top layer and it makes it seem as if Matilde is disappearing in the middle. Ms. Wagner, the young and perplexed assistant coach, should be on a schedule except that Matilde is keeping her there. The pool can't be locked up, and Ms. Wagner is beyond agitated; she's pacing and putting her whistle in and out of her mouth with a quick thrust of her tongue. Matilde is swimming like a shark in mid-ocean. What a secret thrill to witness my daughter swimming as if she is a captive of the water. She has never had such velocity.

I'm also dutiful and detect the ramifications of the scene, putting my daughter into Elliot mode. At the moment that I bend down and tap her hand as she cuts through the water, Mr. Flaven, the head gym teacher/coach for the school, appears. Matilde flips again and again and again, fierce and expert; she is spellbinding. I tap her back more forcefully. Either she doesn't feel it or she is deliberately oblivious.

"Mrs. Morris, could you please get your daughter out of the pool?" Mr. Flaven is exasperated. "She's been in for more than an hour and a half. She's missing class, I'm missing class. . . . I've never seen anything like it before."

Understandably. How many students at Elliot Middle School believe the water will heal them, make them whole, save the family.

"No, I suspect not." I lean toward the water and would dive in if not for my clothing: Tahari boots, teal blue pashmina, and jeans. The accoutrements of life in Elliot. Being so close is a tease, the desire runs high.

"Matilde! Matilde!" My hand is up to stop her as she slithers past, more frenzied per lap. Both coaches are looking at me, noting that I'm no more efficient than they are, that it was a pointless task bringing me in.

"You see, she won't stop. We can't get to her. That's why we called you," Ms. Wagner says.

"Why didn't anyone jump in and grab her?" I ask.

"Are you kidding?" Ms. Wagner says. "We can't. It might be interpreted as an assault; it's a lawsuit."

I stand up although the pool still beckons me, water whore that I am. What never goes away is the sense that any water will do, any-place, anytime; I too cannot resist water of any sort.

"No, I've never seen her do this either," I say. Useless informa-tion, yet very true. I take a kickboard from the wire rack against the wall and place it a foot in front of where her right arm stretches as it propels her forward to the other side. I straighten the board horizon-tally to effect a roadblock.

"I've tried that, Mrs. Morris." She's staring at me.

"Matilde!" I shout as I thrust the kickboard against the wall where her hand reaches before she returns. Confounded and disheartened, she stops. The kinetic energy in the room dissolves within seconds. Matilde, robbed of her goal, takes off her goggles to make certain that I'm standing there.

"Get out of the pool, Matilde." I sound severe. I bend down and give Matilde my hand. She alights like a dancer, a trapeze artist. Together we move into the girls' locker room, where a mixture of sweat and sports awaits us.

"Mrs. Morris? Can you see your way out and I'll call you in sev-eral hours?" Ms. Wagner asks.

"That's fine. I'll take Matilde home, if you don't mind. She and I will chat there." One of the charcoal pencils holding up my hair topples to the floor, my hair falls to my shoulders. Matilde, who is shivering although she is wrapped up in a towel, scoops up the pen-cil for me.

Alone at last. Matilde opens her locker and taped to the door is a map of the Raritan River, a small-size replica of the one on the board at the Y, where I have completed two hundred miles. Matilde takes a blue Magic Marker from her knapsack and starts to color in a swath of the river.

"Look, Mom, at how far I've swum. I'm almost as far as you are, after today."

"Matilde, what are you doing? What possesses you?"

"You're the one who taught me to swim like that. I'm the one who swims away with you, Mom. I was practicing." Her eyes are solemn.

"My darling Matilde, I'm not planning to go anywhere."

I come close and stroke her face. "There are ways to ·. . . to be okay here, in Elliot."

"I don't believe you, Mom, I don't believe you'll stay in Elliot. One day you'll swim away!" She's shouting and I wipe her tears, salt tears, off her face. I start hunting in my jumbo purse for a tissue. The purse feels false, the locker room a joke. Matilde and I are on shaky ground.

"No, Matilde, I mean what I say." My head floods with the waterfront, Cape May, an empty beach in the long stretch of the off season. A nor'easter that blows for three days straight without surcease. Or the view from our apartment that faced the Hudson, those brackish parts of the river, best viewed on a gray day. To the south, the Narrows.

"I have my children, I don't intend to swim away." I put my arms around her; she clings to me, her wet bathing suit soaking through my clothing.

She begins to cry. "Promise, Mom, okay? Please swear on our lives."

"Oh, dear Lord, Matilde. Oh, dear Lord."

PART SIX

Jess

NINETEEN

O n the Tuesday morning after the nanny incident and what
seems months since we danced together at the club,
Charles's cell number comes across my screen once more.
"Jess?" That voice again. "Have you ever been to the Gansevoort
on Twenty-ninth and Park Avenue South?"

"The restaurant?" What is the name of it . . . Asellina. "Yes, I have.
At a recent business dinner with too many gastroenterologists and
their spouses."

He laughs one laugh in one breath. "No, Jess, the hotel."

"The restaurant is in the hotel." I'm not only coy, I need evidence.

"I'm in the city for a meeting . . . several surgeons . . . a seminar.
The lunch with a few colleagues just imploded."

I wait without speaking. I've had invitations before—what distinguishes the call is that it is Charles on the line. Fortunately, my
entire day is free—I haven't a committee meeting on the calendar,
not a lunch date with any grand dame. The day is designated to desk
work and belongs to me alone.

"Jess? Let's meet there."

"What time?"

"One o'clock."

"One o'clock it is." Already I'm considering my wardrobe, my lingerie, my hair, whether I should drive, take the train, or book a car service. Calls to other mothers for my children's pickup have to be placed immediately—the chits called in at any cost. I'm a marathon runner, an opera singer, a rock star; the epinephrine peaks for the performance ahead.

While the world turns in its ordinariness without me, Charles opens the hotel room door. I expect the river view that radiates from the large window behind him. The thought that it is Lainie who loves water enters my mind. It isn't exactly a pang of compunction, rather an observation. I'm conscious of how the bones break when we fall and what must be kept secret, kept safe.

Up close Charles's face takes on another shape—his jaw is longer and his flecked eyes are wider and lit up. His hair is brushed back off his high forehead and his eyes have turned greenish as if the blue in them no longer counts.

He stands there very fit. I know beneath his shirt he has a washboard stomach and Popeye-style biceps. His chipped front tooth that he should have capped, can afford to cap, looks boyish, rather than a reminder that men don't take care of themselves and that wives only do so much.

He pushes me hard against the wall and we begin to kiss teenager kisses, a sword fight—tongue against tongue. Every kiss squeezes my heart; the oxygen swoops in and away from my lungs. He's an orthopedic surgeon and lifting me to the bed is easy; he's stronger than men half his age.

I actually giggle when Charles undresses me, while he frowns, that intent on the journey, the illicit sex that we crave. We could live in this room and it would sustain us. He becomes gentle, although he moves fast; the clock is ticking. My hands are on his forearms and his hands are on my breasts. "What are you thinking, Charles?"

"I'm not thinking," he laughs. "I'm lusting."

He kisses my eyes shut, his heart is against my heart. An unfathomable thirst, nothing I've never known. *Eros.* He puts his mouth on my neck and I sigh, his mouth is on my breasts, I thread my hands across his back, a surgeon's back, where the muscles ripple and tighten.

"Jess? Jess?" He is ready to be inside me.

I open my eyes. "I would like the passion without the longing."

Charles tilts his head. "Passion without longing. What an idea."

When we're spent, I wonder if he will be the type to retract after the act is over, to jump up and flee. Those men who dress in silence, buttoning the starched shirt (less starched and crisp after having crumpled it onto a chair) and tying the limp tie. The deed is done, the man moves on. Not Charles. He turns me on my side, then spoons me. He passes the test by treating me as if he is my boyfriend, my lover, as if he cares.

I'm sentimental, gawkish, unaccustomed to myself. I'd like to believe him, to take it on face value—forget that we have six children between us and two spouses. There's a remedy for the guilt that is about to enter my psyche. Guilt? Isn't my feeling for him enough to dispel the ghosts? Apparently not; I push Lainie away as best I'm able, then I see her. First in Cape May the summer we were nineteen at Poverty Beach. She's in a one-piece navy tank suit while the rest of us are in skimpy bikinis. Yet everyone is watching her—the old men, young men, lifeguards, and the boys line up for her every move. She is oblivious, skipping out to beyond the markers to swim those goddamn laps. What about Lainie today? Try when she asked me at the pool last week about cheating wives.

"Would you ever have an affair?" she asked.

I professed it to be a profound question. "I'd rather come clean. Get a divorce, start again."

"Me too," Lainie said. "I couldn't do it to Charles." *Charles?* Is she delusional? Am I special, the only one he chooses outside the marriage bed?

"Let's make a pact, Jess. Let's promise that if we ever are tempted to have an affair, we tell each other," Lainie said. Intense, almost optimistic.

"Sure, Lainie."

Lainie held out her left hand and insisted that we pinkie swear. A pact seemed a good idea, a method of keeping me honest and away from Charles. I squeezed her pinkie in mine. Seven days later my self-deception knows no bounds.

Charles pulls me closer, naked. I could remain here forever. I knock Lainie out of my brain except the next mind game begins. *William.* I try to push him aside but he looms in front of me, as he looked on our wedding day at the Plaza Hotel. The party is over and we are alone at last in our wedding suite. I go to the window, believing that he'll follow me, but instead he starts to cry. I agree this is a sorry occasion; we have taken our vows and have committed to spending the rest of our lives together, faithful until the end, in two-step for a lifetime. A chilling reality for a man of William's temperament and desires. And terrifying for me, since I have bought into the deal by ignoring his nature. William and I, partners in the public eye.

Then I see past lovers, those who were playthings and boy toys, trinkets, a method to leave the tyranny of my marriage for a few hours. If the here and now with Charles, Lainie's husband, is forbidden, it is also irresistible. I know the stirrings of love and war—I know the conflict ahead. I also know that for me it is not a one-time event, the result of a physical attraction, a flirtation. Isn't this what I've been waiting for since the night we were introduced? I sign on—I will go to great lengths for the stolen hours of our future. An addict for her drug, the drinker for her drink, the robber for her heist. That is why I let Lainie go, I let William go, I let the one-night stands and passersby, faces I cannot recall, all go.

Charles flips onto his back with his arms over his head. We are about to begin the conversational portion of our afternoon. Our appetite momentarily sated, true confessions are about to kick in. I resist the urge to sit up, naked, and pull the sheet up to my chin in order to explain: *I don't want you because you are Lainie's, I'm not interested in seducing you because she and I were girls on a beach together. We fought over the boys, she had a better body, better profile. She is kind and I am mixed. I want you because of you. It is a misfortune and sheer coincidence that you are Lainie's husband and that I'm fastened to my own unmerciful mess.* Can I take the Charles out of the Charles Morris, husband to Lainie? I wait.

"Your husband is a very smart man. An excellent administrator, Jess." Charles speaks first.

"You like him? I thought that surgeons despise the CEOs."

"Despise?"

The thought never entered his mind, too consumed with the stance of a savior.

"William is . . ."

"William is very dedicated, Jess. I came to Elliot Memorial mostly because of my meetings with him."

I burrow my head in the hollow of his shoulder and move my body closer to his body, trying to melt into him, shut out the conversation. Jesus, what is wrong with me?

"Yes, he's very dedicated. Plus, Lainie is my friend. My dear friend from when we were kids. Summers. College. You know, right?"

"Jess . . . Jess . . ." He is kissing the back of my neck, his arms around me. "You fill my head."

"And you mine, Charles."

Together we are over the line.

"We'll work it out, Jess. We'll figure it out."

I decide to do my best so that Lainie shall never find out. Then he starts again. There is nothing else in the world except this moment.

TWENTY

I'm becoming a soapy sort of person, one who thinks in platitudes and on occasion has a few scruples. A relatively recent occurrence that began when the Morris family became my pet project. Many ways to skin the cat, from charming Tom, the only child of theirs with the good sense to value me, to pleasing Lainie, for myriad reasons. The most obvious being that my discovered compassion makes me aware of Lainie's need for help. A fish out of water, a woman on the verge every time I see her, especially at the Y pool, I realize how she struggles with the unremarkable: food shopping, school meetings, driving children around. She travels with a map, the kind purchased on the Parkway at a road stop, rather than her GPS. What does one say to someone who doesn't see the forest for the trees?

Finally, the Charles factor. Charles, who sends chills up my spine, who lingers where no man has gone. *Charles*. I end up on the busiest of days as the prissiest, most consequential Elliot wife (the one who weighs in on the shade of the cocktail napkins at the hospital benefit), aching for him. *Passion without longing. Too late.* I go no further with these thoughts and feelings. I'm as removed from a solution as I've ever been, in the moment as I've never been in my life.

When I drive up to the Morrises', Mrs. Higgins, the find of the century, lets me in and directs me to Lainie's studio. The original plan was to come at one o'clock because Lainie believes that in mid-November it is best to observe her work in the "purest daylight." I'm delayed due to Matilde, whom I consider Lainie's child, not Charles's. Apparently she has cannonballed everybody's morning by professing to be an act at Waterworld.

The door is open and Lainie is looking at a pair of pastels leaning against the wall. The colors are gorgeous and the rawness is uncharacteristic. Not the Lainie I used to know.

"These are striking." I startle her.

"Jess! I'm glad that you're here."

I point toward the pastels. "How unlike anything you've ever done before."

"Not mine, Matilde's."

Despite my newfound empathy that bubbles over in enough circumstances to believe there is to be a special place in heaven for me one day, I'm green with envy. Someone else's child did these pictures—Matilde in particular.

"They're exquisite," I say.

"Well, talent is one thing, but today was wicked at school," Lainie says.

As if I haven't heard already. Nonetheless I sigh for her, with her, and engage. "What do you mean, Lainie?" The sympathetic tone rolls off my tongue.

Lainie is rueful, hesitant. "I'm worried about her, Jess. She's not making friends—it could be my fault. She's trying to be me and she's not acclimating. Maybe on purpose."

"Since you don't fit in?" There, stated, out in the open.

A normal person in a normal universe would blush and defend herself. Instead Lainie tilts her head and ponders, as if it is meant as a real question rather than a jab. My goodwill quotient diminishes slightly and I'm my usual self again. I'm in Lainie's studio to look at her art and to inquire about Mrs. Higgins.

"How is Mrs. Higgins working out?" I choose the better method of starting off.

"Mrs. Higgins . . ." Earth to Lainie.

"Mrs. Higgins. You know, the nanny who is more than phenomenal? She may seem drippy after Candy, a popcorn blond bombshell if I ever saw one, but Mrs. Higgins is skillful."

"Skillful?"

Not certain if Lainie is doing her "lost in translation" act or if she should know more. It occurs to me that I only told Charles of Mrs. Higgins's accolades. "Well, Mrs. Higgins is much more than a nanny. You said that Candy had dropped out of Juilliard, yes?"

"When she was twenty. She was a part-time babysitter who became our full-time nanny when she couldn't get any work in music. I kept saying she should go back to school. Every year I would urge her to return or to apply to some kind of college, Hunter or Brooklyn College. Something. She was absolutely devoted to the children, Jess. Really. She wanted to be with our family, that was her choice. I feel awful about what happened."

"Eh," I say. "I'm sure that Candy is fine. For Elliot life, Mrs. Higgins is a better choice. Look at her credentials. She speaks French, spent a year at the Culinary Institute of America, she's worked with children of every age, babies through teenagers. She's the Mary Poppins of New Jersey. Let's face it, Lainie, if you only have one person, not two, Mrs. Higgins is the answer."

To say nothing of how she suits Charles's vision of what should be. That I do not share.

"Two people," Lainie says. "In a fantasy life I have a driver."

"A driver? Lainie, what kind of mother in Elliot would do that?"

Lainie is by the window and I realize what she means about the hour and luminosity. Her skin is flawless and her eyes so deep a blue that the light can't flicker through them. I shouldn't push the conversation toward motherhood since I already imagine the group e-mails and texts that will be flying all afternoon into evening about Matilde's peril at the pool this morning. I'd say to her, "Corral your daughter, Lainie," if I thought she'd comprehend it.

I take a not-so-subtle look at my iPhone. "Lainie, we should start talking about your new work and plans for a show." Besides, she must have asked Mrs. Higgins to prepare tea if not lunch—blueberry scones and tea, I would imagine—the table set with silver and fine linen. A reward for my driving to her part of town. We should make our decisions regarding her art first.

Lainie points to the two white sheets across the large canvases on the right side of the studio. "Well, I'm about to uncover my latest work. What I'd like to show at any venue that you're able to finesse, Jess. The hospital benefit, the library fund-raiser. My first choice would be the Arts Council. . . ."

The Arts Council is the most prestigious, most bona fide exhibit hall. She is no fool. "Let's see, Lainie."

She pulls the sheets away to reveal three panels. She's completed the first and half of the second. They are staggering and unique—gateways to the harbors, water as a life force. The swamps and marshes of the first painting, the piers and boats, catamarans and Jet Skiers of the second. Everything is framed in heavy rotted wood with eccentric sea life attached. Beyond anything she has shown in the city—those delicate portraits of fog over the bayou.

"I've never seen paintings like these. . . . Both you and Matilde are so gifted. . . ." *Freaks that you are in other parts of life,* I think.

I stand close to the canvases, I stand away. In either case, there is an agitation told through women painted beneath what rivals a Turner sky. Kara Walker and Barbara Kruger in terms of scale. Suddenly I'm not doing a favor, I'm discovering a talent, *I'm* bringing the talent to Elliot. She deserves a solo show. Who is to scoff at the irony—that my good deed goes rewarded and my desire for her husband is separate.

"Okay if I take some photos?" I start focusing my iPhone.

"What for?"

"The Arts Council. I'd like to submit a proposal. Perhaps a one-person show if you're able to finish." I point to the panels. "Then produce three or four smaller works by end of March." I take a few pictures.

"Jess, I'm very . . . superstitious about photos being shown at the stage I'm in. I haven't shown these canvases to anyone yet. Not even my sometimes dealer. Charles has seen what you've seen. . . . That's as far as I've taken it. . . . Would you mind waiting? I will commit to the spring. What date are you thinking? I will have the new canvases by then and I'd love a one-person show. . . . I'll deliver photos of everything." She spreads her hands. "In a few weeks. Meanwhile . . . I'm beyond thrilled. I can't thank you enough."

My altruism is exhausting, my patience thin. "Fine, Lainie," I agree. My Longchamp scarf has gotten crinkled beneath my purse somehow, very unlike me and slightly annoying. I remind myself that I've entered the world according to Lainie, one where nothing is exactly what I expect.

"I'll take it up with the committee based on my viewing today, Lainie. I'm fairly confident it will happen for you. If anyone presses for photos, I'll placate them. . . ."

Lainie smiles. "Jess. I'm so excited about the offer. Something special . . . incredible. I won't disappoint you, I promise."

She comes toward me and I flinch. Up close there is the essence of her hair, her body. We are standing face-to-face, a close-up. I pull my coat around me and bend the collar toward my face.

"The weather has turned cold. Mid-November has never been so chilly."

God forgive me that Charles flutters through my mind, Charles's warmth against me.

"Yes, almost winter. A favorite season. I miss the waterfront in winter. . . . There is a melancholia about it. . . ." Lainie says.

"What water in winter? Do you mean down the Shore?" Why are we talking about the beach? I suppose there is little else to discuss. She doesn't seem to have anything left in her that would spur her on to a designer bag sale at Bloomingdale's or a Sunday afternoon en famille at the Elliot triplex, watching the latest *Iron Man*. The ordinary is slipping away. I glance at her paintings again.

"The water in winter? It could be anywhere. . . ." Lainie says. "I mean, it *starts* in Cape May. . . ."

Time to dodge her dramatic gestures. "Okay, I'm off then, Lainie."

"Let me see you out."

We take the steps of the slightly grand stairway. The house, although not elegant, suffices as a rental. Lainie seems content while I suspect that Charles, given his druthers, would prefer a more palatial home with a perfectly majestic vestibule.

"Jess, would you want a Kind bar? I'm about to have one before I go back to painting. No time for lunch with pickup for the twins starting at three thirty."

"A Kind bar?" I follow her into the kitchen. Mrs. Higgins is measuring flour into a bowl and boiling chicken.

"Hello, Mrs. Howard," she says. Then she drops carrots and celery into the boiling pot. "Chicken pot pie for dinner tonight."

"Delicious." Not that I would serve such a caloric dish. "Is that a favorite of yours, Lainie?"

"Tom loves it," she says.

Lainie, at the cupboard, reaches for two bars from a box. A paradigm of how the mothers in New York City conduct themselves.

I shake my head. No protein bar for me, who knows what the ingredients are. "I'll let myself out."

Lainie remains on cloud nine over the plan. "Okay, Jess. I'll text my husband and tell him the good news. I'll sing your praises."

Husband. Coming from her, the word cuts through me. I remind myself I too have a husband. Who doesn't?

When I shut my car door, I check my text messages and with a rush of excitement I read the first one—from Charles. *Rendezvous? Name it.*

PART SEVEN

Lainie

TWENTY-ONE

Ever since Mrs. Higgins came to live with us two months ago, I have devoted more and more time to my art. I'm structuring my triptych, each of the three canvases meant as a scene of the beach, framed in dried seaweed and sea creatures from my salvaged *Trespassing: Driftwood*. I've overscaled the women. Some are in black coats, others are dressed for summer although there is a prevailing bleakness, winter. My intention is a battle between the women and the jetty, a way for the viewer to hear the wind, to find fragments among the whole shells.

Before dinnertime Matilde studies for a math quiz in the studio, half observing me. "What about the third canvas?" Matilde asks.

"Oh, Matilde, you keep asking. I love your instincts, that you already know what I'm after . . . more bleak skies. . . ."

Matilde puts down her math notes and stands before the canvas. "Yeah, well, the ocean will be stormy, darker than the first two canvases. There will be children, right?"

"Yes, in the distance, coming from the dunes toward the women."

"The children will want sunshine," says Matilde.

"Of course, my darling girl." Although I've taught my children that it would be agony to always be in sunlight.

"Those summers in Cape May when you make us sit in the shade, Mom? Isn't it because selkies go underwater except for a few times a year when they sunbathe on the rocks?"

"Too much sun is not good for anyone, Matilde. That's why I insist on some shade."

"Aren't the women in the first part of the triptych really selkies, Mom? Selkies who are too far ashore with too much beach between them and the water—so they worry about where they belong?"

"Matilde," I sigh, knowing she wants more from me, evidence that selkie blood runs hot while mother/wife blood runs cold. "Lately I've been painting furiously, as if there's a shortage of time."

"I know, Mom. Now that we have an old biddy nanny you hardly come into the kitchen or family room. Claire notices that you don't tell stories, and last night I was the one to read a bedtime book to her."

"A temporary situation." I glide my right hand across the pasted shells and splintered wood.

"Remember when the twins were jumping the waves at Sunset Beach when they were about four, Mom? You said you'd capture it . . . paint it. But the twins aren't in any of these pictures. What happened?"

"Matilde . . . it's as if I'm not choosing my own pictures. . . ."

Matilde nods. "Okay, but the twins will be in *my* set of three pictures."

"Matilde, you're very gifted. What more would I ask than for you to be sketching and painting?"

I open my supply cabinet and hand Matilde a brand-new set of Prismacolor graphite pencils. "These are the best."

Matilde balks. "I'm not sure, Mom."

"You are ready, Matilde. Decide, my darling girl, on your technique. Once you are convinced, the work will flow." I lift a large sketchbook from under the drawing board.

"How did you get that? How did you get my art from school?"

"Ms. Lacey called last week and told me your good news, Matilde.

That your work has been selected for the Christmas display for the junior high. I decided to meet her and that's when she gave me these. They're exceptional, Matilde. . . . I hear they are the best in the class. I can't wait to show your father."

"Show me what?" Charles asks as he once again materializes from behind the slightly open door—a cardinal sin. Both Matilde and I jump.

"Charles, you're home." I walk to him and we exchange a small dry kiss.

"Indeed, I am!"

"You're chipper," I notice.

"That too!"

"Well, look at these—by Matilde. Her art has been selected. . . ." I hold up Matilde's two sketches and she frowns at me. Perhaps she isn't fond of how we bond over our children's achievements.

For a millisecond Charles seems puzzled. "Great," he says in a perfunctory way. "Matilde, shouldn't you be starting dinner with your brothers and sister downstairs?"

There is that shadow over the room, the same feeling as when the sun goes down and the afterglow has burned out. "Matilde, we'll talk more about your art . . . other art . . . later. After dinner," I say.

She walks out and pulls the door tightly closed.

Charles pushes me against the wall and starts kissing my neck; his hands travel up and down my body.

"Charles, what has happened to you today? Weren't you in the city for a luncheon? Did you eat oysters?"

"I did. I was there for a preliminary meeting for those of us going to the OMTEC convention, Lainie. Hadn't I told you? Enough surgeons showed up, I'll say that. Yes, oysters, a half dozen to be exact." He holds my hands up over my head and rubs into me. At first I'm silent, holding my breath, and then I start to laugh. "Ah, that trilling laugh of yours, Lainie . . . It's been ages. . . ."

"Charles! Charles!"

"Ah, more of that laugh of yours." Charles puts his mouth on my ear. "Do you know that you're squealing, Lainie?" he whispers. "Like those annoying little dogs squeal if you accidentally step on their toes in the elevator of our old building?"

I laugh again. Charles goes to the cupboard and opens the bottom drawer, where there is an old quilt I sometimes use to cover my work. He spreads it on the floor and he picks me up, carrying me to the middle of the quilt. We start to kiss passionately. Our faces are an inch apart; his eyes are exquisite, I could dive into them.

"Charles . . . how very . . . unmarried." We kiss more and he yanks off my jeans and panties. Charles is inside me and we're on our own raft on a river that only he and I share.

Faintly, in the background, Jack is yelling, "Scum bag, scum bag, scum bag" from the family room and no one is stopping him. Where is Mrs. Higgins? Where is Matilde?

"Charles?"

"I don't care." He pins my arms down and keeps moving inside me.

Jack won't stop screaming.

"Charles?"

He pulls out and sighs. As he hoists up his pants I hear footsteps scurrying away. I look at Charles, who doesn't seem to have noticed. Matilde! Matilde, whom I've always trusted. Charles walks to the door but there is no one there. Jack's screams have stopped.

"Where were we?" Charles unzips his fly and heads toward me, as sexy as in the old days, the pre-children days.

TWENTY-TWO

When Tom and Matilde were younger, before the twins were born, Thanksgiving was my favorite holiday. Charles and I would take them to the Macy's parade along Central Park West and Charles would place Tom on his shoulders. Not so Matilde, who resisted and only chose to be held in our arms. After the twins were born, no one was lifted and the older children took turns pushing the double stroller along the sidelines or we stood together with the other families, watching the floats. Our first year in Elliot will mark the first year that we won't be going to the parade.

In my unending quest to keep the city as part of our lives, we are in the midst of our second "discussion" on the matter. A talk that takes place with all of us piled into the family room before the twins' bedtime, the Sunday night before the holiday.

"Why don't we drive in early in the morning to see the start of the parade, Charles?" I say. "Or we can go the night before, when they inflate the balloons."

"Not the best idea, Lainie. I vote that we skip a hellish ride to the city—especially when we have a big day this year. I'd prefer to be in Elliot the night before, and surely the morning of Thanksgiving is nonnegotiable with the invitation that we've accepted."

"What does Thanksgiving at the Howards' have to do with it?" I ask, knowing that fussing makes it worse. "Why can't we drive at off-hours in a reverse commute—for the children to still have this in their lives, Charles, to have continuity?"

"The traffic, Lainie. That's why." The children are restless and out of the corner of my eye I catch Jack playing with Matilde's mini iPad.

"The Wednesday, beginning at noon if not earlier, is one of the most heavily trafficked days of the year," says Charles.

"Let's take the train," I persist.

"The train?"

"A few of us could go. The girls and I?"

"Another divided family event." Charles is annoyed. A flash of pity and sadness flows through me. Once the feeling starts, it's a form of swimming downstream. I nod, knowing that my recovery will be slow.

"We should bake a pie or two for Jess and William the night before." Charles moves right along. "A family project in our Elliot kitchen."

"What do you think, Mom?" asks Matilde. "Apple pie or pecan?"

"Either way." I stare at the gloaming through the windows, a suburban midnight that starts when the sun goes down. With my canvases I own the picture, while in real life the hours skim beyond me, jumbled.

"If only we were going to the beach house on Friday, even Saturday," I beseech Charles once we are alone in the bedroom. "Charles, I'm homesick for Riverside Drive—yams and brussels sprouts that Candy made, her tasteless gravy."

Charles shakes his head and I know it's a done deal but I can't let go.

The holiday at Jess's will be more tolerable if you would change your mind. I might remind him of that, of how it is for me, how the necessary mitigated by the sublime is a form of survival.

"Charles, we live nearer to Cape May, we are already in New Jersey. Okay, we'll skip the parade. Then let's drive down the Shore on Friday, as a compromise."

"If Mrs. Higgins will join us, we'll go. Only with Mrs. Higgins."

"Mrs. Higgins has three grandchildren, Charles. You must know since she describes her granddaughter, who is Claire and Jack's age, whenever she has the chance. She is with them over the holiday weekend. Besides, we don't really need Mrs. Higgins."

"Another time, Lainie, I promise. Besides, you have paintings that are due. Wouldn't you rather paint in your studio than have us freeze our asses off, bored to tears, for some vista in Cape May?"

I remember a year ago when we were in Cape May, climbing the dunes, trotting toward the bird sanctuary—the only ones near the water's edge. Charles beside me, if not convinced of the poignancy of being there. Tom carried Claire, who buried her head in his chest to duck the wind. Charles carried Jack. Matilde faced me while I prayed that we would never be anywhere else for years on end, the six of us.

For the first and only time since we moved, I start to cry in unflattering gulps and wails.

"Lainie, please, please, I've already promised." Charles is at our closed bedroom door. "Do you hear someone?"

I shake my head.

"Are you sure?" Charles pounces on the door handle and swings the door open. "Who is out there? Tom? Matilde?"

"No one is by the door, Charles." I blow my nose. Yet the thought of Matilde eavesdropping washes over me. I sense that snooping around has become a pastime of hers recently.

After that I stop crying. Charles walks into the master bathroom and back to the chaise with dental floss in his hand.

"Is that what you're wearing?" Charles asks me the next afternoon.

"What do you mean, Charles?" I manage to get a gold dangle

earring into my left earlobe by tilting my head while up close to the mirror. I open a mascara with a wand to serum my eyelashes before elongating them. Matilde bought the mascara for me on my birthday in the summer. Maybe it's a bit dried out, although it has never been used—my lashes aren't any longer or thicker. I shake out my hair, which is piled up in a tortoiseshell clip, and start brushing. If Charles is taking note of my effort, he doesn't seem pleased.

"Beautiful for a funeral, Lainie," he says. "Black on black—your skirt, sweater, boots? Nothing to lift it up?"

"Well, if clothes are a form of costume, please note I'm in a designer skirt and sweater, bought at—"

"I don't doubt that you care, Lainie, but it seems to me that you have more variety in your wardrobe. Thanksgiving today is as important as a hospital dinner, a dinner with a drug company, a business trip."

I turn to face him as he paces the length of the bedroom, more dapper than usual. Not that he isn't always dapper with his lean build, his height and broad shoulders. Charles *looks* like a swimmer, someone who could swim the Raritan River easily and win. If he swam. When I'm kind I describe him as a "weak swimmer."

"I'm happy." I smooth my skirt and check the fit, which is impeccable, although the impact is lost on Charles. I put on lipstick and smack my lips together. Charles is at the doorway, adjusting his tie and blazer.

"What about the children? Will I be disappointed in their attire too?"

"Christ, Charles. We're going to someone's home for Thanksgiving where tons of children are expected . . . and five or six couples . . . the men watching football. . . . Jess said it's a buffet."

"This is business for me, Lainie."

Somehow Matilde has appeared and is sitting on the floor with her legs stretched out and her back pressed to the base of my makeup table. I stand up so quickly that I almost trip over her.

"Matilde. Honestly."

"Charles, would you like to approve the outfits for Claire and Jack?

Mrs. Higgins is dressing them, before she leaves for the holiday. I don't know where Tom has gone. He might be playing one of Jack's video games, although I asked him to read a book. He has my Kindle. . . ."

"I'll check it out," Charles says.

"Matilde, am I that dreary?" I ask once he is gone.

Matilde shrugs her shoulders then starts yanking at her tights as if testing them for the body-paint effect.

"How do I look?" I ask. "We have to leave in fifteen minutes."

"You look fine, Mom. You do." Matilde straightens and glances at herself in the long mirror. "I'm drab too."

"Not drab, exactly; I don't think that a dress that hugs your body that way can be described as 'drab.' Maybe the color?"

"Mom! The color is old lady!"

Matilde starts hiking the dress, which is already well above her knees, up to her thighs. I count the years since I was her age.

"That works, Matilde," I say, secretly appalled while determined to be supportive. "We should have gone shopping—to the mall, both of us. I should have thought of it."

Matilde stands behind me and in the reflection from my makeup mirror, she and I are strikingly similar. Her hair is almost as dark as mine and she has my bone structure. The jetties in the sun by the ocean flit through both our brains, that I know.

"Lainie? Matilde? Let's round up everyone and climb in the car," Charles shouts from below.

⌗

I have been invited to Jess's home three times and every visit an image of a castle in Scotland comes to mind. Charles's dream come true—the apogee of success. That it wouldn't be possible without William's family money is beyond him. Charles, who will someday at best inherit his parents' dairy farm, while the likelihood that I get anything from my parents' marina is absurd.

There is an abundance of mirrors in every room—more mirrors

than in any other house, yet who would dare to interpret that the owners have a serious crush on themselves. The long hallways lead to turrets, double ceilings, round staircases in the back and on the sides of the house. The guesthouse is a mini version of the main house, with an indoor squash court and flanked by a tennis court and a pool. Every room echoes, and as winter approaches, the sound is colder and louder. The five-inch thin-heeled boots that the wives/mothers wear make it worse, as do the rampant children shrieking through the rooms. There is what Jess calls "staff," including a white-gloved waiter carrying silver trays of hot hors d'oeuvres and a bartender who seems overworked shaking the mixed drinks.

Despite how lavish the house is, a strong turkey odor pervades every room, as if there is no escape. Jess, the prison guard of the day, struts by and her Joy perfume almost effaces the scent.

PART EIGHT

Jess

TWENTY-THREE

I am perpetually flattered to be pegged "the hostess with the mostest." Thanksgiving happens to be the pièce de résistance for my talents, a Hollywood set, my favorite time of year. Although some believe it's early in the season, our beautifully adorned Christmas tree is trimmed the night before. I remain the one to kick off the season with a tree that rivals living theater. I've been told that the tree reminds guests of the Christmas tree that grows to a giant beanstalk onstage at the *Nutcracker* ballet—while the children dance around it. My guests dance around me today.

As people arrive, I greet them in a new print wool Dolce dress and Louboutin boots. Deline, who has colored and blown out my hair the past three years, has finessed streaks of blond sculpted into waves that fall across my shoulders. I'm wearing William's grandmother's drop tourmaline earrings and several strands of Van Cleef clover around my neck. The other women today are, naturally, my followers. Except for Lainie, who is not only ultraplain but dreary. How difficult could it be for her to buy a few proper dresses, to radiate a little style? She knows better, we know that. Poor Charles, who appears not to be perturbed, but seems happy as a clam. He's loosened his tie and is drinking Jack Daniel's, entrenched with the other men sitting deep in the leather chairs in the den. They root for the football teams, jumping up and shouting in a surprisingly high pitch. Charles is well situated between William and the head of neurosurgery. Twice now William has clapped Charles on the back.

In the formal living room, where the women and children have congregated, Lainie is acting okay—on her own raft until the day is over. I instruct the thirteen children to go to the playroom. It is no coincidence that among the most savage of boys is Jack, trumped only by Seth, a seven-year-old monster who bites everyone. Then who can blame Matilde, Lainie's protégée, for shying away from two girls who are in her class. I myself overhear Sidney Darvis and Aimee Sax in their blatant rudeness.

"She'd be pretty if she didn't wear such . . . dorky clothes," Sidney says.

Aimee rolls her green eyes and yanks on her script necklace as she assesses Matilde. "Very dorky in every way," she says.

"Matilde." I practically drag her away from her perch half behind the living room door, where she hears every word without being noticed. We face the entrance. "Take no heed of what they say. They are nice girls. . . . Their mothers, one is sitting beside your mother . . . are very nice. . . . You know, I think that one of the fathers was a patient of your father's. Your father is his hero, he made him as good as new. These girls would love to be your friend."

"Love to be my friend?"

"Be all you can be, Matilde," I say. "I'm sure that your mother would agree."

"Why? Why, Jess?" Matilde asks.

"I know you're thinking that I can't remember seventh grade. I remember it very clearly."

"Does Mom remember?"

I pause. Lainie didn't live on dry land back then. She had no best friend, no boy she hoped to be with after school, no popular crowd to follow. She was in Cape May at the family marina where her father winterized the boats every November.

Sidney's voice interrupts our conversation, traveling to us via the airways. "Or if Matilde wasn't so fucking queer."

Matilde is tightlipped, and as much as I'd like to shepherd her, dinner is about to be served. My majordomo is giving me that flashing smile.

"Excuse me, Matilde," I say when Claire comes up to us and tunnels her head into her older sister's thigh. Matilde starts feeding her candied pecans from her palm like she's her pet pony. Candied pecans that she's taken from the crystal bowl in the living room. "Mommy! Mommy!" Claire is off in search of Lainie.

"I'm about to announce that dinner is served." I waggle my small silver bell several times for the room to quiet down. Matilde backs away as Liza appears beside me.

The men begin to filter into the dining room, jovial, inebriated, pleased by their televised Thanksgiving Day football. Next the women stream in, some, such as Lainie, holding tight to a younger child. Matilde is alone, racing through the Great Hall to stand on line for the powder room. In front of her is Diana Reeve, a classmate of Tom's, waiting and arguing with her father. I pass them to access the upstairs wine closet since despite my efforts, I've just noticed that the six bottles of carefully selected Château Lafite 2011 are missing from the sideboard in the dining room.

The lights are dim in the empty pantry. I glance in the mirror and primp although it is too dark for me to be discerning. I'm on my way to the wine racks to open the glass doors when there is a shadow to the right. Charles is behind me, his hands on my waist, my thighs, twisting me around. We kiss one of our breathless, endless kisses. Then we pull apart. "We shouldn't be doing this, Charles. It's lunacy." He puts his hand over my mouth to quiet me, to remind me of our furtive moment. "Imagine this." His hand travels up my skirt.

"We are risking a lot, Charles. I have to get the wine." I start to move across the room.

"Relax, Jess." He stops me, kisses me again, harder. I open my eyes—his face is temptation, raw energy, hope. I see him how he must have been years ago, when Tom and Matilde were small, before the twins were born, what it might have been to have known him. Suddenly there is someone in the room, a swift movement as the person tears out, clanking against the glass doors of the wine cabinets. Charles almost drops me to the ground, he lets me go so fast. "Matilde!" he calls out. "Wait!"

Having found her place card, Matilde is seated at the dinner table before I walk through the double doors to the dining room. Charles too is at his place, angling toward Matilde, trying desperately to get her attention. Matilde's face is ashen, not the pearly paleness of her mother's skin, nor her own paleness that is quite beautiful. She is fidgeting, unsnapping her tortoiseshell hair clip, her black hair falling heavily on her shoulders. Her seat is more than twelve feet away, the length of the table—at the opposite end. Within minutes of the kiss, I take my place, *the hostess with the mostest.* Then Matilde faces Andrew Jacks, one of the more popular, charismatic boys in Tom's class, next to whom she is seated. She presses her teeth against her lips for that bee-stung, bruised effect. Her methods remind me of Lainie, who used to stare down the boys "for an adventure." Before she met Charles.

Matilde turns to catch my eye.

PART NINE

Lainie

TWENTY-FOUR

I pull into our garage at twilight in tree-laden Elliot. The cumulus clouds roll into the night and the stars are almost within reach. Through the kitchen door, I carry bags of groceries. Usually I hate to food shop, but ever since Jess was over last week admiring my new paintings, I feel lighter and the mundane isn't quite as burdensome. Oddly enough the kitchen is empty; I hear the children's footsteps above, emanating from Tom's room. Before me on the granite counter is Liza Howard's birthday cake, a perfect jewel. Emerald green, three tiers with strands of gold. White buttercream flowers with green leaves adorn the top. Although my baking skills are limited and green is inland for me—not part of my palette—I appreciate Mrs. Higgins's creation. I had no idea that she was capable of such artistry. The minute I see her work I know that she can do a beach cake for any of our birthdays, with the dunes, the coastline, beach chairs, and a rainbow umbrella.

Until today I thought of Mrs. Higgins as too dissimilar from Candy to give her a chance. With Jess singing her praises and constantly suggesting what Mrs. Higgins should do next, I mostly miss

Candy and the easy dialogue that she and I shared—a team effort now sorely lacking.

Jess should have such a charming cake. First she produced Mrs. Higgins, next she promised the Arts Council for my work in the spring. Beyond that, offering our family a connection in Elliot, a social standing in a frosty town. Mrs. Higgins's intentions and her talent—shown to me in a birthday cake exquisite enough to rival the work of the best pastry chefs in New York—come from Jess.

Jess keeps referring to Liza's tenth birthday party tomorrow as a coming-out party. She dreads the end of the small-daughter/single-digit tranquility. I know that she is right—how the innocence dissolves and there's no solution, no method of avoiding the reality that our daughters will grow up. Matilde, the most demure young girl, now morphed into a swimmer in turbulent waters who has little mastery, no knowledge.

"What do you think, Mom?" Matilde's voice is in the room before she is.

"I love it."

Matilde snaps pictures of the cake from every angle with her iPhone. I'm aware of what energy is required for "the" day and how the cake plays a part in it. A centerpiece of the weekend, the cake will bestow family birthday tidings that take place tomorrow afternoon at Liza's "family" party. Her "big girl" party that evening, for kids only, will be held in the sumptuous lower level of Jess's home—with a DJ and a few hired dancers. Tom and Matilde are invited to that too and are surprisingly open to a ten-year-old's party. All four children are anticipating the weekend. Charles is pleased and believes in my good fortune in rediscovering Jess. Especially since he works with William. Jess is remarkably preoccupied with tomorrow. If I don't pull off a full throttle on Liza's two parties, it will be seen as a failure. I should be more zealous, I too should be planning my outfit and exhilarated by what is ahead. I should have some gratitude for what it entails to be part of a rarified world.

More surprising is Charles suggesting that I stay at home with the twins tomorrow night to catch up on my painting. He offers to take the older children there and back, fraternize upstairs with a few other parents.

"They have a ride already, both ways, Charles," I said, for the second time.

"Not necessary, Lainie," he had answered. "I'm totally available." *Totally available?* He was knotting his tie and it was only six A.M. Then it occurred to me that Charles *wants* to take Matilde and Tom, he puts stock in the activity, especially at the Howards'. In the city, he never knew where the children were going or where they were to be collected.

I take another look at the cake—the rich green shade is fitting, emblematic of the copious greenery of Elliot in season. The first few weeks after we arrived the trees and hedges were ubiquitous and thick, insular. Before fall foliage, the advent of winter.

"Aren't you taking the birthday cake to Jess's tonight?" Matilde asks. "Won't it be hard to balance in the car?"

"I'm going in a half hour. Does anyone else want to come—the twins or Tom?"

"I'll stay here," Matilde says.

"Really?" I've become too accustomed to Matilde's company in the car; maybe I'm not paying enough attention to her schedule lately. Fair of me or not, with the relentless driving in Elliot, she's become my companion.

"No, I'll stay with the twins. Tom'll go. He'll be glad to go, Mom."

Tom comes into the kitchen with a twin in either of his arms. Tom is getting so tall that I imagine him with a driver's license sooner than he's eligible for it. Then he could put the cake on the floor of the back of the car and he could deliver it to Jess's. It isn't lost on me how much he likes going over there. For tonight Mrs. Higgins might drive over with Tom to protect the cake. If that happens, she can be complimented firsthand for her stylish cake. What I want to do is disappear into the studio.

Tom places Jack on the ground and Claire on a stool. Claire gazes at the cake. "Mommy, I want the green leaf with the flower at the top. The big white flower and one necklace. One necklace."

"No, Claire, my darling girl, the cake is for Liza. You know she will be ten. That makes her five years older than you are, and she will be a big girl! Mrs. Higgins made this cake especially for her birthday party tomorrow. We'll be there for the party and you can ask Jess for the white flower then. That's when you get to eat the white flower, when Liza's cake is cut and the candles have been blown out."

Claire frowns. "No," she says. "No," she says louder. "No! Now!" she screams.

At that moment the landline rings. Matilde picks up the phone and reads the name that comes across the screen.

"Abre." She gives me this look. "Who's that?"

Abre! The name triggers the good that came of Jess's visit and a reminder of Edna Abre's expected call by dinner hour. I snatch the phone from Matilde and dash into the den. I sit down in Charles's favorite leather wing chair, facing the window, as far from everyone as possible.

"Hello, this is Lainie Smith Morris." I am placid, ready. I will myself to have the conversation with Edna Abre. As if I'm in a swim meet where I'm too psyched to lose, where winning is imperative.

"Why, Mrs. Morris," her very cultured voice purrs. "We are *beyond* excited to feature your art for our spring gala. I have not heard Jess Howard quite so enthusiastic about any painter. . . ."

A cacophony of screams interrupts what this woman is saying, first Claire's voice and then a guttural cry from Mrs. Higgins. The screams are pitiless and the sensation that I have no effect on my children seeps into my soul.

"Mrs. Abre? I have to go, I'm sorry, I apologize. May I call you back tomorrow morning? I don't wish to be distracted . . . but it is a bit hectic. You might remember, I have four children and the twins are only five—"

"Yes, my dear. I believe that you are needed," she interrupts. "With your children needing you, a call at dinner hour isn't reasonable."

Astutely, Edna Abre hangs up first.

With the portable phone in my hand, I rush into the kitchen. Claire has climbed from the stool to the counter where the cake sits. She is swiping her hand across the emerald green leaves atop the cake; the entire first tier is demolished. Already her mouth and chin are covered in green icing.

"Get off my cake! Off of it, you spoiled child!" Mrs. Higgins's face is purple and she is wringing her hands in her apron. "Off!" screams Mrs. Higgins. "Get out of my sight!"

Claire regards each of us for a split second. Then she spins herself close enough to put her elbow through the center, sinking the entire cake, a triumphant smirk on her face. I go swooping in and rapidly yank Claire from the counter, dragging her into my arms, holding her too tightly. She begins to howl and with enough green icing on her hands to fingerpaint the walls, she smudges icing on my face and in my hair. I clamp down on her wrists with my hands. She is so forceful I barely stop her. None of us moves, including Jack, who seems fascinated for the first time ever with his twin.

Charles, forever the family phantom, has appeared in the room. He stands close to the counter, watching my anger at Claire. Preternaturally unruffled, he walks to where I stand with Claire writhing in my grasp. With those surgeon's shoulders that lead to those surgeon's arms, he lifts her from me and takes her out of the room. She puts her green face against his ear and plasters it with icing. Mrs. Higgins has not stopped wailing, *"My cake, my cake!"*

The rest of us are watching the tidal wave with a perverse fascination. I swear I hear the water crashing in my ears. Claire pounds Charles's back ferociously as they disappear up the stairs toward the bedrooms. Claire is yelping and crying, "Daddy, the cake! Daddy, the white flower!"

"I'll go to Claire, Mom." Matilde speaks in an undertone. "I'll try to talk to her."

"Matilde, Dad is with her. We should wait."

The crushing sound of Claire crying ends and soon after Charles is back in the kitchen. His twitching jawline reminds me of the first time we were at the beach together. It was Labor Day weekend and we had been dating since the spring before. I had brought him to meet my parents at the marina and I wanted to be at the beach. The lifeguards were flying their red warning flags and the wind was kicking up from the east. Charles had boasted whenever I spoke of Cape May that he too loved the ocean. I persuaded him that in spite of a storm, we should dive in. I ran to the water's edge and the waves were already rough, frothy and high enough for the surfers to be challenged. "C'mon, c'mon! Let's do it!" He took these measured steps, the same kind of steps he is taking tonight. He came near enough that I waited for him. Then he was at a standstill and I knew that he would swim no farther. I dove into the tumbling waves on my own.

"Lainie? Let's go to our bedroom. Let's talk there." Charles breaks into my thoughts.

"Claire is alone," I say. "I'll go to her."

"She's quieted down, Lainie."

Matilde is in a hurry. "I'll go to her."

Charles is about to turn her down, then I raise my hand like I'm a crossing guard. "Go ahead, Matilde."

Charles watches me and the look in his face converts to *failed mother, ruined cake.*

"We have to talk."

"Okay." *I hate my life.*

I lead. Charles's steps behind me are tranquil, almost eerie. I open the door and he closes it.

"What the hell is the matter with you, Lainie?" he hisses. "What were you doing that you missed Claire destroying a homemade cake—an important cake?"

"I was on the phone with the Arts Council. I was in the den. . . . I'd just left the kitchen—the call had come in. It was an important call." I don't turn around to face him. *As opposed to an important cake.*

"Fuck the Arts Council! What kind of mother are you, Lainie? Why did you allow what happened to happen?" His voice gets loud. "What the fuck, Lainie?"

"What kind of mother, Charles? The kind who doesn't want princess parties for her daughters and protects them as best she's able. Someone who is fallible but . . ." I start to cry sloppily, shabbily. Mostly because I have no recollection of once loving Charles, not because I'm defending Claire or the cake. The cake that tells the story.

Our bedroom becomes lonely and cold; it's frightening.

"You aren't *normal*. Why can't you be *normal*? Why can't you be a normal *mother*?" The fury in his eyes.

I don't answer.

"Normal! Normal! You've heard of it, right?" He keeps screaming. I'm sure the children hear, both from the kitchen and from Claire's room.

"*Normal?* What's so fetching about normal, you asshole? What *is* normal?" I ask. Then I open the door and point at the unlit hallway.

"Get out, Charles, get out, please."

Before he opens the door to leave, there is a fleeting question that registers on his face. We both look at the king-size bed, where he and I made love, so recently, so long ago.

"Please, go. Please. Now."

Once there is proof that he is moving away from me, I gather myself into a crouched position on the floor and weep, wondering how it can be that trust turns to scorn.

TWENTY-FIVE

The night long it is impossible to sleep. I tiptoe from one child's bedroom to the next, putting my hand on each of their backs or their stomachs, depending on their sleep position. I do this in birth order, starting with Tom. He lies on his back on top of the covers with the earbuds from his iPhone in his ears. I imagine he is listening to David Bowie or Lou Reed, musicians whom his father has encouraged. I close the door. Next I visit Matilde, who dreams deeply, the covers over her shoulders, her hair in tangles, seaweed on the pillowcase. At the bottom of her double bed are Claire and Jack, wound together. Two puppies in a litter. Claire is beyond angelic, the monster qualities of the day erased in her sleep.

Their steady breathing is a type of elixir. That I could capture my sleeping children's perfection the way a painting captures the perfection of a moment—a memory caught for eternity. A foolish thought; these children when awake are water through my fingers—flowing, cherished, gone.

At dawn I come downstairs to write a note to Mrs. Higgins, part apology for last evening, part a request for her to wake the children if I am a few minutes late. I crave a long, fast swim, one that adds to my Raritan River miles. When I'm about to leave, I hear footsteps. A sickly dread comes over me that it is Charles who has awakened an hour early and that I haven't gotten out of the house first. Instead Mrs. Higgins comes in through the back kitchen door. She begins to tie an apron on. The message is that we are picking up a conversation where we left off.

"You go, Mrs. Morris. I'm sure you need to get to that pool before the sun comes up and anybody notices." Her face has no lines today and her arms seem less flabby.

"I was leaving you a note. I want to apologize. . . ."

Mrs. Higgins pushes my apology away with her hand, dismissing me. "Go on. I'm about to bake a fresh cake before it gets too hectic. Redo and hand deliver."

There is the urge to fall into her arms, to be enveloped in her understanding and acceptance. "Go now. While the moon is up, Mrs. Morris."

I am beside the French doors that face the meadow behind the house. A meadow in dire need of water; a brook running through it would do. The moon is a crescent, hopeful and romantic for those who are believers. I feel homesick for everything that is not in Elliot, starting with Cape May and moving north to Red Hook.

I fish around in my purse for the car keys. "Okay, Mrs. Higgins. Thank you."

"Psshaw." Mrs. Higgins is already filling a bowl with all-purpose flour. She opens the pantry cabinet and lifts a few small bottles of green food dye.

"Do you have enough of the ingredients? Do you want me to go to the store later in the morning and . . ."

Mrs. Higgins waves her hand again. "There's a small window before it shuts tight. You should go."

As if underwater, I press the automatic button on the garage wall, praying the electric door that creaks and heaves open won't wake anyone. I back my Jeep out onto the soundless street.

PART TEN

Jess

TWENTY-SIX

⬯

I cannot avoid rustling around at Liza's party tonight. Upstairs in the conservatory, the popular parents whom I've asked to stay are settling into my inner sanctum for a night of tony tattle. Downstairs in the family room are the ten-year-old girls, sophisticated and self-conscious as they come, with as callow a group of ten-year-old boys as I've ever seen. To add to the mixture are a few family friends' older children, including Matilde and Tom Morris.

Charles is here without Lainie; his eyes are glued to me as I do my best version of the social butterfly routine of wife, mother, friend. My form is impeccable, propelled by Charles's attendance. Why not— the plan has evolved in an organic way. Lainie offered Mrs. Higgins's services several nights ago when I called to ask the favor. "We have to do for each other, Jess," she said. "By all means, Mrs. Higgins must come to you on Saturday night." In reality, what would suit Lainie better than an evening in her studio with the twins asleep and the rest of the family with me? Mrs. Higgins not only arrived to pitch in, she brought her signature hors d'oeuvres, strawberry bruschetta for the adults and salt-and-pepper oven fries for everyone. I'm passing out the bruschetta when Matilde appears. She immediately spots Tom among us, holding a highball glass in his hand.

"Relax, Matilde, it's ginger ale. Dad's putting me in practice mode. He told me that," I hear Tom say.

I walk to where they stand. "Matilde, you're probably bored with the kid stuff. You know that Rory Giffs is having a party tonight and I've called over there. That's the party that you and Tom should be at. I've spoken with Rory and her mother and they'd be delighted if you and Tom could join them."

"Dee-lighted." Tom rolls his eyes at me. "Jess, I'm not sure this is such a good idea. Matilde and I both know how middle-school parties go."

Charles joins us. He smiles. "Matilde, what a lucky break. Jess has just told me that Rory is one of the most popular girls at your school. This could be an opportunity for you!"

Tom becomes suspicious.

"Tom? You'll go too, you'll be your sister's protector," Charles says.

Matilde and Tom exchange glances in what I interpret to be a rare moment of solidarity.

"You'll see, Matilde. These girls are nice," I push.

There is a moment's silence. "Matilde?" Charles says.

"Thanks, Jess," she says. "I'd love to go." She sounds punctured.

Yet I believe that she does want to go, but is intimidated. I sense her upset, her yearning to explore my medicine cabinets again—how else will she endure the night? It's an irony that only adults have access to Klonopin for such occasions.

"We'll drive you," Charles says.

"We?" Tom is raising an eyebrow.

"Tom, your father would be lost for longer than it takes to get there. The roads are dark in Elliot at night and the GPS doesn't always find these estates. . . ."

At the front hall closet, Tom gets on board. He politely holds open my coat.

I insist that Matilde sit in front with me while Charles is pretzeled in the back of my Mercedes next to Tom. Charles is counting the minutes to the ride home, until we are alone.

"Rory and her crowd are awfully fun once you get to know them, Matilde. I suppose it's only natural to be wary of newcomers—anyplace that anyone goes. As you become friends, you'll have entrée everywhere," I say cheerily.

"Fantastic, Matilde," Charles says. "I hope that you've thanked Jess."

"I did, Dad. You were right there. Didn't you hear me?"

"What about me, do I need an 'entrée'?" Tom laughs.

"No, Tom, you don't. You're two grades ahead and you're a boy," Charles says. "The party *belongs* to you."

Matilde traces her finger across the window where the moisture is dissolving. The tall birches and oak trees clutter the moonlight. In my rearview mirror Tom's mouth slips into a tight line. I only hope that he doesn't abandon his sister.

Three hours later Charles and I are back at the Giffs'. "Plenty of fathers will be inside, Charles. Very few mothers come out for a late pickup unless they are divorced with no husbands to do the job," I say.

"Just how did we manage to have the night—out in the open, Jess? Free of innuendo?" he asks.

"We're fortunate that our spouses don't care and that no one dares to talk about me. And that newcomers never find the Giffs' house on their own."

Charles closes the passenger door and heads inside. As I feared, Tom long ago bailed, according to a text sent to Charles. He had hardly gotten there when he left with two brothers who live next door and three girls. Although these certainly aren't my children, I wonder what he said to his younger sister as he walked out of the Giffs'—that he too is in search of a life in Elliot, one that precludes thinking of Matilde first? While I'm the pusher of the evening, Tom's decision has churned up my anxiety about Matilde's welfare. For good reason, it turns out, since as soon as she climbs into the backseat, her stress level hits the ozone.

"Is Mom asleep?" she asks Charles, not glancing in my direction.

"She isn't. She is awake. For you," Charles says.

"Okay." Matilde looks out the window. The rain has begun, falling into icicles. I take the road carefully, slowly.

"Have a good time, Matilde? I know that Tom did. He texted me about ten minutes ago, to say he's staying at his friend's house. Baker something or other. Do you know him?" Charles asks.

"No."

Were she my daughter I would insist that she speak in full sentences. I would say, "Please show some respect." Lainie believes that being polite counts—that I know. Yet when I look in my rearview mirror at Matilde, I read in her face that there's been an incident—her father's and my secret tryst is less a concern than what occurred at the Giffs'.

I ramp up my windshield wipers.

"Look at that," Charles says. "The first snow of winter. Matilde, you always love the first snow."

"In the city." Matilde begins to cry. Not attractive, feminine tears but the tears of those who suffer and their faces are distorted by despondence. Matilde gulps for air, trying to recover from the ugly cloud that hangs over her and exhausts her.

"Tom left right away." She keeps crying. I hand her my monogrammed handkerchief and she tries to hand it back to me.

"No, take it, Matilde, I haven't got any tissues in the car."

"Tom left, Dad."

"We know," Charles says. "I tried to text you when I heard and you didn't text back. I thought you were having a good time."

Matilde cries louder. "The party was in a . . . back room with a back room. A dungeon."

I steer the car toward the house. "Matilde, why don't you come inside for a few minutes before you and your father go home. We'll see if Liza is still up. I know she'd love to tell you about the rest of her party night."

Matilde stares out the window. "No, thank you, Jess. It's late and my dad says that my mom is waiting up."

"Matilde, come with me now." I'm about to yank her arm when I calm myself.

Charles gives me a perplexed look, surprised by my tone. Either he trusts me or he doesn't. He pauses. "Let's go in, Matilde; I'll text Mom to tell her we'll be there soon."

We walk in the through the garage. William comes out of the kitchen as if he's been watching the clock. "Charles, my man, a long night indeed. Let's go and scrounge up some leftovers." He ignores me and Matilde.

I lead Matilde to my small office adjacent to the den and close the door. The scent of young sex, body parts, sweat, and semen emanate from her.

"What happened?" I ask.

"Nothing," she says.

"All right, here's what we'll do. We'll sit in my office until you figure out the advantage of talking to me."

"Nothing happened, Jess."

"Not only do I not believe you, I bet you that I *know* what happened."

"If that's true then you are disgusting, Jess."

"Should I go first?" I won't let her have the better of me, regardless of how much damage has been done. Charles and Lainie weigh heavily upon me. Damage control is the only solution. "If you were my daughter, we'd be sitting here with the same situation, Matilde. Believe me, I have more clout than your parents; I've lived here for years and I've done a few things of my own. . . ."

We sit for a five full minutes while she seems to reflect on the horror at hand and decides that I might be helpful.

"The cutest boy was staring at me and said I was hot. He called me 'new girl,' 'babe in the woods.' We were in the back room—there was music and smoke and joints being passed. I couldn't really see the girls—some were lying on couches and others on their knees in front of the boys who were lined up.

"Then I heard a few girls talking about me, saying that I'd be so pretty if I took my hair down. One of them said she bet I didn't know anything and that I was a prude. Two other girls from ninth grade were saying, 'down on me,' 'come in my mouth,' 'cock tease.'"

I'm sickened by her story, repulsed by what has happened, and afraid for both of us. "Matilde, I'm sorry that you—"

"You're *sorry*? Jess. It was your idea."

"Matilde . . ." I shudder that the crafty schemes of Elliot social life for tweens exists and will continue to exist. "Listen, if we . . ."

"Not one girl would be my friend. It was like this boy was the only one who stuck up for me. And then he pushed me onto the couch and unzipped his fly." Matilde begins to cry hysterically. "He stuck it in my mouth. . . ."

It's awkward the way that I reach out to her, try to give her a hug. She jerks her body away.

"The way he held my arms down, I thought he'd tear them off my body. People were watching. . . ." She's sobbing.

"Matilde," I say, "I will get you through this."

"Like I was drowning . . . If my mother finds out . . ."

"Listen to me." I speak in a terse voice. My body is taut. "Your mother won't know. Nor will your father. I'm going to call you tomorrow morning. We'll make a plan then. Do you understand?"

Matilde stares at me. I take her hands in mine and then press my thumbs against her wrists.

"Do you understand?"

She nods slightly.

"By the way, the cute popular boy who took you to the back room? Reese. His name is Reese," I say.

I call Lainie early the next morning and she picks up on the first ring, as if she's been expecting my call.

"Jess? Is everything okay?"

"Well . . ." I begin.

I hear her pacing about, her feet tapping. Next I hear Mrs. Higgins talking loudly from the kitchen—it hurts my head.

"Pancakes? Bacon? Claire? Jack?" Mrs. Higgins's voice is strident.

"Hold on. Let me close the door to my studio." Lainie would be in her studio already. It could be that Matilde is with Claire in her pale pink bedroom with the blue clouds on the ceiling and too many blown-up photos of the family in Cape May on the near wall.

To prove me wrong, Lainie puts the phone on speaker. "Jess, can you wait? Claire is here and every Sunday morning we sing a song together." Lainie starts playing a YouTube version of Van Morrison singing "Too-ra-loo-ra-loo-ral." Claire can be heard saying, "Mommy, Mommy, I like this!"

"Lainie!" I shout over the din. "Please get Matilde for me. Tell her that she didn't pick up her cell and I decided to reach her through your phone."

There is a flutter of noise.

"Mom? I haven't brushed my teeth yet. I haven't washed my face," Matilde says, slithering out of our phone call.

"Matilde, I've been on the phone with Jess. She wants to talk with you. I will take Claire out of the room." Lainie is apologetic, which translates into "I hate this shit but I'm the mother."

"Matilde, what went on last night, my darling girl, that Jess wants to speak with you? It isn't even eight thirty."

"Nothing, Mom, nothing, I swear."

Good, she must lie. I can only clean it up if she is willing to lie to everyone. To the girls who hate her who were in the back room at the Giffs' to the boys who don't hate her and hope to use her.

"Why is Jess wanting to speak with you? After she arranged for you to be at the party. I'm asking. I'm your mother."

"I'm still on speaker, Lainie, Matilde. I'm waiting to speak with Matilde. Maybe she should call me back from her own phone."

"Would you talk to Jess?" Lainie asks. "Finish up with her, then we'll swim together before Mrs. Higgins leaves for church. We'll swim the Raritan River."

Then I'm not on speaker and I wait on hold as if it's a department store and there is "the silence" before the connection. My phone goes dead. A moment later it rings and MATILDE MORRIS comes across the screen.

"Hi, Jess."

"Where are you? Are you alone?"

"I'm in my room. No one's around."

"Good." I click my tongue. "Matilde. Since I know exactly what happened, I've decided how to play it. I'll do you a favor and I'll back you up on your lie to your mother and what will soon be a lie to your father. Your parents will never know."

Matilde sighs close to her phone, causing mine to give off heat.

"The deal is that I'll defend you and make everything go away. Reese, the other boys last night at the Giffs' home? Whatever they or the girls say, it's not true and people who hear it and believe it, they're *mistaken*. They've got it *wrong,* you did nothing. You were in that back room for one moment and it wasn't a party for you. You left immediately."

"Thank you, Jess."

I pause. "Matilde, there's a caveat. In exchange, Thanksgiving night, what you saw in my pantry—by the wine closet—is wiped from your memory. It never happened. See no evil, hear no evil. Both of us are spotless. *Capisce?*"

When I hang up, I have a sense of accomplishment. Matilde and I are connected by our secrets; we are two buoys in deep waters.

TWENTY-SEVEN

B eing the wife of the CEO of the hospital has its perks, com-
mands admiration, and fills the day. Then there is the other
hat I wear, clandestine, priceless—that of Charles's lover. As
queen bee of Christmas season with interminable invitations and
a "show up" policy, the highlight is a plan with Charles. The twist is
that I'm entwined with Lainie and her children, his wife and his children, ad nauseam. Although I've often considered myself capable of
plots and conflicts, this one beats the band. Every time I'm with Lainie
I want to ask, *How is it with you and Charles?* Yet we operate more
along the lines of husbands are husbands, placate them as best you
can. Children are the glue; cherish them and contort yourself for their
benefit. On occasion we get to chat about wardrobe and a luncheon,
about the pool being empty or the pool being crowded.

For instance, today I arrive at the Y so early that the lifeguard is
testing the water, leaning in with small test tubes. I don't expect that
Lainie will have arrived and I'm in no mood to see her. That's how it
is right before my next assignation with Charles and right after. Too
close for comfort—best to space out Lainie and the trysts with

Charles. What I find are both Lainie and Matilde sharing the third lane, slashing through the water with that combination of velocity and alacrity. They are water dancers doing acrobatic feats—and one has to admit that both Lainie and Matilde have become better swimmers in their four months in Elliot. There is no master swimmer who competes; they flip and turn like big fish. Sailfish or marlins, the ones worth catching to mount on the wall. Matilde, moving through water as salvation, looking more Lainie than the actual Lainie. How extraneous most of life beyond the pool and the canvas must be for them.

The lights are blinding from the interior of the pool and these swimmers appear macabre. One might remark upon how interesting a mother-and-daughter duo they make. Not I. I'm simply relieved that it is a week after the Matilde incident at the Giffs' party. Hosing down that fire required ingenuity that fortunately I have. Each day that passes lowers the Giffs' party/Matilde Morris faux pas on the gossip pole of mid-December.

I sit down at the edge and I'm about to put on my flippers—a form of cheating to some swimmers, a shrewd move to others. They are coming at me, in freestyle then backstroke. In synchrony they switch to the butterfly and the breaststroke. The tenets of professional swimming are obvious: technique, fast turns, the high quality of their strokes. I watch them and suddenly I don't feel like swimming. A nippy day in December isn't the most enticing. I ought to go to my locker and put on my workout clothes. There will be the early-bird Pilates class in a half hour. To boot, it saves my hair and I'm with Charles in six hours' time. I jump up from the side of the pool and head for the locker room, passing the wall board that lists the swimmers in the Raritan River competition. I'm not surprised at what I read, only surprised that I wasn't on top of it sooner. I, Jess, the smartest, dumbest one at the pool. I realize that this is no hobby for either mother or daughter; they are swimming as a means to get through life in Elliot. Lainie has always returned to the water, fought to be the best at it. The top of the roster lists Lainie then Matilde, pitted against each other for first place. Mother and daughter deluded by their mode of flight.

Having fibbed my way out of Elliot for the day is impressive. Then again, I'm facile enough at whatever I set out to do. What's so beguiling is Charles, my lover, and how the hours together take on a life of their own. We have it down to a science: the suite at the Gansevoort, my quick gait through the busy lobby with the dim chandeliers and high ceiling, the wood floors dyed almost black, bleeding hipness into the scene. The titillation of Charles's fictive check-in name, Mr. Ronson, cryptic and exciting texts that lead up to the next afternoon. What we don't have down to any science is what to do with the feelings, the untenable component. My falling for a man would be complicated enough without our particular narrative. I choose to push it to the back of my mind and Charles, Charles alone, remains in the front lobe. He remains there, where he has landed.

From the moment I'm in the room until we've exhausted ourselves there is a yearning that I have never known. We start with kisses that lead us to tear our clothes off, sometimes standing, sometimes on the bed, the couch, the floor. He offers words that are unsuited to his public image while I hold my breath. "Jess. Jess, I missed you. I crave you." Words only for me.

"Ditto." We begin our frenzied, primordial sex, sex that suffuses me with rapture.

That's why I laugh when he settles down after the lovemaking and puts a pillow behind his head. He is in the center of the king-size bed with the sumptuous Egyptian cotton sheets and duvet cover. Each time I try to crawl into him, a first for me—who ever cared about *the after* before—I'm awkward. He *knows* where I should be situated and rearranges me if need be. He's good, he's excellent—then maybe, just maybe, he's seasoned and the women are fungible—and simply up to bat? How unfortunate if I were the one who is hooked. Who would expect it?

"Passion without longing." I repeat my own motto, tracing his shoulders with my fingers. Charles feels my nails, long, polished as opposed to Lainie's, which have always been short and embedded with paint. At this point in our afternoon, my hand is on his heart and my head is cradled in his shoulder. I look up at him. He is more spectacular in confined quarters. Beyond his profile is the weak winter light filtering through the window. We've forgotten to pull the shades—something Charles prefers to do—and I'm rather glad about it. Who wants hidden, disguised married sex when you have the chance to witness every line and crevice. Lovers. *Charles, lover, lover Charles.*

He begins the conversation. "Hey, Jess, what happened with Lainie and Matilde?"

Charles is shifting gears and apparently Lainie is in the ether, in the room, ubiquitous and important to Charles *and* to me. She is exempt only when we are fucking—then I don't feel her, then she doesn't exist. Well, we aren't fucking at the moment. Welcome to the Charles, Lainie, and Jess Show.

"Well, there was some drama." I'm speaking softly, hoping we don't linger on the subject.

"You mean besides when Claire smashed the cake to pieces and Mrs. Higgins made it from scratch again." He yawns, pulls me closer.

"I sort of missed it but Lainie described the scene." I place my hands across his chest that is a map, a journey. Christ, I'm becoming sentimental—very unbecoming.

"All redeemable," Charles says. In his world with myriad limbs and spines that he saves, the patients, men and women, genuflecting afterward and passing along the word, *Dr. Charles Morris, best of the best, savior among saviors,* a family drama is small potatoes. I inhale him, delving into his neck—I have to inhale since the clock is ticking.

"Lainie was a flake." He sits up in bed and stiffens. "I'm out of tricks. I'm not sure how to reel Lainie in, wake her up. There's no excuse for how she acts."

Does Charles believe that Lainie does things on purpose? We both know it is more complicated than that.

"I know that you would have handled it differently, Jess."

"A birthday cake—that's what it was and it worked out fine. The party for Liza was gratifying and everyone was happy. All fine." I'm in her husband's arms, falling for him and defending her. Lately I've begun to surprise myself. To her rescue again.

Charles is upright and his body tightens. I sit up and face him, drawing the sheet under my arms to be less bare. Not that I want to talk about any of these topics, yet somehow I need to convey that Lainie isn't a victim. He and I are not thrown together as a diversion for the long-suffering wife.

"Lainie is there, Charles, in her own quiet way. She's on your arm if you tell her to be. She'll show up at any event for the children, for your work. You know that."

"I'm not worried about Lainie, Jess. She has the art show thanks to you; I'm worried about Matilde."

Do he and I even exist—in a moment, a second, millisecond? The room feels congested, dense. We both belong to Lainie.

Naturally Matilde is next on the docket. Aren't she and Lainie attached by their mermaid tails?

"She saw us together, is that why?"

"Partly," says Charles. "But Matilde *wants* to fit in, her mother doesn't care. That makes it more difficult."

I'm in a dicey place. Elliot society is my bailiwick; Charles is my project. I decide to go for broke, that honesty, when possible, is the best policy.

"Matilde is talked about by the girls in her class. She has to act out, has to be an instigator. She might hear the girls at the party tattling about her—how beautiful she'd be if she didn't dress like a nerd and act like an . . . outsider. The girls in her class call her swimming scary."

"Scary?" Charles doesn't get it.

"Charles, she's at a tough age in a new town, a fishbowl. . . ."

"And then she saw us kissing in your pantry." His guilt. Jesus. For Matilde, not Lainie.

"Right," I say. I wish I had a cigarette to light up and exhale smoke rings. Accompanied by a glass of wine.

"Do you know my daughter? Really know her?" He is taking an interest in the story because it's about his daughter. Child supremacy.

"Just a hunch. You don't have to worry about Matilde. I've spoken to her about Thanksgiving. It's all right. She understands."

"Understands what we did in your house with your husband and my wife at the dining table?"

I shrug. "Want me to leave?" I pull back and his arms no longer reach me. "The door, Charles? Go, go through it. Have your perfect life, your perfect story."

"It wasn't *your* daughter who saw us."

"No, it was *your* daughter. I promise you it is okay. I've spoken with her."

"What did you do, blackmail her? Dangerous stuff, Jess."

I point to the door. "Go ahead, don't let me stop you."

"You know I can't stay away from you." His face is against mine and I smell his skin. "We know that anything could go wrong."

"Yes, a score of possibilities. William, the hospital, Lainie, the children." I kiss his chest. "Meanwhile, it's tractable."

He holds me and before he kisses me, he asks, "What do you want, Jess?"

"To be in your arms," I answer. To trust him, I would want that too. I do or else he wouldn't do as he pleases with my body. When it occurs to Charles how our affair is weirdly amorphous and distinct, he will better accept that he is a husband and a lover. That triangles are treacherous and inevitable, that everywhere there is the pull of three. *Charles, Lainie, and I. Charles, Matilde, and Lainie. Matilde, Lainie, and I. Charles, Matilde, and I.*

Charles is inside me once more. We have an hour left and what is hallowed prevails.

PART ELEVEN

Lainie

TWENTY-EIGHT

I stand alone at the Narrows, wading in the tidal stream that links Staten Island and Brooklyn. The winter sun dances on the pearly water. Only the hard-core devotees enjoy this season. The past two Decembers I came with Isabelle and Cher. The three of us stood under the bridge to sketch and take photographs of the snippet of beach that wasn't visible to the naked eye. The wind was against our faces, our scarves futile in the winter solstice. If I work here today—knowing I might not get to Cape May anytime soon—I will have what I need to complete the paintings for the March show, including the triptych.

I notice the men today because they are not fishermen but patrolmen, perhaps security guards or policemen. They watch me as I snap pictures first with my iPhone and then with my Olympus. If I look to the west, I imagine how this flows to the Raritan River and finally to the Atlantic. The gulls caw overhead; they might or might not make it into the pictures. Once I'm in the water collecting rocks and seaweed in a large white garbage bag, they come toward me. I decide that any scrap of marine life is worth taking back to Elliot and wade knee high in the water. The two men in their uniforms approach me; the first one is like a movie star and young, anyone would notice.

"Excuse me, miss." When he takes off his Ray-Ban sunglasses he reminds me of summertime. They will critique me, *Her palette has changed, her canvases are mammoth to emphasize how women are only part of the story, how place becomes a character for Lainie Smith Morris.* If I have to write it myself and put it at the top of the press release, I shall.

He is at the edge. "Miss? Can I ask what you're doing? No one is allowed in the water."

"I'm collecting shells . . . flotsam . . . appreciating the scenery. . . . I'm an artist." I keep wading and scooping my hands through the water. The seaweed is slippery; I put a clump of it in my plastic bag.

"Lady, you can't be in the water," says the second officer. "You have to get out of the water, now." He is tedious, he needs to be tuned.

I ignore him.

"Miss, please, you have to get out." He is still tedious.

Minnows float by and I try to scoop some up.

The second officer is close without getting his shoes wet. It is obvious that he means it. I should do what he says. Instead I stay; the water beckons me.

The first officer tries to rescue me. "She's an artist," he explains.

"Well, that may be, and so I've heard. She isn't allowed anyway, McCain."

The second officer makes a gesture to McCain, pointing to how I have to get out. McCain practically jumps in. I could fall into his arms. I have always been a Blanche DuBois on some level. In times of need a stranger could have your back. A young man in uniform reminds me of how officers get lost in the suburban shuffle, a place where bankers, lawyers, and doctors rule.

"Miss?" The second officer motions to me. "Let's go. Maybe you don't understand. We can't have ya in the water. It's against the law."

I reluctantly wade out to the bank. My jeans are soaked since the water is higher than my waders. I peer into my plastic bag and I've hit the jackpot.

The second officer nods; he's pleased too, he's gotten what he wants.

"C'mon, McCain, let's get goin'. Nothin' more to do." He looks at me. "You should go, miss. No one should be around, like I tole ya."

"I'll take it from here, Buzz. You go ahead then," says the first officer, McCain. "I'll catch up."

He stays, staring at me. Maybe we were once glued together and our discovery is pivotal. There is the sound of the water lapping against the banks. The second officer plods along, leaving us with the variable tide. In the flickering sun he appears antithetical to anyone I have ever known. While I can feel him waiting, I too am waiting. I want him to be my escort to the Upper New York Bay, taking me from the south, where we are standing, toward Ellis Island and then Liberty Island, in an unending romance with this man and the water. I know everything about him by his posture.

"Is there something you need?" he asks.

"No, no," I say. "Thank you."

In the weak rays of the sun he is a mirage, I'm sure of it.

"Nobody is allowed around this section of the Narrows. That's why we stopped you. That's why my partner got bent outta shape."

"Sure, it's okay." I open my sketchbook for part two of the visit. I take out my camera and snap shots as if he isn't with me.

"Not safe, miss. No one comes around, nobody."

I stop for a moment. "I understand. I won't be long. The light changes and I have to get back to my children."

"Children." He sounds surprised, wistful. "How many?"

"Four. A son, a daughter, a set of girl and boy twins."

Take me anyway, enchant me. Away from my children for the hours you have to spare.

He whistles. "You look young enough . . . I thought you were in school."

"I'm not." It gets awkward. He pauses, then he moves on, turns around in passing me. I could do anything, throw myself at him, tell him the truth, every kernel of the story, how we moved to Elliot, how lonely it is. How Charles's remoteness has turned to ice. How removed

I am from playing wifey and how it matters in a town in mid–New Jersey. Then again, for some reason, the sex with Charles is heightened and that's an unexpected plus. I could describe my upcoming one-woman show and how it keeps me sane, gives me hope, that I'm working on it now, at the Narrows. I could describe how I swim the Raritan River at a Y pool to save my soul. The urge to tell him is tremendous.

"Your name?" he asks. He is standing beside me again. I feel his breath and it is gone, blown far from me. He could put his arms around me from behind and I would lean into him. *Don't go,* I'd beg. *Stay with me.* I know by the width of his shoulders that although swimming is not compelling for him, he does a mean crawl and a vicious butterfly.

"What's your name?"

"Lainie. Lainie Smith Morris." The flurry blows it out of my mouth and into the Narrows.

"Again?" he shouts.

"Lainie Smith Morris." *Take me, Lainie. Take the Lainie out of Lainie Smith Morris.*

He hands me a card, cheap paper, too much design on it. R. McCain is in block letters and beneath the 718 precinct number is his cell, beginning with a 917 area code. Reading his information makes me miss the city.

"We could get a cup of coffee." He smiles at me and his teeth are good. The kind of white teeth that each of us wants. Then the smile radiates toward me through the cool breeze and I smile back.

I don't know if he means at this moment or if he means someday as in "we must get something on the calendar" Elliot lingo. Either way he wants to see me again.

"I would like that," I say.

I believe that I'm in his arms in a hotel room with a low rate where no one I have ever known would go and they short-sheet the beds. His chest is an aphrodisiac. He gets to me and I repeat his name over and over.

I take off my sunglasses. I expect a surprise, a surprise kiss. If

I am doing poorly at this, he is worse. He looks down at the water and his face is pure rugged angles and machismo.

"Well, Lainie Smith Morris, text or call if you ever need anything. Anything. Any time."

I put his card in my wallet and watch his shoulders as he faces away from me. His neck is reassuringly strong and I know instinctively that he would fight to the finish for me. He walks like Charles could never walk, a dense/light/forsaken/safe gait.

The moon rises early this time of year. Tonight it shines through the window directly behind where Tom sits at the dinner table. The children's conversation sounds far off and I'm back at the Narrows with the thick/thin officer and his blue/black eyes. I want to take his card out of my wallet to begin. Begin what? A betrayal of Charles?

I haven't been so much as casually curious about a man for years. Yet within hours of the meeting I reenact the scene; it washes over me and colors the night. Later, as Charles sleeps, I stare at him in shadows that are cast despite the blackout shades, despite the opaque pockets of the house. No matter what his sleep used to be, it belonged to me, his wife. Now it's as if he's not in the room. Maybe I'm not in the room. I feel that I'm watching curtains that don't exist move across the window frames. This is how people lose their minds, I suppose. Then I do hear something, a stealth sound. One of the children prowling around. The wood landing creaks near my studio.

I find Matilde at my drafting board, using my largest sheets of heavy paper, twenty-four inches by thirty-six inches. She's using her graphite pencils, not pastels. She is sketching exactly the scene from the Narrows.

"Oh, Matilde, you frightened me."

"Mom." She is expecting me.

"Matilde, how did you get the picture?"

"You left your phone in my room."

She keeps sketching, keeps switching from blue to green to earth tones.

"There are snapshots in your camera too, Mom. I found them . . . sitting there."

Matilde holds up a drawing and it has a distinctive style—the saturation of water and light. Her interpretation is simpatico with my preliminary sketch from the afternoon.

"Beautiful, Matilde," I say. "Perfectly beautiful." The chill of witnessing your child's unadulterated creativity. "Keep working through till morning, if need be."

"What about our swim?" She looks at my iPad and reads the time. "Less than two hours away."

"Let it go, my darling girl. Sleep in. I'll swim alone, I'll swim for you." I kiss the top of her head and take one more glance at how gifted she is.

Matilde sleeps and I drive alone through the sleepy town to the Y pool. Jess is in the women's locker room, along with a few die-hard swimmers.

"You'd think people would respect the hour," Jess says. "They are loud and it's too early in the morning for me to feel tolerant."

"I'm glad to find you," I say.

"What's up?" Jess frowns. "Everything okay?"

"Yes." I look around. "Let's try to speak alone."

Jess motions to me and we walk with our goggles and caps in our hands to the pool.

"Something has happened?" Jess asks.

"Well, yes, something very strange and dubious. You won't believe it."

"Try me." Jess is practically rolling her eyes. She isn't interested and I should not have begun this with her.

"Oh, never mind. . . ." I say.

"Lainie! Tell me."

"This is so strange, you know. I was at the Narrows yesterday and this patrol cop came over and he flirted with me."

"And you were drawn to him." Jess watches my face.

"Sort of, yes."

"Lainie, that's great!"

"Great?" I'm in despair. I'm about to cry.

"How old is he?"

"How old? I don't know. Young, maybe thirty."

"Lainie, perfect!"

"Perfect?"

"You should meet him for a beer or whatever they do, those guys."

"Jess, I could never do it, never have a beer with him if he asked. I couldn't do it to Charles, to our family. He was unlike Charles, the opposite, that's the thing. Probably what made him . . . interesting. . . ."

"Lainie, did he ask, did he ask you to meet him somewhere?"

I look around to be sure that no one is listening. "He mentioned coffee. I'm almost sure of that."

"Lainie, what's wrong with a flirtation? Elliot isn't your piece of heaven on earth. You acclimate the best you know how. You need a pleasure of your own, you deserve a distraction."

"I would *never* do it to Charles; maybe that's why I stayed up most of the night thinking about it."

"You feel guilty and you've done nothing. *Nothing,* Lainie. Why not do something for yourself? The *idea* of it isn't very satisfying, it would be the deed that satisfies. Remember when Jimmy Carter said he lusted in his heart? Lusting in one's heart is . . . well, a dead end."

A lesson from Jess. "How about the promises that don't exist after a while? Isn't that what you mean?" I ask.

"Exactly," Jess says. We both look at the clock on the wall. We know we only have a half hour to swim before we shower and pick up the kids to start carpooling. "I'm also saying that nothing is what it seems. Who could predict that there'd be a guy? You didn't go after some cop in Red Hook."

"It wasn't Red Hook, Jess."

"Okay! I get it," Jess laughs. "A specific guy in a specific place. Something about it got to you, or we would be swimming already."

"Charles is my concern. That counts. I should be faithful to him."

"Why? Charles is everywhere and nowhere. William, more so." Jess puts her arms around me. "These men, Lainie," she says. "They slip and slide, they come, they go."

TWENTY-NINE

lthough Vermont this year is unlike our previous ski vacations, I feel obligated to a modicum of enthusiasm. Matilde's skepticism, her outright negativity, has to be dispelled. "Matilde," I explain, "the Howard family and our family have always skied in southern Vermont. How serendipitous is that?" I do not mention that we ski neither with the same frequency nor at the same level. Besides, Charles is incredibly pleased that we are staying at the Howards' chateau ski house, more lodge than house, and has conveyed that we are decent enough skiers.

We begin the vacation by admiring the humongus fireplace, three stories high in the main room, with a deer's head and antlers above the mantle. The large, black eyes are glazed, a reminder of how very dead it is, while on the floor there is another dead animal's head, a bear's head on the bear rug around the fireplace.

Jess is in gym coach mode. She practically blows a whistle as she leads us through the rooms. Charles gives me a glance that conveys that I should be admiring of every detail. "Oh, Jess, I'll need a road map to get back to my wing" and "How romantic it is!" and "I love your home!" I say.

Jess is also in a glamorous Vermont mode; her bangle bracelets clink together while she twists and turns as we follow her to the master bedroom. There is a fireplace and a four-poster bed that has a stepstool on both sides. Jess pulls up the shades to reveal the mountains.

"Lainie, it unquestionably rivals the Atlantic Ocean and the Hudson River, right? I mean, seriously, Lainie . . . Lainie?"

"Yes, it's terrific, Jess." Have I ever felt farther from the zephyrs and swift currents, the waves that break and roll to shore?

"That's for sure! That's right!" Jess claps her hands.

Charles instructs both Tom and Matilde to help set up the children's room. Tom carries knapsacks and duffel bags to the finished attic, as Jess says, "for the boys." The girls are to sleep in a large bedroom that is reminiscent of a country-style dorm room. Three single beds are made up with matching white starched duvet covers.

"How inviting," I say. "Matilde, what fun it will be with the younger girls." If she wonders why she is the built-in babysitter, it has to do with Jess's impassioned plea for help over Christmas break. Although she has hired Mrs. Higgins at double the salary—at Charles's behest—and Norine is here, Jess considers Matilde the "big girl" of the group.

Charles and William walk into the girls' room. William is slapping Charles on the back and Charles is laughing at a punch line: "And then they just pass each other in the hallway and say, 'Fuck you.'"

Jess focuses on the men. "William? Where is Mrs. Higgins?"

"Mrs. Higgins is in the kitchen, Jess," Charles says. Then he whistles, which is unlike him. I raise my eyebrows.

"Well, I happened to be in the kitchen with William, looking at their Wolf ranges, six burners each at two stations. Quite imposing. Mrs. Higgins is in her milieu, concentrating on our dinner."

Now I'm stunned. "I'm sorry?"

"Mrs. Higgins is starting a lamb stew as we speak," Jess says. "Peeling potatoes and steaming vegetables, browning the meat."

I look at Matilde. William moves toward the open doorway, an escape artist of immense talent.

"I love lamb stew," Charles says. I'm not sure if it's true or not since I don't make stews and he's never talked about it before.

"I'm about to start a crème brûlée. Would you like to join me, Matilde?" Jess asks.

"Okay." My daughter moves toward Jess as if she's on the field and it's time to concede to the other team.

William arrives late for dinner, having skied Stratton the entire afternoon. He strolls to the head of the table without taking off his ski sweater while Jess starts waving to signal a lack of manners. The twins squirm in their seats while Billy tries to emulate Tom. Liza, who has told Matilde that her friends are at more exciting places for Christmas than Vermont, is preoccupied with texting them. Jess has blown her hair dry and is wearing a heavy layer of mascara. She has changed her clothes for dinner and is wearing a black cashmere V-neck body-fitting sweater and a black wool skirt. Too late I realize that à la *Downton Abbey,* there is the expectation that we will change for dinner every night—and I'm still in the clothes that I wore for the four-hour ride up. No wonder that William annoyed Jess. I feel the hives spreading across my neck and I miss my studio almost as much as I miss the Shore. Both places seem remarkably far away.

"What attractive silverware and placemats." I fill the tension in the room.

"Lainie, how gracious of you." Jess gives me a practiced smile. Claire starts her water dance.

"Mommy? Let's go get a book!"

"Claire, my darling girl, we are about to have a family dinner. A double family dinner with two families. All the Howards and all the Morrises. That means you. So we'll do the book *after* dinner."

In less than a minute I'm up and have returned with the copy of

Amelia Bedelia Goes Camping that is always in the bottom of my purse. "Darling girl, this is your book." I hand it to Claire, who slams it down on the table. "You turn the pages yourself and I'll read it to you later, after dinner."

Claire scowls. "What? No! Read it now, Mommy!"

"Claire, listen to me. . . ." I'm so very tired.

Jess brings in the tureen filled with the stew and places it on the sideboard. "Jeez Louise, Lainie. Let's give your five-year-old an iPad or take her into the kitchen and switch on the TV for a few minutes. You know, to her favorite show?"

"Not necessary, Jess. She's fine. Thank you."

Norine enters with a salad and a bread basket in either hand. Jess moves nervously from her seat to the sideboard and starts to dish out the food.

"Mom, when are you leaving?" Matilde asks.

"I'm leaving tomorrow, in the late afternoon."

"Tomorrow? Mom, we just got to Vermont."

"Yes, Matilde, I thought you knew. I have to prepare for the show."

William shakes his head at us—pathetic fools that we are to him. He leans toward his plate and rudely slurps his food into his mouth. I'm wondering how I will be able to exit gracefully. I brace myself for Charles's onslaught: *Lainie, don't leave, don't leave your children.* Instead, Tom sits straight in the chair, shoulders back, and says, "I knew, Mom, that you were leaving tomorrow. It'll be okay, Jess and Dad will be here. We'll ski Bromley those four days."

"*Four days,* Mom? Why can't you come back after two days, for the last part of Vermont?" Matilde asks.

"Your mother is going back with me, Matilde," William sighs loudly. It is surprising that he knows her name. "Your father is a lucky man that his schedule allows for him to take some time. Your mother and I will drive back together and that leaves two vehicles at our house. One for your father to drive and one for Jess to drive. Then Lainie and I will be back early on the thirty-first. New Year's Eve. In time for the festivities."

"The Arts Council show is important to your mother, Matilde," Charles says unexpectedly.

"Yes, that is true," says Jess. "There you have it—that's the plan."

Matilde's face darkens and it causes a shudder through my heart.

PART TWELVE

Jess

THIRTY

C harles and I become the parents-in-residence the moment that Lainie and William, uncommon traveling companions that they are, leave for Elliot. The first evening we roast marshmallows over the hearth. I set up a Monopoly board. "Old-fashioned fun," I say, ignoring Liza's remark about "old-fart games in the middle of nowhere." Meanwhile, Billy is influenced by Tom, who is already bluffing about the "fun." In fact, Tom is bluffing about everything. Mrs. Higgins returns to do a final straightening, humming "When Irish Eyes Are Smiling," and abruptly exits before I make any other demands. Charles stokes the fire, handing over the poker while Tom stands beside him, although the fire is in fine form.

I watch Matilde, who would sleep for days, if it were allowed, to escape her emptiness. Instead she languidly turns the pages of *The Hunger Games,* stealing glances at Charles and me. In return, my eyes are on her and I feel an odd sensation—a true concern.

"Matilde, can I borrow your book?" Liza asks Matilde.

Charles is giving Matilde a thumbs-up.

"Well, I'm reading it, Liza," Matilde says. "I can give it to you later or tomorrow."

"I left my Kindle in Elliot and I don't have anything to . . ." My daughter does a pathetic voice for the benefit of the adults.

"Matilde?" Charles says. "You must have some other books in your bag, I know you. Mom mentioned that you're enjoying *A Separate Peace*."

"Enjoying it?"

"I know you're fine with handing over *The Hunger Games* to Liza for a few days," Charles says, mostly to please my daughter, which would please me. Matilde walks to Liza and gives her the book. The message in her action is that she is not only fine with this gesture, but that Liza can't be responsible for her wretched mother. It is an act of sympathy.

While we are closing up the house for the night, Charles presses me to the wall beneath the floating staircase and starts kissing my neck.

"We can't do this," I whisper.

"Why not?"

"You know why not. We have six children in the house and only two are asleep."

"All the more exciting." Charles rubs his groin against mine and slips his hands under my sweater. He unsnaps my bra. "All the better to eat you, my dear."

"Charles! We can't."

"So you've said." He takes my hand in his. "Unzip my pants. Who will ever know? Then I'll lead you upstairs and we'll lock the bedroom door."

We lock the tall, eight-inch-thick oak door of the master suite and I lie on my back while he undresses me. Through the window the stars are lost tonight in the black sky. "Just a quickie, Charles."

He laughs. "High school in reverse, Jess. Those days we sneaked around our parents for sex, and now we sneak around our children."

The pirouette of sex begins. "Nothing heightens you but you," I say. "Wherever we are, whatever the risks, or better still, no risks . . . I could touch you endlessly. . . ."

At midnight I unlock the door. Matilde, in her Ugg boots, is half-way down the hall, padding away from the master suite as if she's on the SWAT team for an important mission. Has she been standing out-side the room while I sighed and moaned, while Charles grunted and our bodies heaved together? I follow her as she sprints back to the girls' bathroom, where I hear her throw up. Twice. Next she cries, most likely in front of the mirror, her eyes swelling from the entire experience.

❈

The third day I corner Matilde in the mudroom, where she's pulling out ski boots and poles for Claire and Jack. Tom should be helping her; instead he's with Charles watching CNN in the library. Matilde, meanwhile, is appraising me, in my anti–Lainie garb, leggings, a plum-colored V-neck sweater with some cleavage sneaking out, leop-ard scarf twisted twice then knotted at my neck. We are in close prox-imity.

"I never realized that you have brown eyes, Jess. I thought most blondes have blue eyes."

"An unusual combination, I suppose."

Matilde edges back and drops her hand to her side. She's in a hurry to get the ski equipment.

"The ski conditions have been fine, don't you think, Matilde? I don't delude myself that we're in Vail—short of that everyone is hav-ing a good time and that's no easy feat. And today you have two solid hours on the slopes once the twins are at ski school. If you pick them up, I'll be down by lunchtime and you can ski all afternoon."

"Okay," says Matilde.

"You like to ski, don't you, Matilde? It might not beat swimming the Raritan River at the Y, but there is the rush down the mountain, how your breath vaporizes into the clear air . . ."

"Claire and Jack are waiting."

"They are eating chocolate chip pancakes with local maple syrup. Norine is at breakfast today. There's time," I say.

"They have to get ready to get to the slopes." Matilde tries to move past me with the poles. I place my hand on her shoulder.

"I said there is no hurry."

"I have to go."

I put my hand on her shoulder again. "Matilde, your mother doesn't *want* your father to be available. I do."

She steadies herself. "I don't feel sorry for you, Jess."

"She doesn't want it. She doesn't want *him*," I say.

"Yes—she does. What do you know about her?"

"I've known your mother since summers in Cape May. . . . I've known your mother since she had her first crush. . . ."

"You are deluded, Jess."

"You, of the entire family, Matilde. You know how it is with your mother, her art, her love of water, her . . ." I clench my teeth. I try to be calm.

"Cut it out, Jess. Please just cut it out. You've made a big mistake. You've no idea about my mother and you're supposed to be her friend! She breathes like a fish, not a mammal bitch mother from Elliot."

Matilde tightens her entire body and, stumbling at the mudroom door, she takes one more look at me.

"Maybe you dreamed up the whole episode, Matilde. Maybe not. Maybe you should hate me, yet I doubt that you do."

THIRTY-ONE

s a spouse I've got my own gig. I'm slipping away quietly and the advent of William, my repugnant husband, and Lainie, Charles's dolphinesque wife, is a form of being cut open. These past few days playing house with Charles and the late nights in bed have washed over me and rendered me fresh, mysterious. Tonight the moon shines through the blinds to the north and Charles and I are kissing, high school style again.

"Your kisses have changed, Jess."

"How?" I'm so locked into him that every time we make love, we share the ether. Sentimental and gushy, yet what I've become.

"Better, more erotic. Your lips, your tongue."

I'm not sure what he means, but I hold on to it, kissing back with fervor while he tugs off my La Perla finest, a sheer black nightie that was once purchased in hope of seducing William and never worn in reality. Maybe I bought it in anticipation of Charles in the sublime fantasy where dreams are realized and prayers answered. Then he is inside me, filling me up. I have never known the sensation. I cling to him afterward, part of me unable to let go.

When I awake in Charles's arms early, before the sun is up, he announces, "Today we'll take the kids to the slopes early and have lunch together."

"And pack sandwiches? Or at the restaurant?" The chaos of it and beyond that our togetherness—an amazing concept. I sit up straight, trying out life as the Brady Bunch.

"Either way. Whatever is easier for you, Jess."

Then we are at it again in that hunger we have for each other. A poem by Christina Rossetti, "Twice," which I've not thought of in years enters my consciousness. A poem about giving yourself utterly to the one you love. I fear for my soul; I've fallen for Charles.

By early evening Lainie and William amble into the main hall and stand under the double-vaulted ceiling. I don't know how to greet them; my skill set has diminished. Yesterday I was looking at stars and today I'm following splintered light. And it's New Year's Eve; we're close to the fragility of a new year while the shit of the last is not yet fading. Nor does Lainie appear any happier than I am, both of us tossed into one more round in Vermont after four days of chance. I ignore William and focus on Lainie.

"Lainie! How is your work going?"

"All good, truly. The time was . . . quiet, easy to paint, to think. . . ."

"And you, William? Was it fruitful?" I sound tinny and loud, my voice lilting to compensate for his flatliner mode. If your partner is the mirror and you are looking into his eyes for a reflection, the news here is that there is no reflection, there is nothing to get from William, he is one long well-educated grunt. Until Charles entered my life, I did the best I could to break free of William without searching for anything more. These wifely duties are a camouflage—none of it quite compensating for a twisted life with William. Thanks to Charles, William has become invisible to me whether he is in the room or not, on the phone, texting, e-mailing, sitting at my side. I am, at last, delivered from his public figure, his private hell.

I'm guiding Mrs. Higgins and Norine in their final hour in the kitchen before they are officially dismissed. I don't know what's come over me that I've conceded that they do not need to work through the dinner this evening. I'm sure that if we fast-forward to midnight when the kitchen is piled high with dishes, I'll be contrite, but for the moment I appreciate the plan, it feels homey and sophisticated at once. Not to mention generous.

"What's for dinner?" William asks in his immense commonness. He sniffs at Mrs. Higgins's station. Norine is counting plates for the dining table. "Simple dishes." Mrs. Higgins shrugs. "Mrs. Howard told me to leave it at that."

"At what? Meatloaf and mashed potatoes?" William is rooting around in the refrigerator. He pulls out the hors d'ouevres that I bought yesterday with Charles, the king of male food shoppers, for tonight. Why is he contaminating everything? In his arms he has guacamole, hummus, wedges of cheese, country pâté. *Fry in hell, William.*

"That's more like it." He dumps the food onto the counter.

"Mrs. Howard?" Mrs. Higgins says. "The roast is perfectly timed, the side dishes are in order, but I'm wondering about the pasta. I have stirred the tomato sauce. . . ."

"No worries, Mrs. Higgins. Lainie and I will do the rest." Why not the two women in the room? This sexist comment comes out of my mouth too fast to censor it. Mrs. Higgins's skepticism arises.

"Who is cooking the angel hair?"

"I will," I assure her. "The one pasta I do to perfection."

Behind me is Charles, who might be the only less capable cook, after Lainie.

"Are you certain?" Mrs. Higgins wipes her glasses with a dish towel.

"I'm on! No worries," I say.

Mrs. Higgins and Norine, her new sidekick, mosey out of the kitchen.

I take the largest pot in the kitchen and fill it up with water. Charles helps me carry it to the stove. He toys with the burner to adjust the flame. I miss yesterday, when Charles and I were alone together and the only pretense was that we were both devoted to our spouses. An old story if ever there was one. I quickly drop fistfuls of angel hair that look like straw into the boiling water.

"Al dente?" I ask.

"Al dente. What else?" William says. What is he still doing here? Sitting at the island, stuffing his face with pâté and lacerating the French bread. I'd rather starve than watch William eat. I take two potholders and carry the giant iron pot to the sink. Charles is suspended, not exactly sure if he should help again. My body language tells him to stand aside as I splash the entire contents into the colander in the sink. I wash the angel hair in cold water, as even the most feeble of cooks have been taught, to remove the starch. The steam rises, ruining my hair. Lainie is stirring the tomato sauce with a certain precision.

"Charles? Could you please check the tomato sauce? Am I forgetting an ingredient?" Lainie asks. To my surprise, Charles has already positioned himself on the couch in the family corner of our eat-in kitchen, glued to the Georgia Tech–USC game. He claps his hands and jumps up and down when they score a touchdown.

"Charles?" Lainie holds on to a large saucepan. She shakes her head at me to convey that Charles is entrenched in the game.

My attachment to Charles makes me root for Georgia Tech too. As I recall, William prefers the opponent and is terribly glum, still gorging on the country pâté.

I slide the angel hair into the Crock-Pot and Lainie pours the tomato sauce over it. That's when William turns away since his team is tanking, William of the living dead and disenfranchised, William of the lost-husband brigade.

"What the fuck, girls!" he screams at Lainie and at me. "What is going on?"

Lainie and I lock glances. I try to stop Lainie by putting my hand on her arm. "Lainie, let me do the sauce."

"I made it, Jess, let's finish this dish and move on."

What I needed to have whispered in her ear earlier—an hour ago—is that she *mustn't* pour all of the tomato sauce into the bowl.

Lainie, unaware of her foible, is folding the entire bowl of sauce into the pasta. William is stomping the floor six inches from where she stands. She looks at him, perplexed but not as afraid as she ought to be.

"Don't you *know* that you never put the sauce over the entire bowl of noodles?" William's voice is cruel. *"Never?"* He lifts the pot, which has been mostly emptied, and slings what remains over Lainie's cream-colored crocheted sweater.

Neither Lainie nor I move. The truth is out, there is no place to hide. Years ago I married William and bore him these two precious children. Once he loved me enough to hold me until I was fast asleep; once we went to Berlin and stayed up the entire night going to clubs with transvestites and funky music. We danced, we drank, we went back to the hotel and made love. Ages back that happened. Was he barbaric then? He has always had this ugliness that is well guarded and buried within. Mostly within.

"You are *ruining* the pasta!" William is shrieking. *"Ruining it!"*
Asshole William.

Charles has come to the scene of the crime. "Hey, William, it's a dish of spaghetti. A goddamn pasta side dish."

William says to Charles, "Yes and no." William takes Lainie's wrists and yanks them sharply. Lainie cries out, another mistake. He begins to twist her arms painfully. I know it too well—how my husband tightens his piercing grip. How next he might start shaking her shoulders. Back and forth. Back and forth. How he will bruise her and how long it takes for the bruises to turn from deep blue to that yellow that means one is healed. *Not.*

Any minute one of the children or several of the children will come through the swinging doors. There must be an alternate domain where I am not sick inside.

"William, please!" Charles comes over and puts his hands firmly on William's forearms and William drops Lainie's wrists. Charles holds Lainie to him; her heart is next to his. Lainie is crying and in shock. I needed to warn her, to keep her from that goddamn sauce.

The football game drones on while the rest of us fall into an empty shock, a shock that has no end, no place to go. After a minute or five minutes or eternity, I speak up.

"Does anybody know how I can get the fuck out of here tonight?" I ask. "Does anybody have a clue?"

Charles wins for restoring order and a semblance of decency. I am nothing tonight but an abused wife, battered physically and emotionally. One of the stats you read in women's magazines and online, in the newspapers and in posthumous articles about Nicole Simpson. You swear to yourself, *not me,* yet it's you, it's you and you sweat that your daughter cannot know nor your friends nor your family. Lainie witnesses the depths of my despair and she is forced to come through, to stoke the fire in the great room and check that the children are fed. An inch away from fetal position and a bottle of vodka, my heart hurts. Mostly because Charles was there, mostly it is the shame and remorse. I should have explained it, I should have warned him. Not that tragic, I self-soothe, it's my life through lies and secrets.

Mrs. Higgins reappears at Lainie's insistence and helps out with the dinner. William is taciturn but unrelenting; the children collapse at various hours through the night. The twins in a heap on my favorite cashmere throws by the coffee table, the older children in fits and starts in the adjacent smaller den, counting down the minutes until the ball descends.

Per usual, we are together, the damaged foursome. Lainie is cuddled up with Charles, her head against his left shoulder on the green leather couch. I don't wish to knock her out of position, only to lie against Charles's right shoulder. *Let's share him, share him while we watch the Milky Way this winter night.* Charles looks at me and I look back. Lainie's eyes are half closed; William is feigning sleep from where he sits on the wing chair. Only Mrs. Higgins is moving about.

She gathers the dirty glasses and dessert plates, catches the furtive glimpses, absorbs the narrative, and pads out of the room with her heavy tray. I am too sick to cry, too sick to follow her into the kitchen, the scene of the crime, and make some wretched excuse. Instead I consider the consequence of tonight and the risks of a slow fade.

PART THIRTEEN

Lainie

THIRTY-TWO

The children are asleep after a full day at school and Charles has conked out on the sofa in the family room. His head is back too far and his legs are deployed across the coffee table. I open the back door and stand against the side of the house and view a starless night. The bitter wind blows through the trees without the quasi-romance of Vermont, and the extinguished sky is blackness.

When I come back inside Charles has gone upstairs and has already turned out the lights. The past two nights have been surprisingly amorous and I've followed my instinct to be beside him in bed. In a fresh new year, I must do more that is wifelike—beyond the sex—and be more grateful to Charles. Once the paintings are completed for the show, I'll be that person, I'll view Elliot in a better light. I'll not only appreciate Charles, I'll consult Jess. Jess could be Matilde's mentor. A qualm of conscience washes over me. Matilde, who mothers the twins, Matilde, who suffers the curse of being set apart. Again that nagging knowledge that fitting in is a gift—for example, Jess, who embodies every nuance of conformity. Not that

Jess isn't tough or dogmatic, that she prevails. She wouldn't jeopardize her social position, she always knows right from wrong in the social swirl.

The night is before me. I use the hours in my studio to paint sections of my triptych—first the sandpipers, then the gulls, who engulf and devour whole creatures. The shoreline is riddled with debris while the atmosphere above is contoured. I end up there until morning.

<hr/>

"There will be plenty of sales clothes, designer mostly, to choose from," Jess tells me the next morning when after swimming we drive to the Mall at Short Hills. Although I've never been to this center before, it was one of Charles's selling points of moving to Elliot. He had shown me a Wikipedia synopsis of the mall when we were living in the city. "You see, Lainie," he had said, "Short Hills, not twenty miles from Elliot, was founded by a man described as a nature lover. The mall has chic stores—as chic as any in the city, they *rival* the city. Look at this, there is an Hermès, Chanel, Gucci, Van Cleef."

"Then the man must be rolling in his grave," I'd said. "I mean, a high-end mall is not exactly at one with nature."

"I thought you'd want to know the history of the place," Charles defended.

"Charles, it's okay," I had said. "I'll be fine." I was resigned by then and his hoping to induce me to buy high-end commercial goods made me pray for us both.

That's why it took me until early January to agree to go to the mall with Jess.

"I don't need anything," I say.

"That's preposterous. I don't understand."

Jess steers me toward the center of the mall. The antiseptic air blows at us on the top tier where the crème de la crème of designer boutiques are aligned. The sounds of footsteps on glass and marble reverberate as more customers file into the complex.

"Let's stick with Neiman's. One-stop shopping, at least to start." Jess makes an assessment.

"That's a good idea, Jess. It will be faster."

I follow her into Neiman Marcus. We enter on the makeup counter side of the store, where the scent of perfume is astounding. Jess tromps along with purpose.

"I don't have much time to shop either, Lainie, with a meeting for the Elliot Ballet Academy and then the calendar committee at the library this afternoon. Plus PTA council at six."

She leads us toward the designer shoes and out of nowhere there is a crowd of women crushing women.

"What is going on?" I ask.

"Are you kidding?" Jess is already at the size 7 rack, fingering the right shoe of a pair of leopard stilettos. She examines it in the fluorescent light. "Too racy, right?"

"For your life as the wife of the CEO of a hospital?"

She hesitates with her eyes on me and drops the shoe. "Right. A pair that is less feral with the same heel shape and height."

I look around. There are women of assorted ages squeezing their feet into these platform pumps and narrow six-inch-heel shoes.

"Did you tell Charles that we were going shopping?"

"I did. He loves when I do these suburban outings. He said to look for a dress for the Arts Council and for the Spring Fling opening."

Jess drops her purse on the plush lavender couch and collapses beside it.

She starts forcing her foot into the leopard stiletto as if it's an important matter. She holds her leg up.

"Did you tell William?" I ask.

"Did I . . . hmmm. I usually do."

A short bald man, about fifty, in a baggy suit, comes over to us.

"Would you need some assistance?" he asks. The question is more directed at Jess. I try to focus on his life, helping the women who pepper the shoe department. I never thought about it in the city; I never considered shopping a consuming activity before, it was more a means to an end. There is no hastening in and out, there is a leaden sense of allegiance.

Jess holds up the leopard stiletto and a tamer shoe, a black suede platform. "I'll try these. I'll need the mates, these are the right size."

A woman comes by and pauses in front of Jess, points to the leopard stiletto, and displays her shopping bag.

"I bought the same ones. Fuck-me pumps." She nearly elbows Jess and Jess smiles at her as if they are in the same sorority or they belong to the same secret society. I don't know William well but after the incident in Vermont, I'm confused. Being with William is taxing and sickening. Maybe the purchase is Jess's only way of appeasing him, maybe she needs to do this. As her friend, I should ask, I should offer support, a shoulder to cry on. Jess is being incredibly good to me, and I don't comment. I get suctioned into her denial as if the secret were my own.

The salesman hesitates and looks at me accusatorily. "For you?"

"Oh, I'm not shopping for shoes," I answer. I'm getting antsy—it happens more and more. I know the agenda at a mall, and we've yet to dress shop. I take my miniature sketchbook out of my purse and draw a moonrise over the ocean with one woman standing alone. On her right ankle, I give her an ankle bracelet that reads *Love*. Then I look up at the salesman and see his sorrow. I draw it into the woman's face.

"What are you doing?" Jess asks. She is watching as if there is no hope for me.

"Jess, I'm good. I just had an idea and I'm jotting it down."

Jess sighs in annoyance. I suppose that I should be more into the mall-shopping-spree spirit. She pushes her Neiman's card toward the salesman at the register. Her purchases are rung up straightaway. "C'mon." She grabs my arm. "There's a lot of ground to cover. We both need dresses for the spring events in Elliot."

Again, a surprising distraction—the luster of the fabrics in winter. Jess is a few steps ahead of me. "These aren't on sale, Lainie. These are for the next season, I know you get that." She tips her head and points to the sale section, where I find a teal blue gown.

"Okay." Jess snatches it off the rack and holds it up. "Most every-body will be wearing long. At the auction and dinner too."

"I know. Charles told me this morning. I'm not sure how he would know, but when I said we had our plan, he said to buy long dresses."

"What exactly did he say?" Jess pauses, three sale gowns on her arm and the one I've chosen on her other arm.

"He called you the perfect person to shop with for a splendid dress or two. I never knew him to pay attention, although he always cares about the result."

"Yeah, I know what you mean." Jess leads me toward the dressing room. Along the way I spy a midnight blue dress. "Charles might like it too." I stop to check the size. "Maybe you can take a picture of me in both dresses and I'll e-mail them to him. Or better yet, maybe we should send it as a text."

A saleswoman appears. "My, my." She is staring at my face and then back to the two dresses I'm holding. "Won't either of these be outstanding with your coloring. Those eyes!"

Jess stomps ahead and finds a double-size dressing room. She is busy zipping herself into the first of her dresses. I look at her in the three-way mirror and race to try on.

"Nice, Lainie. The color is nice."

"That's it?" I hand her my iPhone.

She snaps two angles in two seconds and hands it back. I look at her in the long charcoal slinky number.

"Armani, on sale. I don't really want anything too showstopping. More subtle, y'know?" Jess smooths the fabric at her waistline.

"Want me to take a picture for William of the dresses that are top contenders?" I ask.

"Oh, no. No thanks."

I try on the second dress. "Which one, Jess?"

"Either works."

I hand her my iPhone again. "Can you take one more shot for Charles, please?"

A few seconds later Charles texts back: *Buy both.*

I show this to Jess.

"It seems so . . . extravagant," I say.

Jess shrugs. "Not really, Lainie. I'm taking the black dress. The one that's not a gown, the one I haven't put on—I'll do it at home. Returning is easy." I detect a slight coldness that reminds me of the wind in late October at the Shore, not yet winter, not yet sharp.

A half hour later Jess is driving on the highway like she's a tourist on a Jet Ski.

"Jess, all okay?"

"I'm fine. I have to stop at CVS. If you don't mind."

"I have to as well. I think I have a yeast infection."

Jess veers the car haphazardly, steps on the gas. "From the pool? From standing around in a wet bathing suit?" she asks.

"I hardly ever do that," I say.

"When you watch Matilde and you're finished first you do," Jess says. "That could be it."

"I should call my gyno. The new one, who you've introduced me to."

"You could," Jess says. "Yeast infections are the worst. Yuck."

"I'm pretty sure it's from Charles, though. The gyno will recommend no sex for a few days or a week, right? Along with Monistat cream . . . yogurt . . ."

Is Jess tensing up, am I giving too much information? She keeps speeding.

"I could call now." I take my phone out of my bag.

"I didn't realize that your sex life is so active, Lainie," Jess says as she pulls up to the CVS and parks, furiously, too close to the curb in front of the store.

"Lately it has been, Jess. Very active." She misses my confession, already halfway out of her seat and staring straight ahead.

THIRTY-THREE

W hat were you *doing*, Matilde?" Charles is screaming
while we sit in a cubicle at the Elliot police station. In the
next cubicle are Matilde's supposed friends, Nick and
Stephanie, with their father and mother. Abigail is the friend who is
placed across the hall, alone with her mother. According to Jess's as-
persion of the week, Abigail's father left his wife and family ten days
ago for his girlfriend in Philadelphia. Abigail's mother is crying—
painful wails that none of us are able to ignore.

A half hour later, on the ride home, Charles is in his agitated state.

"Charles, I'll ask Jess for a lawyer," I say. "Please just concentrate
on the road."

He swerves fast into the slow lane, then changes his mind as if
the car is too heavy for him, as if we might not make it to our desti-
nation.

"I don't know what has happened to you, Matilde."

He looks at her in the rearview mirror.

"Dad, do you wish you had another kind of daughter?" Matilde
asks sadly. "Are you sick of me?"

Charles doesn't reply.

"Charles! Charles! Say something . . . please." It sinks in, what I've always found disquieting. That you never know who you're married to until there is a problem or a crisis.

The three of us walk into the house through the garage door and stop in the kitchen. I take off my full-length puffy coat to reveal a pale blue sweatshirt and flannel pajama bottoms in a blue plaid that are tucked into my boots.

Matilde is aghast. "Mom? You're wearing an Elliot Lady outfit. You wouldn't have worn that in the city."

"You know . . . I only wear it to tool around before bed . . . in my studio. At least it's my favorite color."

"Jesus, shit, Lainie! Matilde!" Charles is apoplectic. "Are we talking about pajamas when we just left the police station? Matilde, have you forgotten that you were arrested?"

Matilde and I stand still without speaking.

"You deal with her, Lainie," Charles says in a purposely level, deliberately emotionless voice. He leaves the room part pissed, part disgusted. *Your daughter, your creation.*

We are alone, Matilde and I. The night is slipping into morning; elsewhere the sky meets the sea, shells are brought in with the tide.

"Nothing will ever be okay again. I did it, my fault. I was stupid, Mom," Matilde says. "I know you always say, *Think before you act, think every second of every day or you'll be sorry, you'll pay for it.*"

Matilde starts to cry; has my daughter developed a tremor? I place my hands on her face. She is beyond pale and that frightens me. I see my own reflection in the Thermador double-wall oven and we are the same.

"My darling girl, what happened?"

Matilde looks away.

"Matilde? You might be ready to explain. Or . . . if you wonder who would believe you anyway—well, I would. I'm ready to hear. I'm open to your version of tonight."

"My version?"

"Please . . . tell me what happened . . . for everyone's sake," I say.

I climb onto a kitchen stool and motion for Matilde to do the same. "Go on, Matilde."

"I have no real friends in Elliot. In the city I would have had a friend who would have said my plan was a mistake. I asked Stephanie and Abigail 'cause they're best friends and Nick is older, he drives a Honda CR-V. He told Stephanie that I'll be a 'ten' one day. I figured he'd do it if he said that about me. I didn't think we'd get caught since everyone goes to bed early in Elliot."

Matilde takes a breath. I pour water out of a Brita and hand her the glass.

"Mom? I once saw this TV show about a police state where everybody had a curfew. That's how it is in Elliot. Plus, everyone is plain miserable."

As I listen to my daughter I miss the city too much to let it go. If we still lived there, none of Matilde's antics of tonight would have happened. The lack of choice in Elliot is rendering us joyless and dispirited; Matilde and I are woeful.

"While we were driving to the Y, Stephanie talked about how much trouble we could get into, and Nick said we'd go to prison. I was afraid but I was trying to be cool. The reason they said they'd do it was because I promised the girls I could get them into a Justin Bieber concert. I'm not sure why Nick said okay. . . . His sister bribed him, I think. . . . Something about drugs and what she saw. He told us to hurry once we pulled up at the Y and we got in fast. I had gotten the second set of keys from the lifeguard, who didn't notice that they were missing."

"Wasn't there an alarm—a burglar alarm?" I interrupt.

"No, there wasn't. I checked. Not even for the double doors to the aquatics center."

Matilde puts her forehead against my palm the way she used to when she had a fever. She feels hot. I move away and start to pace up and down. "What were you doing there?"

"I ran up to the big board with the list of swimmers who swim the Raritan River. My name was third and yours was second. I took the eraser and climbed the ladder. I wrote *Lainie Smith Morris* as number one and *Matilde Smith Morris* as number two. I took the name *Larry Spence* that was number one and move it to number three.

"Stephanie said what I'd done wouldn't help—everyone would know it had been changed. I said you had the most points and only twenty miles to go. . . . You had to be ahead with me right behind, and the guy shouldn't be first."

Matilde is crying again. "That's when we heard a siren and two cops came into the pool . . . with handcuffs. Everything is my fault. I just wanted you to beat everyone, to win the Raritan River race," Matilde says. "To like it here."

"I believe you," I say.

Matilde stares at me as I take a step toward the Sub-Zero. She nods, she waits. The Sub-Zero starts making a noise; perhaps it is the freezer churning new ice.

"Jess called and she's found an attorney, a local lawyer who will make the mess—breaking and entering, a misdemeanor at the very least—go away. For you, the girls, the brother. Dad will take care of the legal bills. Do you understand, Matilde?"

"I understand, Mom."

"I'm worried about you, Matilde. First what you do and then the wisdom of my making it go away. I am of two minds. These things happen, of course. I want you to be excused, exonerated. What I wish is that you would not do what you do. That you would be *responsible*."

Matilde is crying harder. "Mom, do you remember the salt marsh safari in Cape May last spring? When you took the four of us to look at the wildlife on a skimmer and we saw the plants on the water floor?"

"I remember. There were the fish who live deep down, almost under the sea. Remember the crabs and the gray seals and sea turtles?"

"The sea turtles were my favorite," Matilde says.

"Really? I'm surprised. The seals were unreal."

"You're right, Mom . . . the seals were unreal that day."

I look at her and I remember the day that we brought her home from the hospital. Charles thanked me for making his dreams come true; he said we had a complete family, a boy and a girl. When the twins were born, he said that we were doubly lucky, doubly blessed.

"Mom, tonight I've ruined everything."

I shake my head. "I know it's frightening . . . but not *everything* is ruined."

"Can we still go to the beach house, will it be the same after what I've done in Elliot?"

"Well, yes, we can, Matilde. But we should talk about how breaking into a building is wrong . . . about how we have to live with the consequences of our actions. We have to have a moral center, even if life isn't always fair. So while Jess is a good mediator and she's really worried about what happened and will be a good fixer, at some point, you have to figure out *why* you do what you do. I have to figure out why Dad and I race to cover for you. Every time."

Charles comes back into the kitchen—in a rush and quite unfriendly. He doesn't look at Matilde. "Lainie?"

I don't answer. Instead I go back to Matilde and stroke her hair.

"You can stop babying her, Lainie. You know it's gotten her nowhere except into piles of shit," Charles says.

"Mom? I thought you said that Dad will cover for me?"

"Oh, he will. He always will," I say. "Piles of shit? Piles of shit? That it were so simple, Charles."

Charles faces Matilde. "What has come over you, Matilde?" He speaks normally, a ghastly sound in our ears. I grip Matilde's shoulders.

"I'm finding out, Charles. I'll speak further with Matilde. You must be exhausted. Maybe try to sleep?"

"Sleep? I have two surgeries before ten. *Two fucking surgeries,* Lainie. Matilde, I won't allow you to be a spoiler."

"A *spoiler,* Charles?" He knows what I mean: *Whatever my daughter has done, she is forever on my side.*

Charles looks at Matilde before he storms out of the room. I lead her to the couch in the corner and we sit down together. We are by the window that faces east; the sun is rising, the morning is moving in.

"I miss Cape May. I miss the city," Matilde says.

"I know. I know." I sigh. "Matilde, tell me why you *really* did what you did tonight? Why you thought it was okay—why it needed to be accomplished?"

"I wanted you to win, Mom. I wanted you to win the Raritan River contest, to get there first, before any other swimmer."

"That's why you broke in? Not to see if you could get away with it, not to cause trouble in a place that you haven't quite fit—"

"No, Mom. I changed the board to move you to first place. . . . I took the risk to make things better for you. That's the only reason."

"Oh, Matilde, you didn't have to. . . . Matilde, I would have gotten there anyway, don't you know?"

"I wasn't sure. I only knew it has to be that you win, Mom. For you. So you never leave, so you stay. Because a selkie—a sealy can't be stopped . . . from returning to the . . ." Matilde lays her head in my lap. She looks up at me. "I love the water because you love the water. Cape May is the best; ever since I was little I've loved it the way you love it, Mom."

"Matilde, let's go to Cape May soon, in a few weeks. We'll go when it's cold and the wind is off the ocean. You know how it is, the dunes high and strong."

"Mom? I learned in science class that everyone's DNA has a memory. I remember *your* memory. That's why I love Cape May."

I smile at her. "What could be better—my memory bank is yours, Matilde. I've passed it on to you."

She starts to cry again. "I'm the only one, Mom. Tom and Jack don't have it. Who can tell about Claire . . . yet."

"I know. I know precisely what you mean. You have it, Matilde, the DNA of memory."

PART FOURTEEN

Jess

THIRTY-FOUR

The break-in at the Y has been kept quiet. Thanks to me, pro that I am at mopping up the spill, sponging up the tears. Lainie and Charles are relieved as well as impressed by my skills. Matilde too appreciates my help, mostly because miraculously she is not kicked out of the Raritan River competition. That result, more than anything else in the latest Matilde drama, amplifies my power in Elliot. Not only did I ghostwrite her letter to the director of the Y apologizing for following a "dare," I made sure that the Y board viewed her as repentant. Charles is pleased because he goes under the radar—thanks to my ability to save his reputation. I've even kept the story from William. Lainie and Matilde are more skittish, more flustered.

"If the kids know, then their parents know," Lainie says, when we meet at the Elliot Library by happenstance. She is carrying three heavy art books in her arms and I twist my head to see the titles.

"These are for my triptych. Research."

I glance at the wall clock. Ten o'clock and I'm planning on an eleven o'clock train to the city. "How is Matilde?"

"Some days at school people talk about her and ignore her in the hallway. I try to convince her that slandering someone becomes old quickly and since no one got into any real trouble, it isn't that interesting. Charles keeps reminding her that no one is ever ruined—that you are defamed and then it blows over. We are in your debt, Jess. Both Charles and I."

Ah yes, I'm always in the room with them, always on their minds. After bailing out Matilde for what can only be described as rebellious, insane behavior, I am indispensable to the Morris family. Kudos to me for finding the best defense attorney this side of the Hudson to clean up Matilde's morass. Matilde remains at large because of the team lined up to ameliorate her carelessness. Before that, did I not help Lainie with her freedom to paint *and* a one-person show? Let's not forget finding Mrs. Higgins or the guest country club membership at Wintergreen and early access to the Y on a "sunrise pass," ahead of the crowd.

"What have you been saying to Matilde?" I ask. "You know, to move through the fallout . . . the awful days that follow an episode?" What I could do with that girl if she were under my tutelage. I have never met a mother/daughter duo more nonsensical, an aiding and abetting more obvious.

"I tell her to move through the halls without looking around. To lay as low as the jellyfish when the tide goes out."

Honestly, will it never end with the water metaphors? "Hmmm," I say. "Is she swimming, keeping up with the competition?"

"She is. She swims the Raritan River competition almost as much as I do—she has only twenty-four miles to go."

"What about you, Lainie? How far are you?"

"I have sixteen miles left."

Sixteen miles before she notices that Charles and I are an item, that what I do for Matilde is actually for Charles, to protect and preserve Charles. She and her children are the by-product. "I'm glad that Matilde is adjusting," I say before slinking away without mentioning that I've got to get to the station.

At the Gansevoort Hotel a crude cold blankets the lobby. Snow is in the forecast for the evening and I count my blessings that I have stolen time with Charles this afternoon. Being with him fortifies the day and the three hours ahead will be transformative. I wrap my black pashmina tighter and move with purpose toward the elevators. I'm checking my iPhone for the room number when I read a text that stiffens me with dread. *Meet me at the restaurant. I'm waiting.*

I make the left turn away from the elevators and through the atrium to a public place that evokes more risk than a hotel suite. Charles is sitting patiently in the corner. His looks are deceptive; there is nothing about him that is simple or open except his smile. And he's not smiling. The low light puts his face in silhouette. I miss him unless we are beside each other, at the very least.

"Jess." He won't kiss me in public, not a peck on the cheek. I slide into a chair; I'm waiting for his explanation. A second round of appreciation, beyond the text *thank you at dawn for the female defense attorney with the fire hose.* That would put us on the right footing.

"Jess. Not that I don't want to be in your arms at this moment . . . it's that we need to talk, we should talk." He clears his throat. "You know how I feel about you. . . ."

That he were mine, that I could read his lips and know his every body signal, every twitch of his lips, that the rings around the irises of his eyes would become familiar. That we were a pair, that the children, the hospital, our marriages, didn't trump us. Us.

"My twins are very young, Jess. And Tom and Matilde have a very long way to go. Liza and Billy do too."

I nod. *Remember that you love me.*

"I know how much you've given of yourself to my family. . . ."

I'd like to wish away the scene. The day is slipping by, the hours I've counted on, my irredeemable, irretrievable, not-to-be-exchanged hours with Charles. The hours that make William endurable are

230 | Susannah Marren

generated from Charles. My defenses are not as strong as one might expect. A server comes to the table and Charles waves him off. "We're not quite ready yet," he says. He might have said, *Never come back here since I'm in the midst of breaking her heart.* The server prances ahead, indifferent to his chance with Charles. Not so I.

"Charles . . ."

He holds up his hand and is about to tell me something I don't wish to know.

"I wanted to do this . . . 'this' meaning us. Please don't believe otherwise, Jess, for a minute."

"Then why our conversation?"

"I guess I'm meeting you, Jess, to relay that I can't leave Lainie, not today, not tomorrow. I can't leave my children, I can't break up my family. Lainie is my wife."

Wife. The word rattles around in my brain for want of another word, for a reason to fight for the wife. I too am a wife. A thankless task if there ever was one. I might say to him, *Where does it get Lainie, being your wife? Where has William taken me?* And then I shudder at that truth. From where I stand, Lainie has a nice husband, a sexy husband, a husband worth having. A shame that it means so little to her and so much to me. What complicates it is that she and I shared those summers at the Shore and freshman year in the same dorm. Yet Charles is too meaningful for anything else to have weight or consequence. If only the affair were merely physical. If only I didn't care. If only he didn't matter.

"You can't break up your family," I say. He most likely considers my calm tone a sign that I comprehend that—I'm uber-accepting and in complete agreement with him. That what we do in bed is forgettable and our pillow talk a long-ago dream. He's wrong, that isn't it. I'm simply repeating the message of the afternoon to let it sink in, which it doesn't.

Lainie owes me, Lainie owes me her husband. What else would justify what I do? The good Jess/bad Jess fighting for what is right, what is fair. I'm exhausted from the disarray, from sharing the one man left on Earth with a woman who would go out with the tide in a heartbeat.

"Nor are you in any position to break up your family," Charles says. "Your children, William . . ."

"Not today," I say.

He leans in to hear, expecting that I'll encourage him, that I'll agree, that we are of the same mind-set about spouses and children. That I too view our afternoons in the hay as one thing while a dedication to what we *could* share is another story altogether. That's what he'd like—for me to be a patient person who wouldn't turn the world upside down for him, who wouldn't risk that. A person who doesn't mind doing her best—even when her best has been tested lately—for the crumbs. I do what I do to have Charles, who thanks me profusely, who texts, *You are a genius.* A world I crafted too carefully for any glitch. Except for what happens when you fall for someone. When your pheromones are at a premium and there is no handle on anything—and you toss caution aside. In a world that both parties navigate based on control, containment. The days that are not with Charles become confusing, less defined, rote. He obviously isn't quite in the same space.

"I've been thinking about us very seriously, Jess. Since Matilde's last antic."

Matilde, ever present although she is absent. A ghost of her mother.

"There is something about that daughter of yours, Charles."

"Exactly. There is . . . something. . . ."

"She can't get in the way, Charles—" I start to fight for us, for me.

"We are, alas, at an impasse, Jess," Charles interrupts.

It is remarkable heartache. I'm turning into the sort of woman I disdain, where love rules and she'll lie, cheat, and steal for a man outside her marriage, not for the life she has carved with her husband, the father of her children. If Charles might float away from me one day, he isn't actually mine to float away from. I determine we aren't there yet, not for him to drift, not for me to lose him. I want to say, *I know the game, I'll play by the book.* Instead I lament that I care, that

I have feelings. I've tried both ways and the psychic rewards of loving a man, any man, husband or not, are many.

"Sometimes I believe that if you put Lainie and me into a milk shake you would have what you want."

"Except that she is my *wife*."

"Ah, Charles, the loyalty factor. Tell me that you love her, that you're in love with her, and I'll go."

Charles's jawline twitches. "I am responsible to her, Jess. A complicated connection."

An arctic chill through my soul. "I'm not sure what you mean, Charles."

His jawline twitches once more. We are awkward together; between the sheets is a lifetime ago.

"Charles, I would see you any way that is offered, whenever I can, however I can. However we can manage it. I can simply be Lainie's friend, no more, no less."

"You and Lainie, William and me. These are unrelated issues, except there is no solution. No resolution." His head is bowed. Who might have predicted a triangle that makes no sense to anyone beyond us?

I'm consumed with his socks, his boxers, how he tosses me against the door when I arrive in the hotel room.

"It's okay. Charles, I swear it is." Next I start to unbutton his shirt at his waist, right there in the hotel dining room. I put my fingers against his stomach, familiar and titillating at once. The place is growing busy and people are nosy. I distrust them. My limbs are being torn from me, severed and replaced. This is a fluke, this meeting here today instead of in our hotel suite. Crazy that it ever happened; I cannot divine a word that he has uttered.

THIRTY-FIVE

M y knocking is frantic. Through the glass trim on the sides of the double front door, I spy Lainie at the top of the stairs. I ring the doorbell several times.

"Charles? Charles?" I hear Lainie. "Charles!"

Next Matilde is beside her. I press the doorbell again.

Charles opens the door. He is holding his iPhone and frowning. "It's Jess. I'll let her in."

Lainie tenses. "Jess?"

I plunge into Lainie's arms, making gulping sounds. Lainie is soundless, a thin paintbrush in her right hand. My children are sad and tentative, huddling together. Charles opens the door as wide as possible, letting the night in and motioning with his hands. His voice is high-pitched. "C'mon, c'mon, Liza . . . Billy."

"Oh, Lainie. Do you fucking believe this?" I look at Lainie, not Charles, as I roll up my sleeve to reveal an ugly cut and bruise on my wrist. "William, he . . ."

Lainie puts her arms around me with her paintbrush held above my shoulder. "Matilde?" Lainie talks in that "Matilde knows younger children" voice. Aren't Liza and Billy too old for that? "Matilde?" She's desperate. "Matilde, please take Liza and Billy to the kitchen for some of Mrs. Higgins's banana bread. Go ahead," Lainie says. "Jess needs our help tonight."

Charles flinches. I wish that I could apologize to him for the timing, especially after our afternoon together, for barging in on his surprisingly tranquil home. It's obvious that Lainie and Matilde were as cheery as clams in high water, working side by side before I arrived. Whatever Charles believes about Matilde being sequestered with Lainie, about how she should be with new friends, girls her own age, rather than working on her art, there is the bond they share. How fortunate that Charles is so busy doing those surgeries—"Today I did four knee replacements. Tomorrow will be hip after hip," he said only this afternoon. Thankfully, because ironically it is Lainie's support that I seek tonight and Matilde's trust—that my secret remains safe with her.

Matilde gives her mother a quizzical look and Lainie is on top of it. "Or to your room . . . no, not your room . . . Claire is asleep there. . . . You could go to Tom's room."

Tom shows up at this minute next to Charles, and while he is my fan, he senses right away that I've contaminated the house—the whole place feels sick, a plague that I and my children dragged in.

"Jess, let me check on things with Charles." Lainie flutters about. "Privately, for a moment . . ."

She and Charles are walking to the den when Charles turns to face me. I know what he is thinking, that I'm everywhere, that the three of us might never end. "There's no need for a private conversation, Lainie. Let's talk among the three of us."

"I'm worried, Charles," Lainie says. "I mean, Jess, you should stay at our house with your children for as long as you need to. But the William business is political."

"Beyond political." Charles sounds awful. "It's a disaster."

"I know, I'm sorry. . . ." I say.

"Whatever you decide, Jess, we have to help. You've been my friend since we were—"

"I know that, Lainie. What I'm talking about has little to do with the length of the friendship." Charles sounds short-tempered, pissed. He looks at me.

"And remember, William is my boss. We live in Elliot because of your husband."

"That's why I've kept it so quiet. . . . That's why I came here when I had nowhere else to go," I say.

"What can I ever do for all that you have done for us in Elliot?" Lainie says.

She means it, that's the thing. After a while Charles answers, "Jess, what can we do for you tonight? Set you and the children up in the guest room?"

Tonight. I don't answer. I nod to convey my gratitude for a temporary calm, a fisherman's dock at nightfall.

PART FIFTEEN

Lainie

THIRTY-SIX

T hat's when there is the second knock, again followed by the doorbell. Charles and I know it is William before he comes into view through the pane of glass to our right. Charles opens the door; I stand behind him and Jess is behind me. William pushes through, reminding me of the garbagemen who plow through our comingled newspapers and bottles on Monday mornings, then load their trucks. Their heads go first, bodies second. I'm the queasiest that I've been since we moved to Elliot.

William is in the foyer—his hair is combed, his face is smooth. He wears an L.L.Bean coat in a caramel color. There isn't much that distinguishes him from the other husbands and fathers in the neighborhood.

"Charles, I regret that you are party to the drama," William says.

Charles doesn't answer. Jess and I are holding hands—Jess's fingers are white.

"I'll need to speak to Jess alone," William says.

"No, Charles, we won't leave Jess alone," I say.

Charles and William exchange a glance. "Five minutes of Jess's time," Charles says. "We'll stay with her, however. Jess?"

Jess lets go of my hand and steps up. She and William face each other.

"You'll never get away with this, Jess." William's voice is angry. "Never. You'll pay the price, you'll see."

"I'm going to press charges, William. I have pictures of what you've done to me."

"No, Jess, you won't. Perhaps in the moment, at your friends' home with Lainie and Charles surrounding you, you believe that you will. Remember, I'm able to prove how deficient you are as a mother. I'll take our children from you, both of them. You'll be sorry."

I feel Jess's terror. "You're an abuser, William. I could ruin your reputation. People think you are head of the healers, head of the physicians and staff . . . head of those who save lives. I know who you are, who you really are."

"Don't you dare threaten me, Jess." William's voice turns low.

Charles steps between them. "Okay, c'mon, guys. That's enough said, in our home anyway."

"Who the hell do you think you are, Charles?" William starts to yell. Somehow his raised voice is a relief since it is what we've been expecting.

"William, I advise you to—" Charles speaks reasonably.

"You *advise* me? I made you and I can unmake you. I brought you to Elliot and made you a head of a department, and I can fire you too."

Charles is standing like the garbagemen, headfirst. "I know what a contract is; I signed one. I am as able to sue you, I know lawyers too. A few who walk around without hobbling after I've operated on them. Don't threaten me, William, in your hour of need."

William rubs his temples and stares at Jess. "Well, Jess, we'll fight it out whether it's in the Morrises' house or in our own home. I expect you to come back with the children. Either you come with me or follow in your car."

Jess has stepped back and squeezes my hand again. I need to be by the shoreline, sidestepping the horseshoe crabs. The surf may be strong, the undertow dangerous—yet I belong there for my survival.

"Lainie? Lainie?" In the years that we've known each other, I've never heard Jess sound desperate, frightened. I force myself back into this wretched scene.

"Whatever you need, Jess," I say.

"Fuck you, Lainie," William says. "I'll expect you at home, then, Jess."

The house shakes when he slams the front door. That's when I realize that Matilde is with us.

"Matilde! What are you doing? Please . . . join the others," I say. "Take care of Liza . . . she is with Tom and Billy. . . ."

Charles nods; he's looking as bleached out as an old white sheet faded to beige. Matilde, who has become a witness to unadulterated domestic violence, spins around and runs up the stairs.

⧆

Once William is gone, Jess and I move like rippling water into the guest room, where we are alone.

"I don't know why I married him. I can't remember why," Jess says.

"Maybe you never knew why."

"The night that I married him my knees were shaking and my teeth were chattering. But William looked so sure, so certain. I thought, why not, what have I got to lose?" Jess laughs. "Hey, Lainie, he went to Harvard. The family had money, lots of money."

"Well, yes, Harvard. Family money . . ."

"He's in the Social Register. . . . They're known in the town. . . . They *appear* to be solid citizens. From the outside," Jess says.

"They don't advertise that they're sadistic?"

"Worse than that, Lainie. They're emotionally abusive. I mean the whole family. Not just William; his parents, his brother . . ."

"Jess . . . I'm surprised. I'm sad for you . . . living a lie. . . ."

"I know. I know, Lainie. Do you know that I've volunteered for clinics in other towns, Kendalton and Highgrave, to help abused women?"

Jess laughs a bitter laugh. "Let me tell you what happened one Thanksgiving, Lainie."

"Jess, you don't have to. . . . Talking about it could be making you worse."

"No, I have to. I have to tell you; it's a confession of what William and I really are."

We wait for a minute and get more comfortable in the room. I turn on the desk lamp. There is the scent of a kill; something will be dead soon. A whale that washes to shore on the barrier islands of the Jersey Shore. A sparrow that flies into the glass door at the beach house. A rat in a rat trap in an Elliot basement.

"Five years ago over Thanksgiving we went to New Hampshire to visit William's parents. William didn't want to go and I convinced him it was the right thing to do. I've always made every effort to be a good wife and good mother—roles I've come to play quite well. This trip was about being a good daughter-in-law. It was unpleasant from the start, distasteful and ugly.

"At least if I had hosted the holiday in Elliot I would buffer the event with friends, strangers, anyone to divert the venom of William's family. Odd how at the start of my marriage I couldn't reconcile William with his horrid parents and lemon of a brother, Ned. After that Thanksgiving, I viewed them as peas in a pod. My in-laws weren't any better to the children, and Liza was ready to cry most of the meal, and she was little, she was Claire's age. After a while, William stood up from the table and said to me, 'Jess? Might we chat for a minute? Confidentially?'

"'Why, William,' gasped his mother, Belinda. 'We are in the middle of dinner.'

"William came to where I sat and put his hand on my upper arm, squeezing it. I tried to squirm away. 'Jess?'

"I pushed my chair back and stood up. William rubbed his face against mine and the red veins in the whites of his eyes were sickening.

"'Excuse us.' William spoke to no one in particular. Liza had begun to cry and Billy wouldn't look up from his plate of dried-out turkey.

"William led us out to their indoor porch. I tilted my head and shook my arm free.

"'Is it too much to ask that our children show a little respect for my parents?' He was hissing at me.

"'Are they disrespectful?' I asked. 'I haven't seen that, William.'

"'Fix it. Now, Jess.'

"'Meaning they won't listen to you.'

"William put his hand back around my arm and squeezed again.

"'I said, *fix it.*'

"That's when he hit me for the first time. He simply lifted his hand and slapped me across the face. He hit me with such force I thought for sure I'd get a black eye, that he'd broken my nose. 'Let's go back,' he said.

"Belinda was watching us return to the dining room and I knew that my face was abraded on the right side, streaked with pain. She was drinking scotch and there was a glint in her eyes. She seemed almost pleased. Later on, I went into the kitchen to get some ice from the freezer. Belinda followed me. Their housekeeper, Grace, took a look at my face and was about to fill a Ziploc bag with ice when Belinda said to her, 'That won't be necessary, Gracie. If Jess needs something, she'll find it herself.'

"Then Belinda said to me, 'Get in the game, Jess. There is nothing so special about you except being the mother of my grandchildren, and my son doesn't like anything messy. You'll stay with William because he has two things you want: money and prestige. He's done very nicely and the money came first. Keep a smile on your face and buck up, my dear.'

"'How dare you, Belinda,' I said. I opened the freezer door and she stood so close to me it was revolting.

"'How dare you provoke my son. Learn *not* to provoke him. It can't be news to you that he has a temper. Think of your closet filled with designer shoes. That might help.'" Jess starts crying.

"Jess, Jess." I don't know how to react. After Jess's confession and vile secrets, her pile of shit, I reconsider Charles, who is slightly crabby yet decent. Charles, who loves being a surgeon and has fallen for the suburbs. Charles and I, who may not be in sync at the moment but are . . . attached.

"Lainie, I dread every morning. I wake up and look to my left, and whether William is there or not, he makes me ill. If he is in the shower and I hear the water running, I despise him. Whether he still has a towel wrapped around his waist and is starting to dress or is already dressed and at his most regal with his hair slicked back, in a suit and tie, he is a stranger. When he gropes around on the dresser for his wallet, keys, and Swiss Army knife, left over from his supposedly happy childhood, I have the urge to knock his belongings to the floor and bolt.

"Our being together seems like a monstrous joke that I have to keep alive. If our children aren't in the room, if they're asleep, if they're at a friend's house, I'm at a loss. I have stayed with William to raise the children, offer them the best. We are a bullshit set of parents who encourage them to have good grades, to play sports, play piano, and be on the debate team. William and I are an excellent example of what we are *supposed* to be in Elliot. When he leaves for work and I hear his Lexus first running in the garage, there is more air in the room. I ask myself how it would be if he's not coming back."

"Jess, no more!" I start to cry. "Please no more. I can't listen, it's too horrifying . . . too ugly . . . what you have gone through." I start to sob uncontrollably. I need to swim it off, to decamp.

"I need a drink, Lainie."

"What do you want? I'll go get it. Chardonnay? Port?"

"No, don't worry. I brought my own vodka, straight up." Jess laughs ruefully. "The good ole days. We're on the main beach at midnight with our flasks. Well, except for you—you never had one, did you?"

Jess digs into her purse, pulls out a surprisingly weary-looking flask, and guzzles. "Yah!"

"Jess, you're safe for tonight, and in the morning we'll strategize. . . ." What else is there to say? Charles *works* for William—it's a nightmare. I'm not only shocked and sickened, but also confused about what to do.

"Years of suffering . . . years piling up before I had the guts to leave him," Jess says. Then she shouts, "I wish he were fucking dead. *Fucking dead.* That's the only way out for me."

I look at how the lightbulb seems too naked in the Italian pottery lamp that Charles and I fought over. I thought it an unnecessary purchase while Charles thought it was worth buying. Tonight it reminds me of our bedroom in the city, where we kept it on my side of the bed and we had no guest room.

Jess takes off her sweater. I gasp, looking at her upper arms.

"Black and blue," Jess says. "That's why I look for dresses with sleeves when I'm at the mall."

"Jesus, Jess, to live with this. Of the many charades, the many lies to tell about your life, the worst lie of all. You have nothing with him, nothing that's yours. I don't care how popular you are in Elliot, how big a deal William's position is."

"No, Lainie, that's not true. I have our children, I have this perceived perfect life. I have a successful husband. He isn't *always* miffed with me. In the beginning when these . . . incidents would happen, William used to say, 'What's the difference, Jess? Don't you have the life?' Then he'd warn me not to dare confide in anyone."

Jess starts to cry—wrenching wounded-animal sounds come from her diaphragm. Charles has said that I cry in perfect pitches while my face crumbles. Clearly Jess has waited too long to cry; her crying is beyond crumbling. It isn't recognizable.

"Remember those summers in Cape May, Jess? The cute lifeguards who liked us?"

"They liked *you,* Lainie."

"No, they liked us both."

"Whatever." Jess sniffles.

"Why don't you find a good lawyer, Jess? You can file a report. You should report it. I don't care what William said."

I have never been so self-reliant. If I'm quiet with other mothers, if I feel out of my league, if I'm only myself with other painters,

Isabelle, Gillian, and Cher down at the peers, the Narrows, this is of another order. When we talk about children and husbands, it is within the range of grueling daily life. No one has what Jess has, no one lives in darkness.

"Not yet. One more encounter, Lainie."

"Why?"

"One more chance for William to do the right thing . . ."

"Jess . . ."

"I do, I have to."

"What about Charles knowing, Jess? What does that do to William's reputation?"

"I don't know. We'll ask Charles to keep it among ourselves."

"Charles . . . You and I lost contact before I met him. Now you know him, Jess. Although it is rocky at times with him, I'm thankful."

"You should be," Jess says.

"Charles is . . ."

"I see who Charles is, Lainie. . . ."

I stop. I know she does. I'm silent. The heater rattles down here in a way that it doesn't upstairs.

"I think about Cape May," Jess says after a few minutes.

"Me too," I say. "Let's go down after the show opens. With the children."

"Christ, Lainie, I haven't been there since college."

"How could that be, Jess? I couldn't breathe if I didn't go. That was what Charles had to accept . . . my roots, the Shore. . . . We'll go. What a magical place, it could help you."

"A Band-Aid on my mortal wound," Jess sighs.

"We should catch some sleep; it's late. I'll go upstairs to Charles. Tomorrow we'll swim the five a.m. and get back before the kids are up."

"I'm glad that you moved to Elliot, Lainie. I know it wasn't your choice, but for me . . ."

Jess has gone gooey on top of beaten up and I'm unable to leave her alone. I'm trying to digest the Jess-as-victim revelation when she turns down the lamp while trying to turn it off. Without a word, we crawl into bed together, snuggling closer than most couples would be. I wrap my arms around Jess and she wraps hers around me. We are facing each other. Out of a lost friendship or a history that might never have been resurrected, we share tonight.

An hour later I wake up and Jess is not there. I stagger up the stairs to the safeness of Charles, who has never seemed such a prince of a husband. When I get to the front door, Jess is outside, climbing into her car. Liza and Billy are with her. They look as if they're in a dreadful hurry.

THIRTY-SEVEN

ess has a talent for disappearing acts. The latest being what
happened last night at our home, as evidenced by her phone
call to me this morning.

"Lainie, *The Elliot News-Times* is doing a feature and they'll be over
today at noon. I'm giving you a heads-up in case no one has called
from the council to confirm."

"Jess? Are you all right?" I ask. "I mean . . . I know that you drove
back to William in the middle of the—"

"Lainie, will you be ready for them?" Jess asks. "I don't have to
remind you that it's a week before the show. They are sending a team
to interview you."

"Jess? I'm worried about—"

"Lainie, tell me what you've got for them—what you'll say about
the triptych. Please be welcoming."

I pull several paintings together, the latest and most "strident,"
bold and gentle at once, but not my triptych. That must be veiled
until opening night. They arrive, a journalist, a young man in his
late twenties named Keith, accompanied by his photographer, named

Jill. She too is young, with her life ahead of her, and so eager to snap the shots. She stands in the insipid sunlight. Ahead of her is the prospect of falling in love, of mothering children. In the studio she notices my photos of the New York bays and the lighthouse in Cape May.

"Where are these taken?" she asks. She is a living ad for Urban Outfitters, her tan and denim, her hair tousled and her heavy-framed eyeglasses.

"Around the New York waterfront." I imagine the young police officer, McCain, and my heart races. He recedes in a flash, along the walkway in a spring thaw. Done.

I want to warn Jill to stay on course, to be awake, to be true to herself. *Don't let life pass you by,* I'd like to say to her. Instead I stand beside my pictures while she is absolutely enthused, a fan, a callow admirer, and I—and most artists who I know—take our fans as they come.

"Tell us why your work is about water," Keith presses. His straight-ish punkish hair falling too near to his eyes.

"I paint what I long for: harmony, beauty, power. I paint the world as it should be." I am dauntless.

Keith is recording the interview and typing in a shorthand on his iPad, quotes, some that will become distorted, half truths. The correct quotes I will post on my new website, quotes as a means to an end.

"What is next for Lainie Smith Morris? More sun and sky? More women in jeopardy at the shoreline?"

"A New York show. Next year. The venue is yet to be determined." I smile at the triumph of predicting my own future.

⁂

The daylight in late March is diluted. I imagine the wind that surrounds Cape May, blowing westward, the damp wood of the pavilions, and it centers me. Of all mornings, the morning of my one-woman show at the Arts Council is both long and fraught with tension. I'm at Bricker's pharmacy buying pressed powder, eyeliner, and Jess's favorite blush-tone lipstick, one she insists works better than my usual shade. Jess had suggested that we go to the mall together to do a special makeup shop that she swears changes one's life. I might have gone as a last-minute distraction except for the fact that I want to stop by the Arts Council. Although the paintings were hung yesterday, I have to view them myself before the actual event.

I stayed up half the nights all week, adding to and subtracting from the third painting in my triptych.

"What is wrong, Lainie, that you won't let the last picture go?" asked Charles two days ago. "Why won't you let it be seen by anyone? They might be your finest work, the new paintings, painted in Elliot. Perhaps better than your masterpiece of yore." His smile is self-satisfied, the message underscoring why life in Elliot suffices. Why my collages have eluded him. He doesn't know that these preferred works are from my stolen hours at the New York harbors. What he disdains most he appreciates most.

Home from the pharmacy, I stand in my colossal, understocked walk-in closet, deciding what to wear. Why play with my wardrobe at a late hour except that the dress color is meaningful for tonight. I never am able to envision what style will become me until the day arrives. This day, my one-person show, my long-dreamed-of comeback. My dress selection is narrowed down to two favorites and the midnight blue that I bought with Jess at the mall.

<hr />

The Arts Council knows how to paper the room, pad the audience, convince the town. Mostly I see mothers from all four children's classes or after-school activities, birthday parties, the Y pool. These slightly familiar faces converge upon me as if I am fresh prey. They speak about me and I hear every word. I grab the first fluted glass of champagne that I see go by on a tray.

"Not so imaginative," says one woman.

"That isn't the problem," says another. "I simply can't find any warmth, anything that draws me in, despite the reviews of her style, her work."

"Exactly. That's how I feel. Let's face it, we showed up for Jess, not Lainie Smith Morris." The woman with her coiffed red hair deceives the crowd by baring her teeth.

"Word has it that Jess would do *anything* for the Morris family," yet another woman, a blonde in turquoise, remarks.

They cling to each other, their bodies huddled together, their necks straining for more action while their heads are pulled apart, reminding me of a set of Siamese twins. I force myself to nod hello and then to cruise the room at Jess's instruction. I embrace the strangers, those who have come for my art and not for the curiosity of it. I notice how the crowd inevitably floats and becomes the social animal it is. I almost don't mind since six guests have asked if I'm selling my *Triptych*.

"Your *Triptych* is your comeback." Anthony Laris, the dealer, stops me and presses his business card into my right hand. He is close to my ear. "Do not sell anything without consulting me first."

Jess inserts herself into the moment. "Anthony, Lainie? No introduction necessary, either way? Lainie, for the record, Anthony and I have been friends since—"

"Since I moved to Elliot for a short time and milked the Arts Council dry for some culture," Anthony finishes. "Jess is the only person I bother with in the entire town."

"I'm delighted to meet you, Anthony." I turn to Jess. "Jess, how can I thank—"

"Call me your fairy godmother, Lainie," she interrupts.

Charles appears. "Or your guardian angel," he says. Which strikes me as odd for Charles, and no time to ponder why. A surge of guests propels us forward and there is Jess, ready to introduce me to Samantha Hall, another New York dealer.

"Lainie, Samantha," Jess begins.

"Lainie, you have outdone yourself," Samantha says. Anthony is observing us and that is why she waves her business card before pressing it into my palm. "We should meet for lunch, and I hope that you won't negotiate any sales before that." Her mouth is next to my ear too.

Anthony Laris and Samantha Hall liquefy into the corners of the exhibit, *my exhibit*. William is lurking about too, not around the perimeter but in the midst of guests, not only on his iPhone but schmoozing. I watch him—he doesn't glance at the artwork; it's as if it doesn't exist. Jess strides up to him, poses for a photo of the two of them, his arm around her waist, their smiles radiant. More guests arrive and gravitate to the triptych and point at the framing, at the pictures. I look away from Jess and William. I am lifted upstream tonight; it is a most extraordinary sensation.

⌇

Halfway through the cocktail party Jess holds her champagne glass up and with a swizzle stick bangs against it for attention. The two hundred guests settle down and are her captive audience. She is elegant, beautiful in black, her diamond drop earrings, her long smooth legs in the sheerest of stockings, her blond hair in an up-sweep, her lips pursed in concentration. She is my friend; she has given me this. I'm so intent on Jess that I follow her gaze before she begins the introduction and summons me to the wall where my triptych hangs. Jess, positioned in front of my beloved three canvases, the narratives that have carried me through these months when I've been an outsider. Yet perhaps being out of the loop was the answer. *Triptych is your comeback,* Anthony Laris said minutes ago.

Jess stands in front of the third of the three, what I have not disclosed before tonight, not even to Matilde. My third canvas, of the jetty without a soul around. Whether Jess knows it or not, she is obliterating the black rocks, the salt sea and arch of sky. She is cluttering my work.

"Welcome, everyone, to a special evening at the Arts Council. I'm very proud to introduce the latest work of Lainie Smith Morris." Jess holds up her hands as guests begin to clap. "Lainie and I go back as far as summers in Cape May during high school. Although we were incommunicado for many years, these past few months that we have been reunited have been a gift for me, and I hope for you too, Lainie." Jess radiates benevolence.

"The art speaks for itself . . . and I ask that you join me in welcoming Lainie to the art world of Elliot and to the good that is generated by her merit."

The applause is authentic, resounding, as I join Jess. We kiss and hold for the briefest time, then I take the microphone. However she and I connect, whatever we yearn for, the night is mine—the culmination of my work. Beyond this oasis—the exhibit tonight—Jess has softened the blows of suburban life and engaged my children. Jess is self-satisfied as she slips into the third row of the crowd after her introduction. She walks to where Charles stands blockaded by guests. Although Charles is waiting along with everyone else for me to begin, I watch how he and Jess almost sink into each other. Their shoulders touch and linger in a pose. Then his right hand laces with Jess's left hand, their fingers weave together. The crowd, the critics, the dealers, and the patrons fall away. It is simply Jess and Charles and I. Charles, who I have forgiven for my long hiatus from where I belong. Jess, who mounted my comeback tonight. Jess and Charles, Charles and Jess. A dam bursts in my brain and the pouring water threatens to decimate life as I know it.

My husband, my best friend.

My eyes scan my paintings before I begin to speak. I know that tonight I soar, and this knowledge is too rewarding to be sidetracked by anyone else's spectacle. I have no choice; I push Jess and Charles further away—into silhouette, then outlines. I swat them out of my sight. I clear my throat; the room silences.

"I want to thank everyone for coming tonight, and a special thank-you to the Arts Council for hosting this event and presenting my most recent seascapes. As some of you may know, I'm new to Elliot, and had it not been for Jess Howard's unflagging commitment to my work and Edna Abre's tireless support, I would not feel so welcome. The response tonight is overwhelming and my gratitude is complete."

There is a round of applause. I count to ten before continuing.

"The atmosphere of water is a mystery to me, to any of us. Though I have devoted my craft to its nature—the tidal streams, surges and crests, the surreal quality of gale winds forcing the currents, impacting our lives—water remains elusive, water gives, water takes away. What we seek is the restorative quality of water, of healing and forgiveness."

The champagne leaches through my mind and the room gets slightly muddled. Jess and Charles stand in the same spot, no longer touching. Their joining was so brief, I could convince myself it never was. I remain engaged with the guests; their last round of applause is my salvation.

PART SIXTEEN

Jess

THIRTY-EIGHT

ho is able to ascertain what Lainie knows or feels? The event tonight was stellar from anyone's point of view. Yet there seems an intangible frost from Lainie once we are back at her house. The two of us are in the living room, where I feel tipsy enough that I might be misreading her—how could she not appreciate the show, the results, the potential for her paintings? Or am I simply overly concerned that she might know, know something. Beyond the house, it's as if winter has not dissipated. Lainie faces the windows, where the blinds remain up.

"I'm searching for stars while I check out the moon's position," she says without moving.

"Tonight is endless," I say.

"How endless, Jess?"

"Infinite and with a bitter end. I've got about forty-eight hours to figure out what to do about William. He's given me this ultimatum."

William, who has just driven home after trying his best tonight. William, who is beseeching me to forget, to overlook our latest episode. To this end, Liza and Billy are at Lainie's for a sleepover: an arrangement I made in order to be at the Morrises' after the opening, after the after party, into the wee hours. The idea would be that Charles has to drive me home at some point, or that I too will crash here.

I unlatch the new pearls that William gave to me this morning. Three strands, Mikimoto, ten millimeter. I received them with a note that read, *Forgiveness, Jess? At any cost, forgiveness.* I finger the pearls, more fitting for Lainie than for me—a gift from the sea, aren't they? Then again, what would Lainie do with this type of status symbol?

"He's asking for forgiveness," I say. "These pearls are the olive branch."

"Forgiveness . . . well . . ." Lainie looks at the pearls, then starts one of her contemplative faces. "Maybe . . . Jess . . . you're right. . . ."

I'm not in the mood. "Let's not go there, Lainie. Let's talk about the Arts Council. Let's talk about it for the next two days . . . my forty-eight hours!"

"Tonight was quite a hit. A hit, right, Jess?" Lainie washes down another glass of Perrier-Jouët. Quite the celebration.

"Sure it was. I put you on the map—what a show!"

"Unbelievable!" Lainie agrees. She burps a small burp. "And I put you on the map!"

We both start laughing as if this is humorous—a throwback to those coastal summers when we were in college.

"We should get some rest, Lainie." I pour myself more champagne from the bottle that we uncorked a half hour ago. I like that everyone is asleep under one roof—Lainie's children, my children, our Charles, despite her ignorance. Quite an occasion to be drunk, and since neither of us drinks often, we're sloshed.

I'm not anesthetized, and the undrunk part of me has my ears peeled for noises, movement, any hint that Charles is awake, which is not likely. So what that Liza, Billy, and I are here? There is a tacit understanding that Charles and I will be appropriate. Immeasurably appropriate: no covert glances or stolen kisses under their roof. If he doesn't confirm this Wednesday at the Gansevoort, I might just goddamn lose it. Charles returned from the exhibition hours ago and told me he has rounds early tomorrow for patients who must be discharged. The life of the surgeon precludes any languid Saturday mornings.

"Nothing like the Cape May shoreline in early spring," Lainie says. "Not any other water will do. I haven't been there since we moved to Elliot."

"I know." I know the drama of it, that she's always been "the artiste" since we were teenagers. Her face is close to mine. Her eyeliner and eyeshadow are blurring together and that makes Lainie seem young, more vulnerable than ever, and in need of a cup of black coffee. I place my hands on her cheekbones; they are ice cold and satiny. I blow on the hair that is across her forehead and it automatically falls into the right place. She blows back at me.

"Hey, Jess, we should go to Cape May, you and I. We should forsake Charles, right? I mean, he's no William, but let's go without him for a road trip. *Tonight.*"

"Lainie, you're drunk."

"I might be. Still, I want to go down the Shore." She comes within three inches of my face and I glimpse how her face must be when Charles is kissing her. Her eyes dilate; the dark blue of the iris is showing, there's little white. In return she sees how my face looks when Charles is kissing me. I pull away.

"No, Lainie. It isn't a good idea."

"Really, Jess, I *have* to go. I owe it to myself, to us, after the show's success."

"And leave the children?" I am clearheaded for that part of the plan. "Besides, it's glacial in Cape May this time of year. Virtually Siberian."

Cape May. Smooth waters, schools of minnows, flounder, the sea floor, sailing in a Hobie Cat on the open bay.

"No, no, let's take the children. We'll leave soon, drive through the night. Get there by early morning. Who cares if it's cold?" Lainie plunks down on the couch and pushes the mohair throw to the floor.

"You tell Charles, Jess. He'll be okay with it if it comes from you."

"What's that supposed to mean?" I ask her.

"Tell him. Tell him the plan, Jess."

We put it into play and before daybreak I'm completely coherent and warmed up to the adventure. We scurry around, packing a few necessities per child, and load our own vehicles. At the last minute we decide to take Mrs. Higgins. Charles comes down to the kitchen where we're grabbing every wrapped food from pretzel sticks to protein bars from the pantry, any unopened bottle of green tea or Smartwater that we can manage.

"I'm appalled by this idea of yours, Lainie," he says.

Lainie keeps hurling the snack foods—hummus, bags of carrots and celery—into a white canvas tote bag that is seasonally unchic and may be wishful thinking for summer. Use it early and the months will be upon us.

"This is *our* plan, Charles," I say. "For old times' sake."

"The older children have assignments . . . schoolwork for Monday," Charles insists. Hey, he's not my husband, but he's as irrational as if he were.

"It is four o'clock on Saturday morning, Charles. We'll be back by Sunday after dinner, at the latest. The kids know to bring their assignments. There won't be any distractions there; it's a good thing." I take the risk, I say what I think.

Mrs. Higgins is behind me, an overnight duffel dutifully packed. She is my conscience, in her mind at least. She may feel secretly smug with her knowledge from Christmas week in Vermont. I give her a tight insincere smile that gives credence to my lack of agency.

"Why exactly is Mrs. Higgins going?" Charles asks as if the woman doesn't exist, isn't standing in front of him.

"To start sorting out things at the house for May, June, July. . . ." Lainie says. She sounds exhausted. Sober too.

Charles is displeased. Obviously he isn't planning much summer time in Cape May this year and surely not until the warmer weather.

"Charles." His name echoes through me. "The solitude will be yours with everyone gone. Including Mrs. Higgins. A nice respite." I spread out my hands to convey the house. "You'll have two SUVs' worth of children off your hands."

How did I become the referee for Lainie and Charles? How did I turn into her advocate?

⬭

Our caravan heads south, breezing along the Garden State Parkway with few vehicles in sight. The night lifts and there is the drive across the causeway to Cape May, a homecoming for Lainie, whose desire to be here is palpable. The dusty beach roads, the historic district, the Fisherman's Memorial, each reminds me of the days spent together with Lainie decades ago. I'm not quite prepared for how exquisite Lainie and Charles's home is, a revamped Victorian house. Lainie has said that she honored the old from the outside while the inside has been gutted into fresh and open spaces. I follow her up the driveway to her house facing the open bay—Lainie's water garden. The ground is dank with the promise of green to come and beyond it the waves are volatile.

Lainie's crew are already on the porch, jumping around gleefully. Alive at last in some twisted reality where I hide from William in my lover's homes and suspend time. Lainie is at my side, dreaming of sea glass, starfish, and seahorses—her newly famous palette, thanks to me.

Her children are graceful, lily white and lithe. Lainie alights up the brick steps to the clapboard house while they follow—as if one squall could change everything. I should not have doubted her, I should not have made the slightest noise to Charles about her deficiencies. She opens the door and motions to us. I'm standing on the pavers at the bottom of the steps, my arms around Liza and Billy.

"C'mon, Jess, check it out! C'mon!" We walk into a stunning house on the waterfront.

Her kids are running bonkers and she is opening the blinds with Mrs. Higgins, who is a quick study. She yanks a bit too roughly, in my opinion, on the cords of the Hunter Douglas shades. The exposure is more fabulous, the kind of water and sky and land that meld until the hardest of hearts, including mine, are transformed.

"Lainie," I say. "It's wonderful."

I put Mrs. Higgins to work at a crackerjack speed since the house is coated with a thin layer of salt and sand. I poke around, checking out the contemporary living room with a stone fireplace and the dark wood bookcases. Although I search the family room and then the kitchen for signs of the prosaic or something to criticize or find deficient, there is nothing of the sort. I admire the eat-in kitchen with the titanic window, which faces the bay side and the eddies. Lainie has placed printed children's bedsheets atop the couches and chairs, including the cherry dining table, to protect them from the sunlight that streaks through the highest casements of the double-height ceiling. The sheets are themed: lions and tigers in a jungle cover one couch; an ocean theme, her favorite, covers the other, larger couch. Over the first wing chair is a meteorite theme of bursting stars, and on the second wing chair she has placed a girly print of hearts and flowers.

Together Mrs. Higgins and I open the sliders and crack open the smaller windows a few inches so that the rimy sea air fills the rooms. Then we raise the heat to dry out the moisture. Lainie is immutable; she has opened the double doors from the living room to the deck and is bundled up in a sweatshirt and jeans. She and Matilde face the foamy water. Tom is upstairs with the twins and Liza and Billy, holding court. An unforeseen realization that I could live like this, women and children, for much longer than an overnight escapade. The Lainie sway has superb force.

A half hour later we climb up and race down the deserted dunes with the children. Claire and Jack scramble sideways on the wide beach, howling and giggling. Matilde and Liza jump off the highest dune while Tom and Billy are at the top, staring down. I swear Tom's scowl is rubbing off on Billy. The boys next in line to become men.

We are wrapped tightly in scarves and boots, jeans and gloves, bucking up against the blasts off the ocean. Lainie and I lead as we head north to the state park and the lighthouse. Lainie, her black hair tangled around her face, is ecstatic. She alternates her iPhone and her Olympus for shots that seem too close together, almost redun-

dant, of the horizon, of the children too. Hasn't she always had a camera in Cape May, has there ever been a day where the churning sea
wasn't enough to alter her mood?

"I'm a feather!" Lainie does that laugh. The day is taking a direction that happens only in the cleanse of water, not in Elliot. She is
near me again—triggering memories. Has it not occurred before, on
this very beach with Lainie—the boy talk of yesterday, the winner
takes all. Confusion over who the winner is, who the winner was.

I befriended her early on. Call me courageous or a show-off, call
me curious. I figured that Lainie was unlike the others, a Cape May
native, for chrissake. It turned out that despite her unfathomable ori-
gins (who grows up year-round in a place like this?), there was something about her. Obviously neither of us got the beach boy or the
summer love, neither of us married the man of our dreams. Or did
she?

"Remember Clark?" I ask her as we leap together across the wid-
est expanse of beach.

"Clark." Lainie stops us. The children travel farther north. Their
hoods are flying off their heads, their laughter ringing in our ears.

"I loved how much he loved Cape May, how he came down every
summer and winter weekends."

"Right. We used to watch him from the marina, from your father's
office. He'd get off the ferry those muggy Friday nights," I say.

"Yeah, that curly light hair. He was slight, boyish I guess. I mean,
compared to Charles, who is taller, sturdier. The first night that Clark
got here we'd have sex anywhere we could. We were always sneaking around."

Here is the moment to confess that I liked Clark because she did;
there was no one special in my life that summer and the lifeguards
weren't as attentive as they might have been. If Lainie and Clark went
to the gazebo and I was with a crowd on the dunes, I could hear her
noises—her moans and sighs unintentionally wafting in my direction. I watched Lainie pull it off seamlessly, sex with a boy who also
promised his devotion. Back then she was from another stratosphere,
transcendental—how did she manage to ensnare him? Not that I

remember him as alluring in any manner, more that I wanted him *because* Lainie had him. Clark himself was irrelevant. My attempts to entice him were about Lainie. When I couldn't take him away and he remained faithful, I let her know he wasn't worth it, I made Clark into less and sabotaged her hopes.

"What never goes away, y'know, Jess, is the last one before the husband. Clark . . . always somewhere in my being. That's how first love is. I googled him when Charles was adamant about moving out of the city."

"What did you learn?" I'm all ears.

"Predictable news. He lives on the water in Seattle. Remember, he loved the water. He has two sons. A wife. He's a scientist. She's a social worker."

"A scientist?"

"Yeah, well, he had that brainy side," Lainie laughs. She takes off her Ray-Bans. I follow suit as if she's directing me in a film. Or maybe it's reality TV—with a local spin. *The Hapless Housewives of Elliot.*

"You did me a favor with Clark," Lainie says. "Or else I would never have met Charles. There were days when I loved Charles to the point where I couldn't breathe without him. Back then I loved him so much that I put my work aside . . . half aside. There were the children— that is the life we built together. Then the light dimmed, clouded over . . . too much shadow."

"I know what you mean, Lainie."

"No, Jess, how could you? Did you ever love William?"

"William," I sigh. "William is . . ."

Lainie flicks her head to indicate that William is not part of the conversation. "I'm starting to get who William is, Jess."

"Sometimes I wish that we could do it over again," I say. "Then I remember the children, the children we have with the men we married. What we endure for our children."

The children are set loose at the jetty and have strung themselves together by holding hands. Tom is leading, then Billy, then Liza, who holds Jack's hand, then Claire and Matilde at the end. I admit it's a photo op of nature, children, and family. They are lovely together.

"Look at them," I say. Matilde waves at Lainie, who waves back. Lainie and Matilde and their secret society.

"This time it's different, right, Jess?" Lainie says. Her voice is peculiar. "Different. Right? With my husband, not my old boyfriend. Another kind of allure. Charles isn't about taking away my chances or about competing for the prize. It probably started like that . . . the first time that the two of you met. . . . You always seem to want what I have. . . ."

I stand still, immobilized. Not only does she know, but she sees it—the nuanced level of thievery, the idea that Charles is her ultimate prize. Except there's much more to it. "Lainie, Charles and I . . ."

"Then you fell for him, right, Jess? You're in love with my husband." What she says sends a shiver through me.

"I suit Charles. We suit each other. We *belong* together, Lainie. I *choose* Charles."

Lainie begins to cry quietly, and even in a moment of peril I notice how delicately she weeps. The waves crash and the children become smaller as they approach the next beach. We're quiet for a moment. I'm thinking about how we've been these past months. I've resurrected her work by orchestrating the exhibition. She's made me someone who can sniff out talent, and that works in my favor. We give each other credibility. Only Charles stands between us.

"Lainie, none of it was planned. I don't forget for one minute that we're friends . . . friends in need . . . friends in Elliot." I sound tepid to my own ears. "But Charles and I, it's almost another realm. . . ."

"Friends, sure, Jess. Friends who both know the best of Charles, a sexy, tender man. I wonder, though, if you really get the good guy once he's cheated *for* you."

Charles, her husband; Charles, my lover. Husbands and lovers—apples and oranges.

"I'm leaving him. I am, Jess." That's when she stops crying. "I'll tell him on Sunday night, after the weekend, when we're back in Elliot. After *our* Cape May weekend."

"Cape May weekend," I repeat. She means what she says, both

the idea of leaving Charles and the promise that the weekend remains intact.

"Then you can step in, Jess. You can have what I leave behind."

It's as if we are saying good-bye after a summer at the Shore; we're twenty years old and smitten with our defective friendship. Yet her stupefying present-day decision pounds in my head and reminds me of how high the stakes have become. The sun capers across the ocean and both of us blink to adjust to such radiance.

PART SEVENTEEN

Lainie

THIRTY-NINE

In the entranceway I take my iPhone out of my bag, having missed the entire morning of praise and accolades. Could the art show have only been sixteen, seventeen hours ago? I skim the hundred-some e-mails and more than eighty texts. Mostly about my work described as filled with sorrow, the randomness of the sea, the marvel of water and sky. Four New York galleries are interested, and a *HuffPo* blog from a guest whom I never met writes that my triptych "conveys what lurks beneath."

The recent texts are from Charles and from the Elliot Y and are minutes old. Charles writes, *Rounds to finish. Will arrive by late evening.* I would tell Jess except that makes it old news. Charles's plan, a surprise to me, was most likely hatched when we collected the children for the journey. That he's coming down completes our Cape May sojourn, the latest chapter in our shared history. On these beaches where I first fell for him, missing the signs of what might go wrong and catching only the drift of love ever after. *Jess.* I close my eyes to annihilate their tryst, a penetrating ache, similar to stepping on several men-of-war.

The latest e-mail is from the Y and reads, *"Dear Ms. Smith Morris, We are pleased to inform you that you have achieved first place in the Y competition to swim the Raritan River."* I reread it and am reassured that they are naming me the winner. *The swimmer of the year.*

"Matilde! Matilde!" I go hurtling through the house. "Matilde!" I shout her name.

Mrs. Higgins appears, wearing an apron that has clamshells and oyster shells painted on it. While we were on the dunes she has finished dusting off the house and ushered out the must and mold of winter.

"I'm looking for Matilde!" I've never been so loud in my life.

She adjusts her glasses in order to control my decibel level.

"Whatever is it, Mrs. Morris?" She is concerned, confused. "Shhh."

"Where is Matilde, Mrs. Higgins?" My shouting continues.

"The children are on the sundeck on the garden side." She has adapted quickly.

I take the stairs two at a time and Jess finds me halfway up.

"Lainie? What's going on?" She sounds anxious, or perhaps I'm imagining it after our denouement.

"I'm looking for Matilde!" I insist. "Matilde!"

"Mom!" Matilde appears at the top of the stairway. The door to the roof garden is open and frames her. Today her eyes are the color of the ocean when the breeze flows from the east. "Mom, what is it?"

"I won!" I shout. "I won the Raritan River swim at the Y, and it's the day after the art show!" Everything is changing—my voice feels light enough to be on angels' wings.

"That's incredible, Mom!" Matilde says. Claire comes into her orbit and then Liza flanks her other side.

"Is there a runner-up? Maybe two runner-ups?"

"I don't know, Matilde. I honestly don't know."

Matilde takes her iPhone from her jeans pocket and checks. "Mom! Mom!" she shouts. "I won too! I'm the second runner-up! *Whoo-whoo!*"

Jess is behind me on the stairs. "Girls, come down and ask your brothers to come. We should have lunch and celebrate the news."

Matilde and I are motionless. Then that mothering instinct kicks in. "Yes, lunch is probably a good idea. Jess packed up lots of food and Mrs. Higgins is at work."

"Let's go, everyone." Jess turns.

A brightness travels with Matilde as she descends. She comes near, we hug, we squeeze each other. "Mom, we did it! We did it!"

Claire is beside us, at our thighs and kneecaps. "Mommy, Mommy, did you and Matilde swim to the other side?"

"Of course we did, my darling girl." I pick up Claire in my arms and she is heavier than the last time, than she felt only yesterday. I am amphibious and suffused with thoughts of water . . . tempera paint, the breaststroke . . . daylight to the onset of night.

At sunrise I wake up and stand at the windowsill, staring at the pink and orange streaks across the morning sky. I turn back to face the bed, where Charles's arm is sluggishly stretched out in search of me; his surgeon's hands lay across my empty place. I could say to him, *Charles, I saw you and Jess. How could you?* Yet there is no longer the need. Instead I open every blind and look at the water, mythical and telling. Next I wake him up. He squints, perplexed, and watches me carry my iPad back into bed. I start scrolling through for Cape May marinas.

"Charles, listen, I think we should go on a boat. Let's rent a boat. The marinas should be open today."

"I don't want to rent a boat, Lainie. In March on the open water? It's plenty cold enough in our house. Doesn't the heat work?"

He has taken the covers and pulls me to him without knowing what I know. I shudder at how the air is too thin for the three of us— Charles, Jess, and me—*but no worries now.* I say nothing except, "Please, Charles, we could do a sailboat with a motor. Or a fishing boat. A fishing boat might be easier to find. They're used the year long, they're already in the water."

"I opt to stay at the house and clean up hundreds of e-mails." Charles props himself up on his elbows and takes his iPhone from the night table. "Jesus, Lainie, it's six o'clock. I didn't get down until almost midnight."

As I watch him fall back to sleep, I reel off the pluses of the morning, beginning with the fact that I'm in Cape May, a place that is a love affair for me. There is no deadline today, no art show pending. There is no need to get to the Y pool, I've won the competition. I only need to find a boat for us, one large enough for our fleet of children and three adults.

FORTY

⌾

Mrs. Higgins has opened the blinds and the bay water dips and swells while she mixes batter for blueberry pancakes. I'm the only one who is awake and I'm on the landline when Matilde comes into the kitchen. I put the person on mute and smile at her. "Hello, my darling girl. Runner-up and fellow water maiden! I'm trying to get us a sailboat for today. As I suspected, they're all goddamn dry-docked since it's not season yet."

I unmute the phone and say, "One sailboat for nine people. There will be two small children, five-year-olds, and two medium-size children and two teenage children." I wink at Matilde. To my own ears my voice is singsong, chatty. I'm euphoric that we are at the Shore, near the rocks and real water, not feeder canals and rivers.

"Okay, sure." I put the phone on speaker. The third time I've been placed on hold. "Cowgirl in the Sand" plays during the wait. "I love Neil Young," I say to Matilde, who has no reaction. "Matilde, do you remember my father's marina from when you were small? I might call the new owners next—although they tore down the original building and I've never liked them. I don't know how else to get a boat going."

Matilde sits at the corian counter in the middle of the room and Mrs. Higgins places a plate of blueberry pancakes in front of her. "That's more like it. Sitting down for a meal is the rule." Matilde pours the maple syrup in a circle, around and around.

"Thank you, Mrs. Higgins. Civility is a goal, my darling girl." Matilde and I laugh, knowing that I'm half serious.

"Mom! You're laughing like you did in the city. Like the summers before Elliot."

Through the windows, the water is lucid and feverish. "If we were in wet suits, we could swim in the bay," Matilde says.

"Except it's very icy. That's why I'm trying to rent a boat instead, to be on the water. . . . For everyone. Well, obviously *not* William. But Dad and Jess . . . Tom, the twins, Liza . . . Billy."

I hang up with almost a whack. "Jesus shit, why can't I find a sailboat? I suppose there's one last shot." I scroll down on my iPhone. "Okay, I've got it."

A moment later I'm speaking with Dougie, a local who has a few fishing boats. Dougie was in my class from nursery school through high school.

"Dougie, let's catch up on the last two and a half decades of our lives!" I say.

Matilde frowns at me.

"Nine. In total." I cover the phone. "Matilde, Dougie says that's too many people. Maybe I'll leave the twins at home with Mrs. Higgins. That will bring us down to seven."

"Claire will cry if—" Matilde says.

"He's not buying it, he is insisting on no more than five passengers. The boat is a thirty-one-foot commercial fishing boat. My old pal Dougie is a deep-sea fisherman, he's the captain."

At the window I squint at the slippery shoreline, the gulls gliding on their wings rather than flapping them in the strong gusts.

Matilde keeps pouring maple syrup and watching how the whitecaps have come up on the bay. "I want to go, Mom, but isn't it kind of rough today? And what about Billy and Liza?"

"Dougie is adamant. Five passengers at the most. Don't you think that Billy and Liza will be okay without the ride, Matilde? Maybe we'll do the beach with them afterward, like yesterday." I take a breath.

"Well . . . that might work. . . ." She pauses.

"Thank you, Matilde," I say. "Thank you for understanding how happy I am today, finally. . . . Who wouldn't welcome our plan, darling girl. . . . It is in triptych! First my paintings at the art show, then the Raritan River win, and now we're in Cape May . . . sorting life out . . . about to be on a boat! A boat—the third part of it . . ."

That's when Claire springs in with her face puffy from sleep. "Mommy! Mommy! We're here and I found a secret beach in my room upstairs."

"A secret beach?" I ask, already worried that I haven't yet awakened Charles about our excursion.

"Yeah, up in the corner. It's the Sealy Mommy's house. The selkie." Claire speaks softly. Matilde bends down to listen, more devoted to Claire this morning than I am.

My iPhone rings and I walk to the window, my finger in my other ear. The girls are watching as I start to jump up and down. When I hang up, I say, "That was a dealer. He has a client for my triptych. Someone who will pay quite a sum. I'm stunned."

"Is the triptych for sale, Mom?" asks Matilde.

"It's for sale. That's why it was shown at the Arts Council. The triptych is my first large work in almost twenty years, Matilde!"

"We'll celebrate." Matilde smiles. "It's super news."

I realize that I haven't asked Matilde the entire week about her sketches.

"Forgive me—between mounting the show and our frantic trip to Cape May, I haven't asked you about your work. How are your sketches coming, Matilde?"

"I brought my sketchbook to show you. I'm almost finished with them."

"And from that sketchbook, anything is possible: large canvases, your own triptych, a picture book," I say. "Truly, Matilde, your pictures have their own narrative."

"I can show you, I'll bring the sketchbook on the boat."

"Yes, my darling girl, I would love that. We'll do it on the boat ride."

PART EIGHTEEN

Jess

FORTY-ONE

The marina is crummy, although Lainie is oblivious, running ahead of us down the old crooked dock to Dougie. She calls Dougie the savior of the day. I haven't any recollection of him from my time spent in Cape May and today he is a waterlogged man who appears twice her age. His white shadow beard and torn flannel shirt over his big stomach are repellent. He walrus-walks to Lainie to give her the kind of hug that she avoids assiduously. He has tobacco in his mouth that he spits into the bay.

The rest of us retreat, except for Matilde, who is halfway between her mother and Dougie and the rest of us. Lainie backs up the planks—her gusto is second only to Claire's when she performs what the family calls her "water dance."

"Time to board!" Dougie jumps onto the boat and yanks on the ropes. "C'mon! Let's go."

"Not many boats are around, Lainie," I say. What I want to say is, *You go with your older children. Charles and I will concentrate on the others, hold down the fort.*

"The commercial boats are in the water, Jess." Lainie points to ten or twelve tired wooden boats that must smell inside from fish and brine. "And any minute, we'll be on one."

Jersey Girl is the name of the boat, scrawled in chipped black paint. A "year-rounder," according to Lainie, who has suddenly become an expert on boats, northeast winds, and inlet fishing.

Tom is half asleep until Dougie revs the engine and hands out life vests. "What are these for, Mom? Didn't you guys win that swim competition? Isn't Matilde an awesome swimmer?" he asks.

"Everyone is wearing a life vest." Charles tugs on the clasp of his puffy, soiled version. I avoid his eyes when he checks that we buckle up.

Dougie maneuvers toward the inlet as the waves slap at us.

"Are we going fishing?" Tom asks.

"Too choppy for newcomers," Dougie says.

"What would we catch if we were fishing?" Even Tom is slightly irritating. He moves to where Dougie pilots the boat.

"Since when did you care, Tom?" I ask.

"Since I got forced to take a boat ride."

"Well, yer mom wants a nice boat ride, that's it, a short cruise," Dougie says. "But today the flounder and striped bass are jumpin'. I hear the blackfish came in fast yesterday."

"Well, what if Tom and I fish, Dougie?" Charles asks. "The two of us?"

Dougie keeps his hands on the helm with his eyes on the inlet. The water rises higher against the sides of the boat.

"Can do it, y'know," he says. "I got bait and rods for my next ride out with a fisherman. If ya go below, you'll see ma stuff; the rods are on the floor by a bucket of iced bait. 'Member, the boat holds twenty thousand pounds of fish. Better catch sumpin'!"

"Oh, Charles, I don't know," Lainie says. "It could be very unwieldy and frustrating too."

"They could try it and see." The least I can do is defend Charles. "Look, Lainie, other boats have people fishing."

Lainie is skeptical, not convinced of what I mean since there are no boats near us at the moment. She takes out a small set of binoculars from her anorak and looks around, then hands them to Charles, who surveys the coastline.

"I'm up for an adventure," Charles says. "Lainie, Jess?" He smiles at both of us—his cheerleading squad.

"I suppose it would be fun, Charles." Lainie caves in. "Tom, you'll have to hold the pole tight, and when the fish bite you'll have to move fast to reel them in because of the wind."

"Are we expecting to catch that many fish?" I ask.

"Mostly throwbacks," Lainie answers.

"Throwbacks?" Charles asks.

"Yes." Lainie sounds serious. "You remember, Charles . . . fish that are too small. Or the wrong kind."

"You would know," Charles says.

"I grew up here, Charles."

"Fishing?"

"Sometimes," Lainie answers. *The parts he'll never get. He'll never imagine either.*

"She could be wrong, I tole ya, there's tons out there. Let me getcha to the best area." The boat turns starboard and we bounce wildly.

Charles's baseball cap that reads ELLIOT MEMORIAL blows off when he and Tom start to bait the rods. I'm relieved when Lainie and I laugh together at how Charles tries to catch it in the wind.

"Thanks, ladies," Charles says as the bait in his hand blows into the water too. Lainie opens the tackle box and takes a chunk of cut bunker. She baits the line without a hitch. I am on Charles's other side, noticing as always how my blond hair contrasts with Lainie's black hair against the bluest sky. Hers swirls around her face in a bizarre halo—an Edvard Munch *Scream*.

The bay is wide open—nothing else counts, nowhere else exists. Dougie steers us near enough to the jetties that the gouges in the rocks show in the grayest and the lightest of the stones. Lainie takes Charles's fishing rod out of his hand and casts the line for him.

FORTY-TWO

A narrow trail of rocks juts into the sea. Charles is so relaxed it's a joke, unlike those times that we've been together, sneaking around the city for an afternoon in each other's arms. Those clandestine meetings were more stressful than I care to accept, and I loathe the comparison, the weightlessness of Charles today, on a boat. I move to where Lainie stands facing into the wind.

"Strange how much fun this is," I say.

"Yup, quite something," Lainie agrees.

Dougie shouts, "What about the jetty game?"

Is he suggesting it because we're vigorous and daring? Lainie shakes her head. "Not smart, too risky."

"What's that?" Charles asks. "What's the 'jetty game'?"

"When the boat bounces on the rocks. A fisherman's sport," Lainie says. "Not a good idea—it's too dangerous."

"Let's watch the horizon," Matilde says. She's been quiet, clutching that portfolio of hers as if it will be swept into the current.

"We can do both," I say. "Fish and watch the horizon."

"Yeah, let's catch some big ones!" Tom says. He has his fishing rod in the water and is clueless as to what's next. Charles, rod in hand, steps toward Dougie. "Dougie, are you a good captain?"

"Have to be," Dougie says. "I do it every day. Jetty jumpin'." He steers the boat into the heaviest waves. "We're almost there, almost jetty jumpin' ourselves. That's what we gotta do!"

"Charles," Lainie says, "let's skip it. We've already added fishing to the trip and we've stayed at the estuary even with the velocity of these winds. Let's leave it at that."

"C'mon, Lainie. What's up that you're so cautious?" Charles turns to me. "Jess?" He has a stiff upper lip that's impressive. Why not—we're on a fisherman's boat, for chrissake. How ironic that I'm not as squeamish as Lainie; *I'm* the one who is enthralled by what Homer calls "the loud resounding sea."

Matilde tugs on Lainie's arm with a sense of urgency, her portfolio in her arm. "Mom, we'll go below."

Yet Lainie is mesmerized by the billows. "Jess, you realize my concern. The waters are too rough. Very sloppy waters," she says.

"Mom, let's go below," Matilde insists.

"Wait, my darling girl, a few minutes is what I need." Lainie is watching Dougie, who is turning the boat into the waves, head on. We bump and jar, rise higher, and are dropped with a bang. It's exhilarating, actually, breathtaking. Until we are too near to the jetty and Dougie is immersed in a game he knows, one that we have never played before.

"We're courtin' the waves!" Dougie screams. The boat lunges forward toward the outer ridges of the jetty. "Closer to the rocks!"

Tom's fishing rod falls into the water and disappears, washed away in seconds.

"Let it go, boy. Ain't cheap, but there's nothin' to be done." Dougie yells louder than the crashing waves. He steers us to the rocks. Lainie arches her back and steadies herself. Matilde is beside her, grabbing her hand.

That's when Charles's pole starts to vibrate with a huge fish on the hook. The pole curves and almost busts under the weight.

"Holy shit! Bring it in—it's a striped bass!" Dougie yells.

Charles tries, his surgeon's hands winding the line tighter as a squirming fish is raised out of the inlet and flops back into the water. Charles is tugging at the line while we lurch toward the rocks. Then, in the blink of an eye that changes your life, he is gone. Charles tumbles into the churning foam so quickly that none of us sees how it occurs. There are no witnesses, only the desperation when he doesn't bob up and his tattered life vests surfaces. In the seconds that count, I look at his children and not at Dougie, who must know what to do. Matilde is stricken and Tom is leaning over the edge, screaming, *"Dad! Dad! Dad! Daaad!"*

Lainie pries her hand out of Matilde's and kicks off her boots. She dives off the side of the boat inches from where Charles has fallen. She is wedged between the rocks and the side of the boat before she pierces through the water with her famous crawl.

Matilde, Tom, and I wait. Lainie emerges with Charles's head in the crook of her arm, holding him up and keeping him safe. She swims to the boat like a pro, a deep-sea diver, pushing Charles forward with the strength of Hercules. Dougie has tossed an anchor and is waiting to bring Charles over the rail, dragging him as he sputters and spits water, then opens his eyes. Tom holds his father's head while I wrap him in a boat cover.

"Lainie?" Charles is limp; I barely hear him. "Lainie?"

I stand up and there is Matilde, gazing at the jetty as if in an Indian trance.

"Lainie! Lainie!" I shout. "Matilde, do you see your mother? Do you see her?"

There are egrets, white as snow, on the black rocks. The seagulls swoosh downward and drop the clams to their death and the fish leap over the waves. A Coast Guard boat pulls up behind us. Dougie gestures crazily toward the water. "She's in the swells!" he shouts. "She's in the goddamn swells!"

"Woman overboard, woman overboard," a voice announces from a megaphone. Three men in wet suits dive to exactly where Lainie saved Charles.

"Lainie!" Charles's voice crashes over the wind. "Lainie! *Lainie!*"

Tom moves beside Matilde and wraps his arm around her shoulders and she pushes it away. She stands there, facing the brink.

FORTY-THREE

Claire sleeps on top of Matilde as she has for the last three nights. Her head on Matilde's stomach and her hand knotted in her hair. In her sleep Claire whimpers, "Mommy, Mommy." When she is awake she is with Jack, who shrieks, "Mommy, Mommy, come back soon." Nonstop, a broken record that sears through my distress, stirring a trepidation deeper than anything I have ever known.

Since the search began for Lainie, the divers have combed the inlet and tributaries that filter into the sea and the bay. Her life vest was found not three feet from the end of the jetty. Her scarf with the printed birds was discovered a few feet into the inlet. Matilde stared at the gray and blue birds of assorted sizes, spellbound. "She bought that at Urban Outfitters last year in the city. She called it 'inauthentic' but she loved it. 'The birds are flying toward the ocean, Matilde,' Mom said at the cash register. 'I know it.' That was the day she bought my sixth-grade spring clothes—the two of us . . ."

We sit vigil in Cape May with our six children. Charles is not operating and I have not left his side. He and I speak together in the den that faces the bay and open the door only when a Coast Guard officer or local policeman comes by. The authorities are unable to report anything and are senseless to how much worse that is for us and for the children. Matilde constantly feeds Claire and Jack chocolate that she found in the freezer, old mints that someone once brought Lainie as a gift, no doubt. Although possibly not stale, they couldn't be anyone's favorite, either. Charles is on the phone with the Coast Guard, the local firemen, and the local police between their visits. A few journalists have come over with their photographers and Charles has surprised me by allowing pictures to be taken. "Maybe someone will see these, someone who has spotted her," he said. I overheard the last journalist say to her photographer, "So much anguish."

Charles hasn't brushed his teeth or washed his face in days; his hair is unkempt. Matilde gave him a quizzical look today, confused by his appearance, his affliction.

"Your father will be neat and clean again," I try to reassure her.

"You mean what Mom calls 'the surgeon image'?" she asks.

"Yes, exactly, Matilde. The way that your mother likes it."

Mrs. Higgins fixes food that only Claire and Jack eat and wipes her eyes constantly. She loads platters of leftovers into the refrigerator, meatballs and spaghetti, fish and chips, roasted chicken with red bliss potatoes, with these long moans. Wasn't Lainie complaining only last week that Mrs. Higgins's moans reminded her of ambulance sirens and how they distract her when she is painting?

An hour ago Mrs. Higgins was crying out loud and running her fingers over the rosary that she carries in her apron pocket. "It is your mother's fate to save your father; she was born to save him," she tells any of Lainie's children within earshot. How accepting Lainie would be of her thoughts. That makes me miss her all the more. *Everyone has to grieve in their own way,* Lainie would say, excusing Mrs. Higgins.

Tonight Matilde finds me in the guest room at midnight, taking out my lenses. Everyone else is asleep. She stands behind me in the bathroom and we look at each other in the mirror.

"No one bothers with what I know about Mom, Jess. No one bothers to ask me how it could have happened."

"What do you mean?"

"I once saw a *Law & Order* episode where a girl could teach the grown-ups about the accident, a homicide. Why doesn't anyone wonder if I have any ideas? Why doesn't anyone say, *What do you know about your mother's disappearance?*"

"Disappearance?"

"Yeah. Why don't they ask me? My mother is the best swimmer."

"The Coast Guards believe they know the waterfront, Matilde."

"Like my mom knows it? The tides . . . the bends . . . If she aced the Raritan River, the Delaware Bay is hers . . . the Cape May Inlet is a piece of cake."

Matilde leaves the guest room, and an hour later, I find her awake in her bedroom. The lamps are on, casting a wide golden light, and I realize that it is not only Matilde, but also Claire sitting on the bed. I stand outside the half-open door.

"Look, Claire." Matilde reaches for an oversize sketchbook. She flips through quickly—it becomes animation. "You aren't allowed to tell anyone that you've seen my book, Claire. *Ever.* Okay? You're the first person to see these except for Mom."

Claire bobs her head up and down.

"I knew it from the time I was three that Mom is a sealy. I knew she'd die if she wasn't near water," Matilde says.

Claire is sucking her thumb, hanging on to her blankie, preternaturally calm. "Mommy is a sealy."

"Mom's tale about the selkies is the one where the fisherman makes the prettiest sealy his wife; you know the story, Claire. He hides her coat until she finds it one day and leaves her children and husband.

"I told Mom I'll draw my own story," Matilde sighs. "Since Mom is gone I've been looking at my sketches again."

Claire is very still, pointing to Matilde's open sketchbook.

"I drew these—for you, Claire. Because you love the story about the selkies. We haven't done the selkie story at night in a long time, maybe since we moved to Elliot."

Matilde turns to the next page. "Here's a picture of the two sisters with their sealy mother at the ocean. See? I've made the sun too big to be real so that the selkie and her girls are . . . helpless. . . ."

"Helpless?" Claire cries. "What, Matilde?"

"That's enough." Matilde closes the book and wraps her pinkie in Claire's pinkie. "Pinkie swear that you won't say a word." Claire nods solemnly and Matilde takes another sketchbook from under the bed.

"Here's my new book, what I was supposed to show Mom on the boat. I kept waiting to show her because she was working on her spring show."

"Please get Mommy for me now. *Now! Matilde!*"

"Look at my pictures, Claire, my new pictures. Mom loves the spring winds, right?"

Claire takes her wet thumb and streaks it across the first picture of the mother and her four children, two girls and two boys. Matilde grabs her hand. "Claire!"

Claire stares at the picture.

"Everyone is on a picnic under a beach umbrella, Claire."

"Happy," Claire says. "Matilde, the mommy is *happy*."

"So are her children, Claire."

Matilde shows Claire the second sketch of the mother and father standing in front of Bloomingdale's.

"In my story her husband brings her to the city and takes her shopping. She looks beautiful in whatever he buys for her, but her hair is really made of seaweed and her skin is light because it was covered for years by her seal skin."

Claire is concentrating on Matilde's next picture, where the sealy mother is in the city with her children, along the banks of the Hudson River. Matilde turns the page.

"They take the crosstown bus to the East River, to Carl Schurz Park, to play and watch the tugboats. She takes her children to school and back. She almost floats down the street, not like other mothers who walk or drive."

Matilde turns the page to a picture of the mother in her studio.

"While her children are in school she draws pictures of the sea and sky. Just like what Mom told you, Claire, the father hides her seal coat so she'll be his wife and the mother forever. See the closet in the hallway that I've drawn?

"The mother is okay since she loves her children very much. Then one day she escapes and everyone says she's gone back to be with the other selkies."

Claire becomes hysterical. She's screaming and Matilde puts her hand on Claire's mouth. "Claire, shhh. Everyone is asleep except for us. I'll have to get Dad or Jess if you're too loud."

Claire shakes her head.

"Okay, fine . . . I'll tell the story—what I think is the truth."

Matilde holds up the next sketch. It is of the older daughter in the attic searching for the missing skin.

"Gone, Matilde, gone?" Claire whimpers. "Is the mommy *gone*?"

Matilde kisses the top of Claire's head as Lainie would do.

"Look, Claire, the next sketch is of the daughter by the Narrows. See how she's surrounded by blue and green? Then the next picture . . . here . . . see? One night, months later, the older daughter wakes up and finds a sealy coat left at the back door. The moon is out . . . the stars are out." Matilde takes Claire's finger and traces the picture.

"And here's the final picture. The daughter's hiding the coat. But she knows that one day she will be with her mother."

Both girls are crying.

"Nooo! Nooo! Matilde, there's a coat for me too. Draw the coat for me too. For the same day. To be with the mommy too!"

"Claire, listen, there is one sheet left in my sketchbook." Matilde reaches for her book bag on the floor and takes out crayons and pencils. "Take the black pencil. You start drawing the second sealy coat for the younger daughter. Add it to the page."

Claire is holding the pencil.

"Then we'll do the rocks and the mommy and her daughters together. On this page we can also fit the sky—and I'll do the ocean. We'll use the blue crayons for that, okay?"

Claire squeezes close to Matilde and takes the azure crayon in her free hand. "Okay, Matilde."

The cold air burns on my cheeks. Who will console these motherless girls?

⌘

Early the next night, two Coast Guard officers arrive and Matilde and Claire huddle together outside the den door. The first guard—his name is Chip—sounds nervous when he tells Charles that the day has been unsuccessful. "These bodies, they move with the tide for weeks," Chip says. "Nothing is decided, Dr. Morris. We'll keep searching. We won't make any promises."

Their boots move thickly on the flagstone path outside and the children appear.

"You must be hungry," I say. "If you go into the kitchen, Mrs. Higgins will feed you. It's dinnertime. Come."

Mrs. Higgins is sobbing on her cell phone when we walk in.

"The dead," says Mrs. Higgins, "they take a piece of your heart, they take a piece of you with them."

Matilde slips outside a few minutes later and faces the waterfront to the west. The gale is dying down slowly and the stars are vivid enough to seem alive or as if they've been painted on a sweeping canvas. Dusk has settled and I use the flashlight from my iPhone to walk to where she stands.

"This must be the worst for you, Matilde," I say.

"Mom isn't dead, Jess. I'm okay."

I could tell her that she's wrong, that everyone knows. Instead I place my hands on her shoulders.

"C'mon, let's go inside. There's macaroni and cheese."

Matilde and I walk up the wooden path with the water behind us, slicing at the bulkhead. The kitchen window is lit up and there is Tom standing at the sink and Charles beside him with Jack on his shoulders. Charles moves to the right and next Tom bends down, reappears with Claire in his arms. Matilde and I are almost at the house and we hear Claire laughing. "Put me down. Put me down!"

"They must be dividing cookie dough," I say.

"Claire's smearing it over her face," Matilde says.

Liza and Billy come to the door and wave to us. "Matilde, Mom!" Liza shouts. "Hurry up!"

Matilde pauses as she's about to enter the house, and then Tom comes toward her. "Everyone's waiting for you, Matilde."

Matilde follows him inside.

ACKNOWLEDGMENTS

I am grateful to Alice Martell, my agent, for her tireless and brilliant suggestions; Jennifer Weis, my editor, for her insights and steadfast belief in the story; Jennifer Enderlin and Sally Richardson, my publishers, who encouraged me to write fiction. At St. Martin's Press: Dori Weintraub, Paul Hochman, Sylvan Creekmore, Bethany Reis. Rebecca Stowe, for her wise edits; my writing group: George Bear, James Parry, Jonathan Stone. Those who listened or read pages: Brondi Borer, Helene Barre, Katinka Matson, Jane Shapiro, Meredith Bernstein, Barbara Shindler, Helen Metzger, Meryl Moss, Lindsay Shepherd, Thomas Moore, Mark Shapiro, Judy H. Shapiro, Patti Himmelberger, CB Whyte, Kara Ivancich, Tina Chen, Linda Berley, Sandra Leitner, Sally Robinson, Jessica Soule. Neil Rosini, sage lawyer. Jack Van Dalen for his Cape May expertise. Jennie and Elizabeth—muses. My father, who has always navigated the shoreline; my mother, constructive critic and staunchest supporter. Howard Ressler, truest believer and partner.

ELKHART PUBLIC LIBRARY

3 3080 01584 7463

WITHDRAWN

JUL — 2015

**ELKHART PUBLIC
LIBRARY**

Elkhart, Indiana